Samuel
Son of Jesse

Jesse Stalls Series

Book 2

Michael J Spanhanks

BOGGY CREEK PUBLISHING

ISBN: 979-8-9853968-9-8

Publisher: Boggy Creek Press
For more information or to book an event, contact:
https://mspanhanksbooks.com/

Cover Design by Innovative Presentations
Editing by Editing Innovations

Photo Contributor: ID 33106112 Katalinks
Dreamstime.com

Shutter Stock images
Stock Vector ID: 110487386
Contributor: Robles Designery

Bible References
Job 14:1 KJV
Nahum 1:7 KJV
Philippians 2:3
Hebrews 4:12
Genesis 2:24
Proverbs 15:27
Romans 10:9
Matthew 19:5-6
1 Peter 4:10-11
Ephesians 2:2-3
Proverbs 3:5-6

Train up a child in the way he should go: and
when he is old, he will not depart from it..
Proverbs 4:4-5

RUNAWAY

Chapter 1

Gunfire. Smoke. Three tin cans hit the ground. A rider suddenly emerged in the distance, surrounded by tall, purple sage. Dust billowed from the sandy soil as the horse's hooves pounded against the ground under a misty cobalt sky parallel to the tree line where a gunman stood waiting.

Sweat dripped onto the trail as the black horse snorted. Soon, the rider reduced speed at the water's edge, and the horse stopped and stroked at the parched soil, forcing another cloud of dust into the air.

The rider gazed at the gunman, eyes penetrating.

Gripping the Smith and Wesson Frontier .44-40 revolver, the gunman stayed his ground.

The rider shook his head. "Samuel, what are you doing out here?"

"I'm practicing, Pa. How else will I get good at it?"

Jesse recalled long ago the countless hours spent honing his shooting skills alongside his best friend Billy behind his papa's house, before they left on the cattle drive that forever changed his life. "You're already good enough and will not be getting into any gunfights. You only need to know how to protect yourself from animals and how to bring home meat. There's no need to waste good ammunition shooting up old tin cans. Besides, I've been looking for you to help with old Stomper."

"Stomper? Why?"

"You know I can't nail shoes on that horse without someone holding him. If you hadn't run off after lunch, I wouldn't have to be here looking for you."

"Well, Pa, all I ever do is work around this place. I've never got time for myself. Just figured you had finished for the day since you were sleeping on the porch."

"Samuel, I give you plenty of time to do what you need to on Saturdays, and you know, I nap every day after lunch, but they are never long, and then I'm right back to work. Now we've got horses to shoe and have to gather those mares into a corral to take to Fort Smith. We've no time for shooting and playing around."

Samuel kicked the dirt with his boot. "I just wanted to shoot while you were napping, that is all. Reckon the time got away from me."

"Meet me at home, and we'll start on that horse."

"Alrighty."

✳ ✳ ✳

Shoeing Stomper was a dreaded task and always proved a challenge for Jesse.

The horse fretted throughout the afternoon, forcing them to harness his legs as they cleaned his feet, rasped hooves, and forged his shoes.

Drenched in sweat, the salty secretion flowed down his hips and legs as the gelding voiced injustice for the torture he must endure. Nothing Jesse or Samuel offered comforted him.

Soon, Jesse drove the last nail to the shoe and released the horse from the harness as a black carriage made its way up the lane. "Wonder what this is about."

Rudolph Anchorman grimaced as he called out to the mare. "Whoa, Miss Maggie, hold up, girl." The bay horse reached a stopping place a few feet from Jesse and Samuel.

"Hello, Mr. Anchorman," Jesse said, wiping sweat from his forehead. "What brings you out this way? My note's not due."

"No, it's not Mr. Stalls. You still have a bit of time, though I remembered that a while back, you mentioned you were struggling when you made your payment. At least, that was my assessment. So I came here today to offer you an extension and see if I could help you."

"I don't know. What kind of extension?"

Anchorman stepped from the buggy, hands dragging the wheel, reminding him why he was in the hick town of Booneville. His former boss and the bank president at St. Louis suggested this transfer due to not recovering the money from a robbery.

The banker, a portly man, was always clean-shaven and wearing a suit. He brushed his trousers, gray tweed coat, and light blue shirt with his hat, removing the dust that had settled.

Smiling, he stepped closer, grinning and gazing at Jesse. "Mr. Stalls, I'm here to offer you an extension at a lower rate. I hoped my offer might help you in these hard times. As you know, the original loan was for fifteen cents on the dollar. What I'm proposing is a six-month extension for ten cents per dollar, besides your balance due. To be clear, the loan will cost you slightly more and give you another six months to pay the full debt—a small price for that time, don't you see?"

"And I suppose with this new extension, the ranch remains collateral?" Jesse asked.

"Well, certainly. This arrangement changes nothing about the original contract but gives you more time to pay at a cheaper rate."

Jesse's first years of ranching were great for the horse business. A friend, Montgomery Roe, had offered for his work, select mares for foundation stock when his wife, Hanna, and he left Kansas.

In the good years, Jesse borrowed money from the bank to buy more horses and build a lovely house in Booneville County for Hanna and their children. Months later, he borrowed again to build a stable for training horses, but then the horse market fell due to the nationwide economic state. During the downfall, few buyers opted for quality horses, and training them for others had also fallen.

"So let me get this straight," Jesse replied. "I would have about a year to pay the note—with the extension, but it will cost me another ten cents on the dollar?"

"Yes, that would be right. Sorry, I don't remember the exact due date of your loan," Anchorman said.

"Yes, you do because you remind me every time I come into the bank. So, let me ask *you* a question, Mr. Anchorman. What happens to a man's place when he can't pay the note? What do you do with the ranch he has worked hard for all these years?"

"Um, well, it goes to the bank."

"No, what does the bank do with it from there?"

Anchorman scratched his head. "Most certainly, it will go up for auction. Now, the bank could, in some instances, offer it to one of the good citizens of the County, you know, those with guaranteed money who *can* pay off the note."

"And you would sell it for the remaining debt?" Jesse asked.

"Well, now, that all depends. Banks have only so much currency to operate with during the month. We borrow money to make our loans. We might offer such a place at an auction, but often, we must take an offer from an individual to pay off what we owe. That's how the banking business works."

"So, if I can't pay the note, I might as well sell the ranch myself. I could then make a profit."

Anchorman's chest rose, and his eyes zeroed in on Jesse. "Mr. Stalls, that *might* work, but let me tell you. Folks may not be so happy to grab a ranch like this if they determine you are selling it to pay off a huge debt. Most folks want a bargain. Since I've dealt in real estate, I can testify that it's a competitive business." He turned and stared at a pile of old wood from a shed Jesse had torn down, pointing. "You'd have to clean up this place. Folks won't buy a dwelling if it has piles of trash like that sitting around. You should do that, anyway."

Samuel had been quietly absorbing the conversation. Jesse never involved him in the ranch's finances, but he couldn't stand by and let the banker tarnish his pa's reputation. "Mr. Anchorman, we will pay off the note. My pa is good for the money he borrowed. Don't you trust him? He doesn't lie. Pa is the most honest man I know."

"I'm sure he is, Samuel, but a contract is a contract. I am only trying to help your pa. He doesn't have to accept the offer. Everything's optional. This is business."

Jesse grinned and peered at the banker. "I know it's business, but *your* business puts more money in the bank's pockets. Samuel is right. I *will* pay the note on time. You need not worry. I thank you for your visit, but I must refuse the extension. Good day to you, sir."

Anchorman turned and stepped into the carriage, visibly displeased. "You don't have long, Mr. Stalls. If you go one day beyond the due date, I will have no choice but to confiscate your place, and the sheriff will remove you." He prodded his horse and turned his buggy towards town.

Samuel stepped beside Jesse. "Are we going to lose the ranch?"

11

"We still have time, and we know how to pray. Thanks for your comments, Samuel."

"I couldn't allow him to make you seem dishonest."

Jesse patted Samuel on the shoulder. "Come on, let's head inside. Your momma will want to know what Anchorman said. Need to warn her what lies ahead."

Chapter 2

The bronc reared and then gave a buck, tossing the cowboy against the corral fence. The rider dusted himself with his hat and headed toward the opposite side of the corral.

Samuel strolled to where Howdy lay on the ground. "Good ride. That old horse has some grit."

"I'll get him next time unless one of you fine bronc busters thinks you can do better. He's a stinker."

"I'll take him on," Tye Morgan said with a smirk. "Anyone care to wager against me?"

Grant Boyd waved. "I'll take that bet. I've got five dollars that says you can't ride him."

"You better have that five dollars handy because it's mine. Boys, get that bay ready for the ride of his life. Here I come."

Samuel tossed a rope over the horse's head and drew him in as Tye readied himself. The nervous bay hopped desperately, unsure of them.

Tye laid his hand on the horse in a calming manner. "Hold on, horse. Going to be worse for me than for you." Then he reached for the saddle horn. "Well, here goes. Hold him tight, Samuel, until I'm on."

"I'll try."

"Alright, here goes."

"You said that already. Get on."

"I got him." The cowboy stepped into the stirrup and swung his leg over, planting his right foot in the opposite stirrup. The bay darted sideways and then reared, pulling Samuel with him.

Samuel let go of the reins. "I don't have him, Tye."

The bay raced toward the fence line, bucking, tossing Tye above the saddle. The cowboy refused to yield, holding the saddle horn, but the horse gave a twist and delivered Tye to the open air and to the ground with a sounding thud.

"Oh, man. That had to hurt," Howdy uttered.

Tye pulled himself from the ground and limped to his friends. "I twisted my back like barbed wire. Ouch."

From the porch came the sound of hand clapping.

Tye turned to see Frank Bartlett strolling toward them. "Hello, Mr. Bartlett. I hope you didn't need that one today."

"You tried, Tye. No one has ridden that horse."

"Where'd you get him from?" Samuel questioned.

"This bay horse is from Oklahoma and is a mix of Mustang and Thoroughbred. If we can calm him, I will use his bloodlines in my breedings."

"That one's resilient," Howdy said. "Tossed me in two minutes."

"You should not allow the scars from Ramrod to damage your pride. He's tossed many cowboys, but one of these days, someone will ride him. When that happens, we'll see the power he possesses."

"I hope you're right," Tye said.

"Listen, men, I didn't come to the corral to discuss Ramrod. What I need are my riders finishing out those mares. The army will purchase them from me, but they must have time in the saddle. We have to prove they are more than green broke."

Samuel knew Frank Bartlett was pushing the horses too hard without consideration of proper training. According to his pa and brother Kendall, it takes months and even years to make a horse ready for a quality ride. Bartlett's rushed approach would have the army dealing with unruly horses.

Howdy nodded. "Yeah, we will get on them tomorrow. What do you have, eight?"

"Eight or ten, I don't recall. See my foreman. I'm sure he knows how many and will point them out to you."

Barlett strode to the porch, turning once to gaze at them before going inside.

Samuel stood, shaking his head. "You men know we'll need more time to break those mares than Bartlett's giving us."

"It doesn't matter, Samuel," Tye said. "Bartlett is paying us to put a saddle on and ride 'em. If he doesn't want to spend time with them, there's nothing we can do. I just want to get paid."

"The army will not be happy with this batch, and I expect they will complain. Bartlett will blame us for not getting the job done."

"We all heard what he said," Tye uttered.

"That won't matter."

"Samuel, stop fretting. We need a payday," Grant said. "Let's just do the work and get the money."

"Fellows, there has to be something better for us than breaking horses for some old lawyer."

Howdy pushed his hat back on his head. "I don't know what it'd be, Samuel.

"Reckon there are any cattle drives around? At least that would give us a chance to get away from home."

Tye climbed the fence and sat on top. "I'm sure there are some out of Texas or Kansas, but you got to sign up early."

"Hey, my pa knows a man who ramrods the herds. He's a friend from his childhood days. Pa once worked a cattle drive with him, and now this man ramrods his own drives. Maybe Pa knows how to find him."

Grant leaned against a loose fence post. "Go ahead and ask, Samuel. I'll work a cattle drive with you."

"Yeah, me too," Howdy said.

"I'll ask when I get home."

Chapter 3

The sound of a horse whinnying roused Samuel from sleep. Confused about its direction, he hurriedly yanked his clothes on and headed to the kitchen.

"Hello, Samuel. You slept in today," Hanna said.

He collapsed into a chair beside the table as Hanna placed a breakfast plate in front of him. "What am I hearing?"

"Oh, you mean the horses?"

"Your pa is at the corral, working on one to sell."

"I thought he'd wait on me."

"There's no time, Samuel. We need the money the horses bring to pay off the loan. Howard Perkins wants four, but not all mares."

"We don't have any geldings ready. Wait. Pa's not selling Buster, is he?"

"Howard wants Buster."

Samuel darted for the door. "I told Pa I wanted that horse when he got old enough."

"Samuel, come back and eat your—"

Samuel spotted Jesse working with Buster in the round pen. They circled in one direction and then reversed as

Samuel approached. They could trace his lineage to Montgomery's ranch and those they purchased from his Grandpa Everett. Buster was the pick of all the horses Samuel wanted.

Jesse spotted Samuel coming and slowed the horse's pace. "Good boy, Buster," He rubbed his neck. "You came through for me."

"Pa, why are you selling Buster?" Samuel shouted. "Can't you make enough money from those mares to pay off the place?"

"Doubtful. No one wants mares. The only reason Howard is taking the three mares is I told him if he wanted Buster, he had to purchase them too."

"But Buster is mine."

"Samuel, I never agreed with that. Where did you get that idea?"

"Last year, when I was with you to move the horses to the other field, I told you I wanted him."

"Maybe you mentioned your wish to have him, but *I* never said he was yours. Samuel, saving this ranch is the priority, and Buster and those three mares are the price to keep it out of the hands of the bank. We can't have a note hanging over us and the sheriff riding here and forcing us out. You heard what the banker said!"

"Pa, you could have paid it off without selling Buster. I bet you never even heard me say I wanted him, *did you*?"

"Maybe I didn't, but remember, Samuel, the horses aren't for us. We raise them for money to support the ranch."

Samuel called out as he stomped away, "Just forget it!"

Jesse had returned to work when he saw the barn door opening and Samuel leading his horse, Sadie, outside. "Where are you going, son? I need you here to help with the horses."

"No, you don't need me." Samuel mounted the mare and kicked her into a run.

Hanna caught the commotion and rushed from inside. "What's going on, Jesse?"

"Oh, Samuel is upset that I sold Buster to Howard, but I can't help it."

"We could lose this place if you don't?"

"I explained it, and it didn't seem to matter."

"Are you going after him?"

"No, Samuel needs to simmer. He would never listen to me."

"He'll be back later, Jesse, I'm sure."

"I have to get these horses worked before Howard comes to inspect them. I've got to show some progress, or he may back out."

"What do you mean?"

"Howard will be here tomorrow."

"That's too quick, Jesse."

"I know, and I don't know how long Howard's allowing me to finish the job, only that he'll expect to see progress. I warned him they needed a lot of work. He told me his workers could take turns riding them and that I only needed to familiarize them with folks and a saddle. Basically, I have to green-break them."

"Do you need help? Rebecca can help."

"I'm sure she's busy."

"She's writing a book."

"Writing a book? What kind of book?"

"Said she was taking notes for a novel about frontier women in the West. Rebecca hopes to reveal how they survived the pioneer days."

"That sounds interesting. She takes after my sister. Mary Beth loved to write stories."

"I read some of Mary Beth's, and they were wonderful," Hanna replied. "Rebecca's will be, too. I only hope she isn't expecting much. I don't want her working at the local newspaper because men dominate that occupation. Even if she got in, they would harass her."

"Honey, times are changing. Women work in all areas these days. Two women at the bank are tellers, a job you used to see men doing. I saw Dal Caldwell at the barber the last time I went, and he said a woman was working at the hotel checking folks in."

"Jesse, those are jobs few men want. Can you see a woman as the mayor or sheriff? And what about running a ranch of horses and cattle on their own? Do you expect to see women doctors or lawyers? Most men frown when women step into prominent roles, and many fight it, hoping they fail. Men prefer keeping women in their place. That's why I believe Rebecca's writing will go nowhere in Booneville. I think someday she should travel East, and we must help her."

"Yes, it's still a man's world in these parts, and we are far short of women finding liberty. Hopefully, that will change in our lifetime."

"Don't count on it, Jesse."

"Well, I've got to pull those mares up whether or not I'm ready. Not going to make money like they are."

"When will you look for Samuel?"

"Let's wait to see if he calms down on his own. I figure he'll be home by suppertime."

"I hope you're right, though if Samuel's as angry as he seemed when he ran from the house, I wouldn't expect it."

Jesse shook his head as he turned to mount his horse. "Honey, just pray for him. Deep inside, Samuel knows that not losing the ranch is urgent."

"You bet I'll pray. Just get your horses done and come to supper."

Chapter 4

When breakfast came, Samuel had not returned.

"Now I'm worried," Jesse expressed. "It's not like him to stay away overnight."

Hanna put her arms around his neck. "What are you going to do?"

"I can't do anything right now. Howard Perkins is coming today to look at those horses and expects to see some improvement."

"Your son is more important than those horses, Jesse."

"Both are important. Our lives depend on this ranch."

Hanna turned to pour a cup of coffee as Jesse sat, peering at his plate. "I can't leave until Howard is gone."

"Well, eat your breakfast."

In a while, Jesse strode to the corral. Though frustrated and concerned, he had work to do. He tossed a rope over Buster's head and walked him around the outer part.

"Good boy. Glad you remembered. Now let's pick up the pace."

Jesse pushed the horse several rounds, observing improvement each time. Soon, he drew him in close.

"Alright, boy. How about a saddle this morning? I know you've had it on once, and I think you can handle it."

He eased a bridle on the gray horse, forcing the bit into his mouth, and then led him to the fence where the saddle hung.

"Here we go." Jesse picked up a blanket and positioned it on Buster's back. "This won't hurt you." He caught up the saddle, placing the stirrups atop. With a firm grip on the squeaking leather, he guided it onto the horse.

Buster bounded forward, eager to take off, but Jesse, calmly and with a soothing voice, reined in his enthusiasm. Lowering the first stirrup, he turned to the other side, dropping the second one. Finally, he cinched the girth, keeping a keen eye on the gelding's reaction.

Buster gave a nervous snort and stomped a foot hard on the ground.

"Hold, boy. Everything is going to be alright. Let's walk so you can get used to it." The gelding moved forward as he tugged the reins, leather screeching at every step. "That's a good boy, Buster. You're doing great."

After two trips around the corral, Jesse peered away at the sound of hooves on the road. Tying Buster to the fence, he made his way from the corral. "Hello, Howard. I'm glad you made it."

"Hey Jesse, we have much to do today, so I thought we'd come early. This is my son, Jack."

"Glad to meet you, Jack."

"So, what do you have in the corral? Anything ready for me?"

"Well, that's Buster. Not ready yet, though."

"I thought it might be the gray gelding. Is he saddle broke?"

"I'm working on it."

"Jack will ride him out if you'd like while we're here."

"He's not far enough for that yet. I'm taking it slow with him. He's only had the saddle on twice. The horse needs a few days."

"Nah, ride him now since you already have it cinched."

"Howard, you know that's not my method of breaking a horse. When I finish with him, he'll be the best he can be for the time I spend with him. Though he will require more riding."

"Well, I suppose I can wait."

"I'll ride him next week," Jesse said.

"I'd like to study him over, if I may."

"Sure, go right on in. He'll be fine."

They worked their way through the corral gate. Howard and Jack inspected the gray horse.

"He's built fine, Jesse. Where'd you say he comes from?"

"I raised him from the American stock I brought from Kansas. Some of his bloodline is Thoroughbred, giving him speed when needed, yet durable for the trail. Are you planning on working him herding cattle?"

"Sure, if he's ready," Howard said. "I'm presently working with other ranchers, assembling a cattle drive we'll take to Fort Worth in two months. Buster needs to work cattle before then."

"You still have time."

"When we get him, I'll make sure he works plenty," Jack said.

"I'll finish with him in a couple of weeks," Jesse said. "Now, those mares won't all be ready by then. Buster is ahead of them."

Howard turned to Jesse. "Do you think you'll have them ready in a month?"

Jesse thought of Samuel, though there was little to go on. How long would it take to find him? "I'll do my best,

Howard. You may come for Buster a few weeks early to get him ready for cattle drives."

"Nah, I'll just wait until you have them all finished," Howard responded. "I've got plenty of work to do and won't have the time for two trips."

"What if I brought them to you?"

"You'd do that?"

"Sure, Howard. As long as you have the payment."

"Okay, that sounds great. You'll get your money. Now, if you will allow me to look over those mares, we'll be on our way."

"The mares are in the next corral."

The three men strolled to the corral.

Howard opened the gate and stepped inside. "You say you've started on them?"

"Yes, I've worked them in the round pen a few days and will again today."

"I don't get how that helps."

"After a horse goes around a few times, you stop them so they will join up with you on their own. What that means is they trust you. Once you have that, you can do anything with them."

"I don't see how that makes for more effective training than just putting on a saddle and riding 'em."

"Without joining up, a horse may always be difficult to deal with, more nervous, and struggle with commands. The joining method teaches them to trust, so you become their alpha, like the lead horse in a wild herd."

"I suppose that makes sense, so I'm eager to see you finish them."

"My method is slower but will be worth the wait. Trust me."

"I *am* trusting you, Jesse. That's why I'm not taking those horses now, but don't let me down."

"I won't."

"Pa, Mr. Stalls, will do a great job," Jack declared. "I want to learn his methods someday if you'd allow it."

"Sure, but not until after the cattle drive."

"That will be great."

"Alright, let's get home," Howard said. "We've got work to do."

Howard and his son mounted and rode away.

Hanna watched them ride down the lane as she walked to the corral. "Was he pleased, Jesse?"

"What would please Howard is the horses being ready to go. You know, I hate explaining my training methods to folks, but sometimes I must. They only have to look at those we've trained to know it works?"

"Jesse, they'll never grasp the method you use to train horses and would only understand if you offered them a before and after illustration—which is impossible."

"You're right, but Howard presented me with another problem."

"What problem?"

"He wants the horses in a month. Normally, that's not rushing it, except we don't know what's happened to Samuel."

"Let's not jump to conclusions until you've looked for him. If he's safe, then there's no problem."

"I'll hold up on the mares until I find something out."

"Let me make you a lunch, and you can eat it along the way."

"Alright, I'll get my horse saddled."

Chapter 5

Montgomery Roe spurred his horse, driving him into the Osage River, and Tom Hensley followed through the rushing water.

"It's deep, Tom," Montgomery said as he slipped from the saddle, bearing only the horn, granting his horse an easier opportunity to swim.

"Yeah, I wasn't expecting this," Tom said.

"We should build a fire and dry our clothes."

"Maybe there's a camp spot at this bank, Monte. Be good to settle by water."

"Hey, there's an area beneath those oaks."

"I like it."

After clearing the water, they commenced setting up camp and discarding their saddles.

"I'll see about some dry branches. Do you still have that flint rock?" Tom asked.

"Oh, yes. Never leave home without it."

"Good."

"Tom, I'll lead the horses to get water while you get firewood."

"Good idea."

When he had reached the riverbank again, Montgomery thought he spotted movement on the other side. *I hope that's not Indians. Don't need trouble from them.*

After the horses had quenched their thirst, he guided them back to the camp as Tom laid down a stack of firewood. "Did you find that flint rock in my saddlebags?"

"Yeah, and I think the fire's about to go."

"We could have company soon. When I was watering the horses, I spotted movement across the river. Might be Indians."

"That's all we need. What kind of Indians live up this way?"

"Used to be the Osage, and I know the Sioux moved here years ago."

"I had hoped to dry off and grab some supper."

"We still have an hour of daylight. One of us can keep watch while the other dries off. Get that fire rolling, and I'll take the first watch."

"Yeah, I'll find you in a while."

Montgomery reached down to his saddle and pulled free his Winchester rifle. "Might need to shoot across the river."

"If you spot more than a few, hurry to camp, and we'll ride away from here."

"For sure."

Montgomery eased to the river bank a second time and settled behind an oak tree, gazing across to the other side but seeing nothing. *Maybe that was a deer moving through.*

After several minutes of waiting, he spotted the lower branches of a tree shake as two men appeared on horses, inspecting the river. The rushing water cloaked their conversation, and then they reined their mounts downriver.

Hmm, they're looking for a place to cross. Better get back.

Tom was putting on his britches as he reached camp. "I spotted two men at the water's edge. Those same two were at Leavenworth when we sold the horses."

Tom pulled a shirt down from where it hung near the fire. "There's only one reason they'd follow us, Monte."

"Yeah, they want the money we got from the sale."

"They'll come here tonight."

"I know."

"Well, maybe we hand them a surprise?"

"That's what I'm thinking. Tom, are you dry?"

"Close enough."

"While mine are drying, let me think about how we should do this."

"Guess I'm heading to the river. Don't need them sneaking up before we're ready."

* * *

The two men sat near the campfire when nightfall came, leaning against their saddles.

"It ought to be about that time," Montgomery said.

"Yeah. We should see those thieves any moment. Reckon we better find our places."

They made their way to a predetermined area behind some bushes.

An hour later, a branch snapped in the woods.

"Here they come," Tom said.

"Ready to get this over with? Should have been sleeping."

"But aren't you glad we can still go on adventures?"

"I kinda miss those days, but I miss my bed more."

A short while later, two men exited the woods with their guns drawn, the campfire glowing against their dark figures. One bore an unkempt beard, a dark hat, and a knife on his hip, the other a brown stained hat and leather vest with dangling shreds of leather. They ambled toward the bedrolls beside the fire.

"Get up, you two," one man uttered, aiming a gun at the bedrolls.

There was no response.

"I said get up, cowboy. Don't you know today's payday?"

From behind the bushes, Montgomery whispered, "Are you ready to ease out?"

"Yep, let's go," Tom replied.

The second man reached down and drew back the bedcover. "Rocks. Eugene, there ain't nothing but rocks here."

Eugene reached for the second bedroll and tore back the covers. "Same. Look around. They got to be somewhere, Mitch."

"*They're* right behind you, Eugene. Don't move a muscle," Montgomery asserted.

"Ah, Mister, our mistake. We thought you were someone else and maybe had a little coffee for some friendly travelers," Eugene said, pointing to a cold metal coffee pot.

Tom stepped closer to him. "Uh-huh, and you, *friendly travelers*, planned on getting that coffee with guns aimed at us."

"Oh, I think there's been a misunderstanding," Mitch alleged.

"The misunderstanding is on your part," Montgomery replied. "Now toss those weapons by the barrel with your left hand."

The two bandits pitched their guns into the dirt.

Montgomery directed his weapon toward Eugene. "Now, the knife."

Eugene reached a slow hand and removed his knife, tossing it by the weapons.

"Now, face the other way."

"Mister, you don't have to shoot us," Eugene pleaded.

"Shut up. Tom and I are Texas Rangers, which gives us the right to hang both of you."

"Mister, we didn't know."

"Don't worry, we ain't going to hang you, but tomorrow, we are taking you to Fort Scott so the Army can deal with you however they want."

Mitch turned toward Montgomery. "You may as well hang us here, mister. Everyone knows Fort Scott is a hanging fort."

Montgomery had not heard this about the fort but decided the Army must determine justice for the men's actions. "Nothing I can do about it, fellows. You did the deed. Now you have to face the consequences."

"You saw us back in Leavenworth," Tom uttered.

"Yeah, mister, we saw you," Mitch said. "That don't mean anything."

Eugene turned to Mitch. "Shut up, Mitch. You're digging us a hole."

"Doesn't matter now," Tom said. "We saw you in Leavenworth, and somehow, you found out about our horses and the money we made and followed to rob us."

"Mister, I don't know what you're talking about," Eugene said.

Montgomery stepped up behind Eugene and poked his revolver in his back. "We caught you here, though, didn't we, trying to rob us? That's all that's needed. Now put your hands behind your back."

Tom bound his hands, then tied Mitch's, walked both men to a tree, sat them down, and bound their feet, securing them to a tree.

"Now, maybe we can sleep," Tom said, peering over his shoulder at Montgomery.

Montgomery threw the rocks out of his bedroll. "Yeah, we can try. Just not sure I *can* sleep with those two tied up."

"Will be better when we get them to Fort Scott. The problem is lugging them for two days. Maybe we should just find some trees and hang 'em here like you said, but I didn't know we were still Rangers."

"Yep, you can retire, but once a Ranger, always a Ranger. Nah, we'll let the Army decide their fate. I was funning with them, saying we could hang them. I'm too old to determine whether a man lives or dies."

"Good thing. I wasn't looking forward to that."

"Guess we better get some rest—if we can."

Chapter 6

J esse set out for Booneville to search for Samuel, riding to several places, yet failed to locate him or his acquaintances. Then he recalled that Samuel and his friends had trained horses for Frank Bartlett.

When he reached the lawyer's place, he dismounted and tied his horse to the hitching rail.

One of Bartlett's hands spotted him and started his way. "Can I help you?"

"I'm wondering if you've seen my son around? Samuel Stalls."

"Those men haven't been here today."

The ranch house door opened, and Frank Bartlett stepped out on the veranda. "What does he want, Manuel?"

"He's looking for Samuel Stalls, his son."

Bartlett walked to the edge of the porch. "Samuel was here yesterday with Howdy and those others breaking a few of my horses. I haven't seen them today, and I'm angry because they have a job to do."

Jesse leaned against the hitching rail, removing his hat to wipe sweat from his forehead. "I'm just trying to locate my son, so would you know where they'd be?"

"I do not know. I'm sorry. If you find them, tell them if they want to get paid to finish the work."

"Sure."

"Mr. Stalls, there is another matter I wish to discuss with you. I would like to purchase your ranch...for a fair price."

The comment surprised Jesse. "I'm sorry?"

"That's right. I would buy your place for a fair sum."

"Not planning to sell my ranch, sir."

"I wish you'd think about it."

"Already have, but if I may ask, why would you want my place? It only has a hundred acres."

"I own the land next to you. Plus, you've built a gracious home and barn on the place. Any rancher would love to own it."

"I could never sell because I built the house for my wife and family."

"Just think about it, Mr. Stalls, and remember, I'll give you what it's worth and more."

Jesse walked toward his horse and mounted. "No need to think about it. Got to go." He reined his horse around and left.

"We'll see about that," Bartlett mumbled, watching Jesse riding away.

* * *

Jesse rushed back to Booneville to speak to Sheriff Ruben Dawson. When he had reached the lawman's office, he tied his horse to the rail and hurried inside.

Sheriff Dawson stood gazing at him. "Jesse, fancy seeing you here. What's happening with you these days?" Dawson then sat behind his desk.

"Working a ranch, but today I'm looking for Samuel. Seems he's left home, and I wondered if you had seen him."

"So, he's missing?"

"Samuel got upset with me yesterday and rode off. We thought he'd come back home by this morning, but we haven't seen him. He runs with Howdy Millard, Tye Morgan, and Grant Boyd."

"I've seen him with that crew. They're all pretty good boys and caused no trouble that I'm aware of. But they will frequent the saloon when they're in town."

"Are you saying Samuel goes in and drinks with them?"

"I've seen him there, but *Samuel* drinks sarsaparilla."

"I'd rather he not go in at all, though he is nineteen, and I can't keep him from every temptation."

"Don't worry so much about Samuel. He's a good kid."

Jesse stood, ready to leave. "I suppose I should ask about him at the saloon."

"Now, wait a minute. I'm not finished. I was visiting earlier with Joe, the bartender, and he said he overheard Howdy in a conversation. They talked about riding to Kansas for work at a ranch breaking horses."

"Kansas, wow. I can't believe Samuel would do that. Did he say which ranch?"

"Not that I recall, sorry."

"That boy has put me in a quandary."

"How's that?"

"I've got several horses to ride out for Howard Perkins. That money will cover a loan payment against the place."

"Now, that reminds me. I overheard Frank Bartlett and that banker, Rudolph Anchorman, discussing a ranch that might hit foreclosure. Strangely, Bartlett expressed the desire to acquire it and pressured Anchorman to ensure he did. Said he'd blame the banker if the foreclosure fell through. Then I heard later they were referring to you."

"That explains Anchorman's latest visit. He offered an extension on my loan. I'm sure he thinks that if he can drag things out, Bartlett stands a better chance of getting me to sell."

"Might be."

"I was just at Bartlett's looking for Samuel, and he offered to purchase my place."

"You're not selling, though, are you?"

"No sir, and don't let anyone tell you different."

"Good, and I'll advise you not to trust Bartlett. He once worked as a lawyer at the bank in Fort Smith until accusations arose about his involvement in embezzling money—their money. The bank couldn't prove it, of course. I've also heard rumors of shady deals he's made with other businesses. Be cautious with that man, and never turn your back on him."

"Agreed. Well, I have unfinished work with the horses, then I suppose I'll head to Kansas and look for my son. Sheriff, I may need your help to check on Hanna and Rebecca. Bartlett is unpredictable and subject to cause trouble in my absence."

"I'll do my best, but it's only me and Craig Stone, my deputy."

"Well, if you can, Sheriff. Thanks for the information. At least now I know where Samuel's headed. But maybe I can visit friends at Humboldt."

"Oh, one more thing before you leave. There's a friend of yours in town staying at the hotel. I think he called himself Eli Cole. He came by and said hello and was looking for your place."

"Wow, Eli Cole. I haven't seen him in years. Last I knew of Eli, he worked for Montgomery Roe and Tom Hensley at that Kansas ranch I spoke of."

"He had a friend with him. Called himself Doc."

"Doc? Just Doc?"

"That's all I heard."

"Alright, Sheriff, let me get out of your way."

"I enjoyed the visit, Jesse, and hope you find Samuel."

"I will."

Jesse untied his horse and led him from the sheriff's office to the hotel.

* * *

The clerk at the hotel desk was busy when Jesse arrived.

Then came a voice behind him. "You scrawny old dog, you. I can't believe they let you into a decent hotel like this. Meet me in the street with that hog leg right now."

Jesse spun quickly with his hand on his gun to a man standing and grinning. "Eli, you startled me. But you're just the man I'm looking for."

"Huh? Me? How'd you know I was in town?"

"The sheriff told me."

"Yeah, your Sheriff will check out strangers who ride in. Come to the dining room with me. Doc and I are having some lunch."

Eli introduced Jesse to his friend as they sat.

Doc was a thick-muscled man with a heavy reddish beard and wore a black leather vest and dark faded hat.

"So, why are you in town?" Jesse asked.

"Looking for work."

"What happened with the job at Tom and Montgomery's ranch? I figured by now you'd marry that Spanish girl…what's her name?"

"Samantha?"

"That's right."

"Wasn't because I didn't try, but I think Samantha knew I'd move on someday."

"But they are great folks to work for?"

"Yes, they are, but you know me. I move on from time to time. When I first left, I rode to Texas and worked as a foreman for a lady rancher for about a year until she pressed me to marry her. Don't get me wrong, she was mighty fine-looking, but I suppose I wasn't ready to get hitched.

"After leaving there, I worked a cattle drive out of Texas, and that's where I met up with Doc. He knew a man named George who raised horses in east Texas at a town called Gilmer. We hired on with him right away, though the job only lasted until he passed. Then Wilma, George's wife, sold every one of his horses to another rancher and moved east to the Carolinas, where she's from. We rode here from her old place. I'm getting old, Jesse, and I hoped I might settle somewhere. Don't know about Doc, but I'm tired of moving from place to place."

"That's quite a change for you, Eli."

"I know it, but I think it's time."

"So Doc, do you enjoy partnering with Eli?" Jesse asked.

"Uh-huh."

"You'll have to excuse Doc. He doesn't say much. Figures everyone else says enough."

"That's okay. Any man who rides with Eli Cole has to be a good man. I'm glad to meet you, Doc."

"He is a good man. Doc saved my bacon a few times. How many times did we run into Indians, Doc?"

"A bunch."

"Once on the cattle drive. Another time, Indians came to the ranch and tried to burn out Wilma. We fought all day and only took control after killing ten. I thought the army had taken care of the Indians. Guess not."

"Hanna and I had our run-in with Indians on our trip to Kansas."

"I remember. So Jesse, what are you doing these days?"

"Trying to keep my ranch going, but now, my son has run off. His leaving has caused me some difficulty."

"You have a son?"

"A son and a daughter."

"Wow, I *am* getting old. So what's going on with him?"

"His name's Samuel. He got upset because I was selling a gelding he claimed for his own. The problem is that I have a bank loan soon due, and I have to sell that horse. The sheriff told me he overheard Samuel's friends talking about riding to Kansas to find work. Now I'm without his help in the middle of training that gelding and three mares for the buyer. Samuel left at the worst possible time."

"That is a dilemma for sure, but what if Doc and I were to pitch in and help you finish those horses? You could then leave sooner to search for Samuel."

"That's a great idea if you haven't forgotten my training methods because I still work the same way."

"I tried your methods, and they work well on most horses. So, no worries there, Jesse."

"Alright then, meet me at the ranch in the morning. I'll pay you what I can. You can both stay in Samuel's room until he returns. Ride about four miles to a road marked Henshaw. Take Henshaw a mile, and we are on the right."

"Yep, we'll be there bright and early."

"Not too early, eh? We're not on cattle drive time."

"Ha, ha, sure, Jesse."

"Well, I've got to go now and break the news to Hanna that Samuel is headed to Kansas."

"I'm glad it's *you* telling her and not me," Eli said. "I remember your wife. Mighty bold."

"Maybe you could say a prayer for me?" Jesse rose and then left the hotel. When he had mounted his horse, he started for home.

Chapter 7

J A McFadden had called for his foreman, Nick Lambert, for a meeting in his office. "Come in, Nick. We need to talk about something."

Nick sat in a wooden chair inside the door to avoid carrying dirt and soil onto the cloth furniture.

"Nick, I want to increase the bronc busting work. The Army is paying top dollar for partially broken horses, and I'd like to take advantage of this to help with our payroll. We've only been averaging three horses a month, which isn't enough to meet the Army's requirements. We have to step up these efforts."

"Maybe you've hired too many cowhands, sir, and not enough bronc busters."

"Don't tell me how to run my business, Nick. I'm the owner and the boss."

"Yes, sir."

"Gather the cowhands into the bunkhouse. I wish to meet with them."

"You mean those running fence, too?"

"All of them. I only want to say what I have to say one time."

"Yes, sir. I'll go right now."

An hour later, Nick returned. "Mr. McFadden, the men are waiting for you."

"I'll be along soon."

"Yes, sir."

The big man paused, gathering his thoughts. If he were too harsh on them, some would quit, yet somehow, he must emphasize the importance of the bronc work. He would make them understand that this task will get done.

* * *

Twenty minutes later, the cowboys sat waiting inside the bunkhouse.

"I might have to look for work after this meeting. Hiring on last, I'll be the first to go," Victor Chapman said.

"You worry too much, Victor," Nick said. "I'm sure it's about breaking broncs."

The bunkhouse door opened, and McFadden entered the room as the men peered at him suspiciously. Most cowhands had come for the payday but realized soon that McFadden was more demanding than any boss they had worked for.

"At ease, gentlemen," the ranch owner said. "I'm not here to get onto anyone, only to express an urgency."

"Yes, sir," Nick replied.

"Gentlemen, the Army is paying a premium for horses, green-broke and above, and our current pace of breaking them is not meeting their requirements. You men don't know this, but this money is helpful for your payday. The goal is to produce at least six ready horses each month.

"Now, I want to hear from you as to why we can or can't meet this goal. Tell me what you think needs to change."

Grady Austin raised his hand.

"Go ahead there, Austin," McFadden said.

"Yes, sir. Well, we seem to be spread all over your ranch. The herds run on six sections, and it takes three to four men to work each section."

"Okay. Does anyone else want to say something?"

Craig Watson stood and lifted his hand.

"Craig."

"Sir, we have to drive the cattle each day to water. Takes us half a day to get the job done. A good water source like Riverview—"

"I know, Craig, and we're getting to that. Anyone else?"

Lee Warner raised his hand. "Yes, sir."

"Tell it, Lee."

"Mr. McFadden, it's my opinion that there aren't enough hands for all the jobs. Takes everyone to ramrod the cattle, leaving only two at a time for breaking broncs."

"Two? Nick, is this true?"

"Most of the time, sir. By the time I divvy the workload, there are just two or three left for working with the broncs. The days are long, and these men spend most of their time moving cattle. We finish up after dark each night."

"I've asked you to listen around town for men inclined to work, but I haven't heard a thing. Have you tried?"

"That's because there's no one available. Most cowboys already have jobs and the ones who don't...I hate saying it, but they don't want to work for you."

McFadden offered a narrow frown. "They say that?"

"Yes, sir."

"Maybe it's time I went to Wichita to locate *better* help. Our operations must run smoothly even if I have to trade off hands. That could mean more hands or...different cowboys."

"Yes, sir," Nick said.

41

The ranch owner peered around the room at each of them. "For now, I want four men on bronc riding every day. Trade them off, Nick, so no one gets the short stick."

"Sir, some prefer bronc riding, and others prefer running cattle."

"Well, you pick who rides, but I don't want loafers on bronc busting."

"Yes, sir. We'll get it done, though more men will help us make the goal."

"I'll consider it. Does everyone understand this now?"

A big round of yes, sirs, sounded across the room.

"Nick, come with me," McFadden uttered. "Let's go outside."

The foreman followed McFadden out of the bunkhouse, where they sat on the porch.

"Nick, I'm working to purchase Riverview. Unfortunately, Cora Rivers has not given in to my offer. But I need you to help our men understand everything is evolving and that it won't be long until we have a new water supply."

"I know the Ninnescah River flows through her place, but didn't I hear her say we could water our cattle any time?"

McFadden stared at his young foreman. "I cannot trust what Cora says. What if we take cattle there, and she saw it as stealing or has sent her men to fight us? Do we want a range war? Nick, you are good friends with most of the hands, right?"

"Yes, sir."

"Would it not be terrible to lose good men because we were overly anxious about the water?"

"I suppose so, sir.

"Let's not hear talk of such things again."

"Yes, sir."

Chapter 8

Hanna Stalls walked from the house to the corral where the men were working the last mare. Eli set his foot in the stirrup and swung a leg over the saddle.

Jesse led the mare forward, and she danced from side to side. "Easy, Sally. You're going to be okay."

Eli felt her sudden movement and guided her into a gracious walk.

"What do you think, Eli? Is she ready?" Jesse asked.

"I suppose we'll see. Turn her loose."

Jesse eased the rope over the mare's head. "You got her."

Eli clucked, persuading Sally forward. The mare made five more rounds, and then Eli pushed her into a gallop.

"She's looking good, Jesse," Hanna commented.

Jesse pulled himself onto the fence. "She's the last one."

"So, when are you going after Samuel?"

"I thought I'd let Doc and Eli work these another day while I ride to Papa's."

"Papa's? What for?"

"I want to speak with Kendall about staying at the ranch until I return and maybe watch over the place."

"But doesn't he have work to do?"

"I'm sure he does, but I'm concerned about what Bartlett might try when he realizes I'm gone. He wants this place awfully bad for some reason."

"Jesse, Rebecca, and I will be fine."

"You don't know that. The sheriff said he overheard Anchorman and Bartlett discussing our ranch. Bartlett expects a foreclosure on the loan, and Anchorman will want to keep him happy since Bartlett owns the bank. I suspect that lawyer will be angry when he discovers the debt paid."

"But what about Samuel?"

"I intend to take those horses to Howard and collect payment in a few days. Clearing off the loan must come first. Then I suppose I'll ride to Kansas."

"Do you think Kendall can come with all his work?"

"That's hard to say. I suppose I'll find out tomorrow."

* * *

As Jesse rode closer, he gazed upon the fields near his papa's place. Memories of the day he left twenty years before flooded his mind. He had joined a cattle drive that ended in Fort Worth six months later. A gunfight took place involving Jesse, resulting in the death of the notorious gunhand, Max Tolliver—the name forever branded in Jesse's mind.

That day, he crossed paths with Montgomery Roe, who offered him a job with the Texas Rangers, his first assignment being to rescue Montgomery's wife and two other women from Mexican bandits.

When they caught up with the bandits, they realized Indians had attacked and killed one of the Mexican captors for the women. The Rangers had no choice but to engage in battle with the Indians. Fortunately, the Rangers emerged victorious.

The women were unharmed, and Jesse met Hanna Elrod that day. They married a year later, and the Lord gave them two wonderful children, Samuel and Rebecca.

Samuel's departure for Kansas brought back memories of Jesse's personal and spiritual struggles that came about since the gunfight. Now, he wondered if Samuel had fallen prey to similar troubles because of being skillful with a gun. But he could do little until he reached Kansas except pray for Samuel's safety.

Jesse rode up near the porch of the old home place, spotting Kendall. "I thought I'd have to search the place over for you."

Kendall grappled with some crutches and pulled himself from the chair. "I'm easy to find these days."

Seeing his condition, Jesse asked, "Did you hurt your bad leg again?"

"Nope, broke the other one about two weeks ago. The doctor said I'd be down for at least six weeks. He put on one of those new castings. Jesse, these things itch me to death, so bad I want to cut it off. I would if Laura would let me."

Dismounting, Jesse tied off his horse and started for the porch. "Six weeks is not so long, and you'll heal properly wearing that thing."

"Now you sound like Laura."

"Takes time to heal, Kendall. If they had those castings when you hurt the other leg, you might not have that limp."

"Yeah, I thought about that. And what bothers me most with this thing, besides the itching, is that I can't get any work done."

"Riding a horse might be difficult. So, how *are* you getting work done?"

"Papa and Jasper and the younger men are pitching in. I have to wait on training horses. Not something they can do. So what brings you home? I'm sure you're staying busy, too."

"I hoped you might help me for a few weeks, though I figured to find you covered with work. And seeing how you are, I suppose I made the trip for nothing.

"What do you need? Maybe I *can* help. The view of the front pasture has bored me silly."

"I've got to ride to Kansas to find Samuel?"

"Why is Samuel in Kansas?"

"The boy got riled up a few weeks ago after he found out I was selling a horse he had his eyes on. Samuel had eyes on that one for himself, though I never promised it. Recently, I made a deal with a friend for the gelding.

"Kendall, we were sure Samuel'd be home later that evening. When he didn't show, I knew something was wrong. After checking in town, the sheriff told me the bartender overheard one of Samuel's friends speak about leaving for Kansas for some bronc riding jobs."

"Samuel took after you with horses."

"Well, Hanna is not happy that I haven't already left."

"So, what do you need?"

"I was hoping you and Laura might come and stay at the ranch with Hanna and Rebecca for a few weeks or until I return. But seeing how you are—"

"I can come, Jesse. Can't do much here but sit on the porch on my backside, though it sounds as if you're holding something back. Are you having problems again with gunfighters?"

"Nothing like that. I'm concerned about a certain lawyer. I borrowed money from his bank a while back to work on the house and add a new barn, for which the bank required the ranch as collateral. The lawyer's name is Frank Bartlett, and he wants my ranch for himself. Horse sales had fallen off by the time I completed the building projects, and money has been low."

"Sorry, Jesse. Yeah, horse sales dropped off to nothing last year."

"The sheriff heard the lawyer and his banker talking about the foreclosure of a certain place, which the sheriff now believes is mine. The lawyer told the banker to make certain we fail on the loan."

"Sounds like this lawyer will make it hard on you to get what he wants."

"Yes, which is what concerns me."

"You can't be sure this lawyer won't try something while you're gone."

"Right, I can't take the chance that he might send someone to kill my horses or burn us out. I have horses almost ready now for their new owner. After I receive the payment, I'm headed to the bank to pay off the note. When that lawyer finds out, there's no telling what he might try. He's not a man to regard lightly."

"Laura and I will come before you leave. With my leg like it is, Jesse, I can stay as long as you need me."

"Thank you, brother. I knew I could count on you if you could get away."

"You bet."

"Now, I better get back and help those men finish the horses. Tell Papa and Momma I came by and that I'd stay longer, but I don't have the time. See you tomorrow."

"We'll be there."

Chapter 9

Kendall and Laura pulled into Jesse's place on a buckboard the following day.

Jesse sees them from the barn and makes his way to them, leading his horse. "You made it, Kendall. Good to see you, Laura. Sorry, I missed you yesterday."

"Yes, me too. So good to get away from the ranch for a while. I'm Looking forward to spending time with Rebecca and Hanna."

"They are, too, believe me. Any time other women come around, they get excited."

Kendall slipped from the wagon and grabbed his crutches. "Where do you want us?"

"I'll get those bags and take them in, brother. You get on the porch where you belong," Jesse said.

Kendall laughed. "Thanks. Just throw me out with the water."

"You know what I mean."

"Sure."

"Hanna changed out the sheets and cleaned the bedroom. I've had a couple of fellows staying to work the horses."

"I hope we aren't intruding," Kendall said.

"Not at all. I believe they have other plans."

"Hanna doesn't have to clean up for us," Laura said.

"Oh, it's finished," Hanna responded, stepping outside. "Jesse, put their things in the room?"

"On my way. Then I've got to hit the trail."

As Jesse headed inside, Eli and Doc rode up to the porch, leading Howard Perkins' horses.

"You got some fine stock there. Kendall Stalls is the name."

"You're Jesse's brother, the one who trains horses. I'm Eli Cole, a long-time friend of Jesse's, and this is Doc."

"Thanks for helping my brother. Are you going with him to Kansas?"

"He hasn't asked, but we would."

"I hear you're good with a gun."

"Don't know how good, but I can take care of myself."

"Would be nice if you went along in case he runs into trouble."

"Trouble? Jesse said, stepping outside. "Who said anything about trouble? Don't plan on finding any, only Samuel."

Kendall nodded. "Yeah, and you're going through Indian territory where there's always concern, and you don't know what you might face at that ranch."

"He's right, Jesse," Eli replied. "We'd be happy to ride with you. What about here if something happens? Kendall looks like a man who can take care of himself but with a bum leg, I don't know?"

"He won't have this place alone," Hanna said as she, Rebecca, and Laura came from inside. "I can shoot."

"I can too, Pa," Rebecca uttered.

"Well, I can load the weapons," Laura remarked.

"See, you have an army watching your place," Kendall commented. "Get on out of here. We'll be fine, but take those two with you."

"Jesse, bring Samuel home," Hanna said.

"First things first—drop off the horses and get paid," Jesse said. "I'll wire when we reach Kansas."

"You wire me before Kansas if you go through a town."

Jesse mounted his horses and took a lead rope from Eli. "There should be money left in the bank after paying the loan. Pray that all goes well on our journey and that I'll find Samuel without delay."

"I've already been praying, and I know everything will be fine," Hanna replied, then kissed him before he mounted his horse.

Jesse, Eli, and Doc rode away, leading four horses.

✳ ✳ ✳

The men soon reached Booneville and turned toward Mill Road.

"How far down?" Eli asked.

"Only a few miles," Jesse replied.

"Do you reckon this man will like the band of mounts?"

"Yes, Howard saw their potential already when he came. He has men who can keep going with what we've started."

"That's great—" Eli jerked when a bullet ricocheted off the dirt, narrowly missing him.

They spurred their mounts into a run as more shots came nearby.

Jesse searched for a safe place for them and the horses. "We'll turn into the canyon ahead and make a stand."

"We better hurry before someone takes a bullet," Eli replied.

Leading them into a section with an overhanging projection, Jesse halted the group.

"Why are you stopping?" Eli asked. "This canyon may go on through."

"I want to find out who's shooting at us."

They led the horses into a crevasse for safety.

"A cave?" Eli asked.

"Not really, but will do."

When they had dismounted, they secured the trained horses to their own. Then, after retrieving their rifles, they found a suitable position to fire from behind a group of large boulders.

"This will work," Eli said.

Dust reeled as four men on horses appeared with weapons drawn.

Jesse and Eli fired the first rounds, hitting the ground before the riders. Doc sent a couple of bullets echoing off the canyon wall. The riders held up their mounts and pulled back.

"Who are you, and what do you want?" Jesse called out.

The riders bolted from their horses and found cover at a dip in the canyon wall.

"We only want your horses," came a voice. "No one will get hurt."

"Not going to happen," Jesse answered.

"We'll see about that," the rider said as he opened fire, bullets bouncing off boulders and the canyon wall near Jesse and the men.

The crew exchanged fire, sustaining the stand-off.

Jesse called again. "I'm telling you, it will not happen."

"Only if you give us the horses will we leave you alone," the rider replied.

"I'm not giving up my horses to a bunch of thieves. Go back and tell Bartlett it's over."

"Who's Bartlett?"

Jesse turned to Eli. "Bartlett has to be behind this."

"And what if he's not? These fellows may just be horse thieves," Eli said.

"Maybe they are both. My bet is Bartlett hired them to steal my horses because he knows I need money to repay the loan."

"You may have something there," Eli said. "What do you think, Doc?"

"I don't know, but they have us penned."

The sound of more horses grew louder from farther in the canyon. Shots echoed, and the thieves ran for their mounts and rode away.

Jesse gazed out and saw Howard Perkins, his son Jack, and three more men riding closer. "Howard, you couldn't have ridden by at a better time."

"We weren't just riding past. There's a particular sound this canyon makes when there's gunfire. I figured it could be you bringing the horses. Folks around here have had cattle and horses rustled of late, so we thought we'd try to help whoever it was."

"You thought right. Thank you. Howard, meet a couple of good fellows. This is Eli Cole, a long-time friend and his buddy, Doc."

"Hello, men. I'm glad to meet you. Jesse, I suppose those horses are ready to go since you got them this far?"

"They are, but remember, they need more riding."

"I told you we can do that. We'll trade them out working cattle with 'em." Howard reached into his pocket, pulled out a wad of cash, and handed it to Jesse. "Take this, and count it. I believe it's what we agreed on."

Jesse thumbed through the bills. "Yes, thanks, Howard."

"Now, about what happened here, Jesse. Just a bunch of thieves?"

"Maybe. Could be Frank Bartlett hired them."

"Why? What would Bartlett want with your horses?"

"I owe money against my place at his bank. Bartlett wants it and knows any day I could settle it."

"Well, I hope he doesn't get his way. Never liked the man."

"The money you paid me for the horses is more than enough to pay off that note. Bartlett can't buy it from the bank, but he *can* make things difficult and try to force me to sell."

"I'm sorry for your trouble, Jesse. If you need me, send someone, and I'll direct my men your way."

"Maybe I will. I'm heading to Kansas to find Samuel. My brother Kendall and his wife Laura are staying, but Kendall has a bummed leg. Not sure he can watch everything."

"How long will you be gone?"

"Three, four weeks, or until I find my son."

"You go on to Kansas then, and don't worry about things at your place. Tell Laura if she needs us to send someone. We'll come or bring with the sheriff."

"I appreciate that, Howard."

"Now give me those horses so you can get on your way."

Jesse handed the horses off, and Howard and his men rode from the canyon.

"One more stop, Eli, before we leave for Kansas."

"The bank?"

"That's right. No more loan."

"Well, I hope those boys haven't figured out that you took payment already," Eli said.

"I bet they are on their way to Bartlett's place right now. I just hope Kendall can handle things."

Chapter 10

Samuel and his friends journeyed on the old mail route through eastern Oklahoma. After a grueling 150 miles of riding and evading Indians, Howdy called for a rest.

"Howdy, can't you ride at least until sunset?" Grant asked.

"Look, men, my bottom has galled since we rode through that river. I'm asking if you'll stop so we can build a fire and dry out."

"Yeah, my feet are burning," Tye said. "Got water in my boots at the river."

"Hey, fellows, look up ahead. Isn't that a campfire? And I hear cattle," Samuel said.

"Didn't know there was a cattle drive through these parts," Howdy said. "Maybe they'll let us dry out around their fire."

"And dry our britches," Grant said.

As the men rode towards the smoke, they spotted a chuck wagon. Several cowhands stood when they heard the approaching horses.

"Hello, in the camp," Samuel said.

"Who are you, and what do you want?" said a husky voice.

"Only to dry a little at your fire, maybe get some grub."

"Come in slow, and don't make any quick moves. We got plenty of guns on you."

Samuel raised a hand to stop his friends before they reached the camp to avoid startling the cowhands. "We mean you no harm, mister."

The man looked them over thoroughly. Besides Indians, the only men they ever met on the trail were cattle rustlers.

The man with a thick red beard wore a leather vest and chaps and held a Sharp's repeating rifle. "What's your name?" the man asked.

"My name is Howdy Millard. To my left is Grant Boyd. The first man to my right is Tye Morgan, and the other is Samuel Stalls."

"Stalls? Hmm. Any kin to Jesse?"

Samuel hesitated, considering the consequences of mentioning his pa's name, who had a reputation as a fast gun. He did not want to cause unnecessary trouble for his friends, but the cowhands bore no resemblance to gunfighters. "Yes, he's my pa."

"You don't say. I'm a friend of Jesse's from way back. The name is Billy Cantrell. We worked a cattle drive together before getting separated. He got married, and I took another drive to Montana. Your uncle Kendall married my sister Laura."

"Yes, sir, I've heard him speak of you. Said you two were best friends growing up."

"That's right. You fellows, get down and warm yourself. Did you all get wet in the river?"

"Yes, sir. We should have stopped and built a fire. Just wanted to make some time."

"Where are you headed?" Billy asked.

"To Kansas for jobs. A ranch near Clearwater is hiring bronc riders, and we thought we'd check it out."

As the men spread around the fire, Howdy turned to his horse and retrieved a blanket.

"Are you cold, mister?" Billy asked.

"No, sir, galled. Thought I might shuck my britches and dry them."

"Felipe, do you have that salve?"

"Yes, sir," replied Felipe Mendez. "I get it from de wagon."

"Bring some here for this man. He's raw in an inconvenient spot. Mister, this stuff will ease the pain and help it heal."

"Thank you," Howdy said.

Tye pulled his boots off and laid them by the fire. "Mr. Caldwell, do you need any cowpunchers for your drive?"

"No, sir, I'm over what I like to use. I had one man who thought he couldn't come along because his momma was sick. Then she passed before we left for the herd, so he's with us. I try to work with those who've done me a good job. Maybe you men can sign for my next drive. We start in Kansas City these days and drive to Fort Worth."

"What about the railroad?" Samuel asked. "Why wouldn't you transport your beeves by rail?"

"Tried it. The railroad charges too much, and I don't trust them. When we tried them, we didn't make as much money. We later heard they were working the weight numbers to suit themselves. We know our cows weighed more than they paid us. We may lose a little weight on the drive, but we make more money."

"I'm sorry."

"Oh, don't be. The cattle drive offers jobs for these men."

"That's a good point."

"Samuel, what's your pa up to these days?"

"He's still raising and training horses."

"Jesse always had an eye for good horseflesh. I remember the black he bought in Fort Worth. He was a dandy, and Jesse had to have him."

"You mean Black Jack?"

"Yeah, that's the horse. Is he still alive?"

"Yes, sir. Pa doesn't ride him now but still uses him in his breeding plan."

"Has Jesse had any problems with those gunfighters?"

"I've not heard anything if he has."

"I was with him and your family when six gunfighters, the brothers of Max Toliver, came looking for him. We ran them off with the Good Lord's help. Your grandpa was tired of them coming looking for Jesse. He prayed, and then we headed to town. He told those boys that we had come for them. They never expected they'd face six guns instead of one. But then, some townspeople stepped out one at a time with rifles and handguns. At least fifteen guns were standing in the street against them. Those men took for their horses and rode away. I stayed a few weeks more until Momma passed. After her funeral, I rode to Montana."

"I've heard the stories, not from Pa, from others in town. Pa never talks about it."

"Jesse struggled about killing that man. He was not a true gunfighter, and Toliver pushed him into the fight. When he saw the man's lifeless body on the ground, it scarred him. Jesse carried Toliver's death on his shoulders while having to face other gunfighters who came looking for him. He had bad dreams, too, many times. Jesse would wake up, sweat dripping down him like blood."

"You know Samuel there is fast too, like his pa," Tye said.

"Samuel, I hope you never get into a gunfight without good cause. If you survive one, you'll carry death around your neck like a ball and chain all the days of your life."

"I know."

"Alright, I heard someone mention grub. Are you fellows hungry?" Billy asked.

"Yes, sir. We could eat," Howdy said.

"Felipe has some deer stew ready. Help yourselves and warm by the fire through the night. But I must warn you, we're leaving at break of daylight."

Chapter 11

S amuel and his friends came to a place near a creek and an overhanging bluff.

"What do you fellows think about this place?" Howdy asked as he dismounted.

"This is great, and beside the water," Samuel said.

"That sign said Kelso was just ahead. I think I'll ride in and ask how far to Clearwater while you men build us a fire."

"That's a good idea, Howdy. How about picking up some grub?" Samuel asked.

"Yeah, if you all pitch in because I'm not buying it myself."

Samuel reached into his pocket and pulled out two bits. The others did likewise.

"Here are two bits more for a bottle of whiskey," Grant uttered. "Anybody else for whisky?"

"Yeah, I will," Tye said, handing Howdy more money.

"What about you, Samuel?"

"You know I don't drink."

"Yeah, one of these days, you're going to have to explain that," Tye said, reaching for a dry limb.

"I'll tell you after Howdy gets back."

"Men, get a fire burning. It's going to be cold tonight. I'll get back as soon as I can." Howdy mounted his horse and rode away.

* * *

Dark was closing in, and Howdy had not returned.

"I bet when he got to the saloon, he did more than buy whiskey," Tye concluded. "Bet he started drinking, and Howdy doesn't do well drinking."

"I'm right here, you buzzard." Howdy rode into camp.

"What took you so long?" Grant asked.

"Well, this little saloon gal wanted to make my acquaintance."

"I told you he went drinking."

"No, I didn't. Only a couple because I thought about you fellows. There's grub in the sack. We got beans and steak."

Tye looked into the sack. "You went all out."

"We got to eat, don't we?"

As they sat eating, Tye brought up Samuel's not drinking again.

"I read the Bible, fellows," Samuel said. "Pa raised me going to church. According to the Bible, it's wrong."

"All this time we've known you, and you never mentioned that?" Howdy questioned.

"I didn't figure it mattered much since we were friends."

"Hey, that Billy Cantrell mentioned your pa killing a man in a gunfight," Grant said. "I haven't seen him shoot, but I've seen you, Samuel. You're the fastest of us all. You could build a mighty reputation as a gunfighter. I've never seen anyone so fast as you."

"I don't know how fast I am. I practice because you never know what you might run into. Look, fellows, I'd never pick a gunfight on purpose."

"Why not? You wouldn't lose."

"Have you ever read the dime novels?"

"Sure, we've all read them."

"You can't believe all you read. Most stories are an exaggeration. What is never told is that there's always a faster gun right around the corner."

Grant took a swig of whiskey from the bottle and passed it to Tye. "Nah, I don't know about that."

"Then tell me, how many gunfighters do you know who made it to the top of their game and lived ten years or more after that?"

"I think Billy the Kid did."

"Nope. Billy only lived two years after he became famous."

"Hmm."

"Hey, men, don't mean to butt in here, but what will we do if those bronc busting jobs aren't available when we arrive?" Howdy asked. "News travels slow these days, and there's a good chance the jobs we want are old news."

"Well, I know where a herd of cattle is," Grant replied.

"Cantrell already told us that he hired on more than he needs," Howdy said.

"Who's talking about jobs?"

"You mean rustle cattle from a big ramrod?" Tye said.

"Yeah, that's what I mean. We could choose the best time to ride in there and take maybe forty to fifty head easy, get them to the railroad, and sell them."

"You know they brand cattle these days, right?" Howdy said. "Not only that, they have numbers registered with the meat folks on them. If any cattle show up that don't match you as the owner, they'll arrest you."

"We could sign his name. How are they going to know?" Tye said.

"That's risky business," responded Howdy. "All I have to say is you better be ready to spend time in prison if you even get that far. Some places still believe in hanging rustlers."

"We better hope those jobs are there," Samuel said. "Cattle rustling is not the answer."

"You'd have it easy, Samuel, with your gun," Grant said.

"Doesn't mean I want to kill someone over cattle."

"Fellows, we best get some rest," Howdy declared. "They told me in Kelso that it was about a hundred and seventy-five miles to Clearwater. We got a lot of riding yet."

"That's three days more," Tye said, "if we don't run into Indians."

"Someone toss more wood on that fire," Howdy said. "I got to get some sleep."

Chapter 12

Cora Rivers sat shelling peas on the porch as her ranch foreman walked up.

"Cora, we shifted those steers to the south pasture like you wanted. The grass there should hold them for a while."

"That's good, Sheldon."

Sheldon Bryant tilted his head downward, closing one eye, peering with the other, a habit he acquired through the years.

Cora looked up as she continued shelling the peas. "Is there something else?"

"Well, yeah. I spotted McFadden's men across the river. I figure he's planning something?"

"Were they on Riverview land or his?"

"They were on his."

"Then we shouldn't have anything to worry about."

"For now."

"Sheldon, what else is on your mind? Just say it."

"Okay. I still believe it was McFadden who killed Stuart. Why you don't admit it, I don't know."

Stuart had poured his heart and soul into Riverview, ensuring it was a secure and viable ranch for his family's future. Cora remembered the neighboring rancher had twice made an offer, but Stuart turned him down flat, telling the big man that he could never offer enough to change his mind. Then Stuart asked McFadden why he still wanted Riverview. The rancher's reasoning, he claimed, was his limited water supply. Stuart called him gluttonous since he already owned more land than most men ever would. "Have you found any witnesses, Sheldon?"

"Cora, you know I haven't, but McFadden wants this place something fierce and will go to lengths to get his hands on it. I heard Stuart right here on the porch clearly tell him that he would never sell. Don't you think those were fighting words?"

Sheldon was right about one thing, she thought. McFadden's evil traits flashed when Stuart presented a map that proved the river split into two forks, one running through his land. The map showed the larger of the two flowed through Riverview, and there was plenty of water for both ranches to grow many heads of cattle. McFadden left that day furious. "Stuart meant what he said."

"And it got him killed."

"Stop saying that, Sheldon. I have children here, and they don't need to hear that a neighbor murdered their father."

"Well, it's true whether or not you care to believe it, Cora."

"If someone could tell me they saw McFadden or one of his men hit Stuart over the head, I would believe it. And don't forget that they found his body at the bottom of a ravine below where he worked on the fence. That we know."

"But that's not all there is. I overheard his men in town talking about McFadden. They say he has a terrible temper and is as ornery as they come to them."

"So what? A lot of men in this valley are ornery. Most of them have uncontrollable tempers."

"They said McFadden *always* gets what he wants."

"Sheldon, listen to yourself. Nothing you've told me is usable in court against JA McFadden. I can't trust hearsay. He will have high-dollar attorneys who will call it speculation. We must have genuine witnesses. Do I want it to be true? Yes, I do. I don't trust the man, but I know the law will do nothing on hearsay."

"That's not what I'm getting at. McFadden *is* dangerous and might bring harm to you or the children. I'm suggesting that if he comes around again, please think about selling Riverview."

"I'm not selling the ranch, Sheldon!" She rose from the chair, staring at her foreman. "I will never sell Riverview!" She raised her arm, pointed her finger toward the barn, and said, "Now go to work."

Sheldon sighed as he turned away. "I'm going."

That man knows I can't do anything about what happened. Why does he burden me so?

The uncertainty of Stuart's whereabouts that day had caused so much pain and worry for Cora, and she hated rehashing it. Knowing of bear attacks in the vicinity, she feared the same for Stuart. Reflecting on it now brought her to the same state of anguish.

Through her mind came those hurtful words she uttered to him at their last dispute—the ones that haunt her still. If only she could reverse time and take them back, but that tragedy robbed her of the opportunity.

McFadden's desire for Riverview was fueled by his demand for more water. But was his push to buy the ranch driven by the need for water, greed, or some evil thirst for more power? Cora believed individuals dissatisfied with their circumstances may covet what others possess. Equally, they can't bear *not* being in a position of authority.

She recalled a scripture in Psalm, Incline my heart to Your testimonies—and not to dishonest gain.

Maggie stepped outside onto the porch. "Momma, what did Sheldon want?"

"He told me they had moved the steers to the south pasture." She and Sheldon had discussed the move earlier.

"I overheard him say something about McFadden."

What else had she heard? "Don't worry about that, honey. It's just business."

"Momma, you should let me help in the business part. What if something happened to you?"

The thought of Jeremiah and Maggie without someone to lead them and McFadden pining for Riverside struck a stern tone. He would crush them for control, and what was to keep him from attempting to take her life if he thought he could get by with it? "Maggie, we will pray that doesn't happen, and God will see us through. I don't know how, but he will."

"You mean like he helped my father?"

Cora fixed her eyes on the pan of peas, a simple task in their volatile life. Everyday routines provided solace amidst the uncertainty. But losing Stuart had left a void, causing her to question why the Lord had not intervened. Her great comfort had been Proverbs 3:5-6 *Trust the Lord with all your heart and lean not unto thine own understanding. In all thy ways acknowledge him, and he shall direct thy paths.* The why in their tragedies did not matter. God always has a plan, and he would see them through. "Maggie, we don't always understand why things happen, but we must go on living and trusting God. Remember, everything that happens is not God's plan. There are bad people in the world who follow sinful ways. These ways can lead to hardship for others. Just don't give up on God."

"But it's hard when I was so close to Father."

"I know, and I'm so sorry that something shortened his life."

"Momma, do you think McFadden did something to Father?"

How many of her people believed McFadden was involved with Stuart's death? Maybe he was, but how could she know? "I don't have the answer to your question, Maggie. We can only do what we see and understand. We can't trust speculation."

"I know that Father would have been more careful around the ravine. I've worked with him, and he always worked safely."

"You're right, but sometimes things happen beyond our control."

"I suppose so." Maggie watched as Cora shelled the peas. "Momma, do you think Sheldon needs me today?"

"I don't know, but I could use you with the peas. There's another basket inside."

Maggie smiled. "Sure, I'd love to, Momma."

Chapter 13

Hanna and Rebecca sat beside each other at the Booneville community church. Kendall and Laura sat behind them. Other members of the Stalls family found a place across the main aisle.

Hanna read the telegram from Jesse and placed it in her handbag, peering at the pastor sitting on the bench, waiting to preach.

An older man led off with *Amazing Grace*, followed by *There Is a Fountain Filled with Blood*, as the organist offered accompaniment.

Minister Jacob Lester stood to deliver his sermon when the songs ended. He emphasized how important it was to love one's neighbors as oneself. At the conclusion, he offered a prayer, and the service ended with the song *O For A Thousand Tongues To Sing*.

Jasper and Emmet approached Hanna as they stood to depart.

"Hanna, it's great to see you and Rebecca again," Jasper said, holding wife Molly's hand.

"Yes," Molly replied. "We don't see you often enough."

Hanna nodded and wrapped an arm around Rebecca. "I know, but at least we can be together at church."

"So, tell us about Jesse," Jasper expressed. "What's going on that you need Kendall and Laura to stay at your place?"

"A man named Bartlett made an offer for our ranch. We heard he hoped we would foreclose on the bank loan so he could swoop in and buy it. Bartlett doesn't know it, but Jesse sold some horses and has paid it off."

"That's great."

Emmet and his wife Delma overheard them. "Hanna, do you trust this Bartlett?" Emmet asked.

"I don't. Bartlett has a reputation as a crook. Some believe he's involved in underhanded dealings with several companies. Others say that's the source of his wealth, and the man is well off."

After exchanging pleasantries with the pastor, the family exited the building and proceeded toward the wagons.

Jasper noticed a man not far away leaning against a buggy. "Hanna, do you know that man in the gray suit?"

Hanna looked upon him and saw he had wire-rimmed glasses, a thick handlebar mustache, and well-trimmed dark hair as he stepped into his buggy. "I don't know him, and it seems odd that he's interested in us."

"Maybe he's working for Bartlett."

Kendall rested his crutches against the wagon. "I bet he's one of those investigators you hear about."

"You mean like a Pinkerton?" Jasper questioned.

"Maybe, or some hopeful wannabe."

"I wonder if that lawyer knows Jesse paid off the loan. That could prompt something from a man like him. Better watch for this man."

"Oh, I'm watching. That's *all* I'm doing these days."

Emmet reached and grabbed his thirteen-year-old son, Jared, as he ran by playing. "Jesse's land is pretty hard to cover from a porch, Kendall. We'll come and help if you want us to."

"Everything is fine for now."

"Send Rebecca if anything looks out of place."

"Let's cross that bridge *if* we have to. Now tell me, how's Papa handling the workload?"

"He's tuckered most days," Emmet replied. "Caring for the cattle and the horses is a lot for a man his age. Jared is giving him a hand when not schooling. Rachel's husband, Hershel, and their boys have pitched in."

"That's great. Papa should try walking in my boots. Well, when I'm walking. Lots of days go by, and I'm eating supper at bedtime."

"Kendall, if you need help, all you have to do is ask," Jasper declared.

"I know, brother, but you have families and lots to do."

"So do you," Molly said. "Maybe it's time Papa cuts back the herd and makes things easier to maintain."

"Oh, and Papa's gonna do that because we ask him to?" Kendall asked. "I asked him for a horse I had trained a while back. Papa said giving that horse to me was like taking money from him and Momma."

"Papa said that?" Emmet asked. "He has plenty in the bank."

"He sure said it. I'm still upset about that."

Molly shook her head. "Why can't families work things out? There's no need for family hostilities."

"You mean like how Jesse worked things out with Samuel?" Hanna asked.

"Yeah, what happened with that?" Jasper asked.

"Samuel wanted the horse Jesse was training to sell to a friend. Samuel declared he asked for it a year ago when it was a yearling. A few weeks back, Samuel spotted Jesse breaking him to sell, and they had words. Stirred him so much that he rode out. We haven't seen him since."

Jasper shrugged. "I didn't know. How can we help? I don't ride broncs, but I can herd horses and cattle and help watch over your place."

"We have no cattle. You brothers, you're doing what you can by being available, and I appreciate that."

"We don't mind helping," Emmet said.

Kendall smiled. "I appreciate the offer, but you've got too much on your plate. You're helping Papa with the corn, right?"

"Stay at home," Hanna said. "Busy yourselves with what's needed. If anything changes, we'll send Rebecca."

"In the meantime, I'd love to know who that man in the gray suit is," Emmet declared.

"So would I. When you get home, Please tell Papa that we all miss them. Hopefully, we can get there soon."

Chapter 14

Samuel and his friends reached Clearwater after a tiring journey. They sought the help of a local cowboy at the saloon who provided them with directions to the ranch.

"I'll be so glad to get out of this saddle for a while," Howdy said. "I got calluses on my calluses."

"You always have been hard-headed." Tye laughed.

"Now, that ain't funny, Tye. You know I got wet, and your feet were hurting too. I bet you can't tell me you're alright now?"

"They are better, but I reckon getting out of this saddle might help."

"Hey, fellows. I think I see the ranch," Samuel said. "Lots of cattle across the river."

"Not another river," Howdy said. "I'm never gonna dry out."

"Maybe there's a better crossing upstream."

They soon came to a shallow area where wagon tracks passed through the river to the other side.

"This ought to be it, Howdy," Samuel said.

As they entered the water, gunshots and shouting erupted. In an instant, three cowboys appeared on the ridge with rifles pointed at them.

"You from Riverview?" asked one cowboy, aiming his Sharps rifle at them.

"We crossed several rivers with a view," responded Samuel.

"Are you trying to be funny? You just came through Cora's property."

"Who's Cora? We're from Arkansas, hoping to find the McFadden ranch."

With a rifle in hand, the young cowboy maintained his gaze, pondering Samuel's words. After a brief pause, he introduced himself as Nick Lambert, McFadden's ranch foreman. He then slid his rifle into the scabbard and inquired about their business.

"We heard this ranch was hiring bronc busters."

"So, I guess Mr. McFadden has spoken to you in a telegraph?"

"Err, no. We saw it in a newspaper."

Nick nodded toward the ranch. "Alright, you men, follow me."

Cattle grazed in the distance as the foreman led them through a vast field. They soon arrived at a barn surrounded by a wooden fence painted white. Behind the barn was a huge, elegant Spanish-style house with a porch running the length of the dwelling and a beautiful balcony held by ornate metal posts. A young woman with dark hair, wearing a lace-covered gown, stood smiling as they arrived. She waved at the foreman as they passed.

Nick stopped them at a long hitching rail. He dismounted and turned toward the main door. "I'll check with Mr. McFadden. Maybe he'll see you today."

Howdy walked to Samuel. "What do you think? Did we make this trip for nothing?"

"Well, it's hard to say until we speak with the owner."

"I'm just happy to have my bottom near the ground."

Samuel grinned. "Your bottom won't like bronc busting if you have so much trouble."

"This is only temporary."

"Right."

After a brief pause, a burly man stepped through the ornate wooden door with a cigar in his mouth. He wore a dark suit, white shirt, black vest, and bolo tie. His gaze landed on Samuel before scanning the other men. "Looking for jobs, aye?"

Howdy took a step toward him. "Yes, sir. We have done some horse breaking and hoped you could use us on your ranch."

"I count four. Are all of you bronc busters?"

"Yes, sir, and we're pretty good at it."

"I guess you wouldn't mind showing that you're *pretty good* at it, right?"

"Um, no, sir."

The man turned to his foreman. "Nick, bring a few horses to that first corral and let them show me why I should hire them."

Nick smiled. "Yes, sir, coming right up. Are you planning to watch Mr. McFadden?"

"I'll take a gander from the balcony. Don't let these men mount until you see me."

Nick hurried toward the barn. "Men, follow me to the corrals. We'll set you up with a couple of participants."

Grant turned to Tye. "What's a participant, Tye?"

"That means a horse."

"Well, I never heard them called that before."

Tye shook his head as they followed Samuel and Howdy.

Nick and another cowboy entered a holding pen with a small herd of horses. Nick twirled a rope to move the herd to one end of the corral. He then singled out the horse he wanted and pressed it to the opposite end of the pen. The other cowboy operated a gate, allowing the horse to enter the next pen.

Tye shook his head. "I bet he's the worst of the lot. This is going to tell who we are, boys."

"We can do it," Samuel said.

"Yes, we can," Howdy replied. "Just get in there and ride like we always do."

Moments later, the other man brought a saddle, bridle, and a rope, tossed them on the fence, and then walked away, grinning.

Howdy grabbed the rope as Samuel directed the dark bay mare toward him. Wasting no time, he roped and pulled her closer, securing her to a center post even as she reared and whinnied. "Grab the saddle, Samuel."

They prepared her to ride in just a matter of moments.

"Who goes first?" Howard asked.

"Wait until Mr. McFadden shows," Nick said. "He's the one who needs to see you ride."

The mare was restless, working and attempting to escape the saddle. Soon, the big man emerged on the balcony across the way.

Tye approached her determinedly, seeing the horse as a challenge. He placed a wad of chewing tobacco in his mouth as he stepped beside Samuel. "I guess they want to see what we are made of."

"You can ride her, Tye," Samuel said.

"I'll do my best."

Tye mounted the horse, and Samuel released the rope from her neck. She bucked and twisted as the cowboy held onto the saddle horn.

Samuel noticed Tye's hat fall to the ground and sprinted toward it, grabbing it and ensuring the horse didn't trample it. "Come on, Tye! You got this one!"

After another round, the mare took an unexpected twist and sent Tye to the ground. He watched from the dirt as the mare continued to buck and work to remove the saddle. Then, after a moment, he rose with a smile and dusted himself off. "Now that was a ride."

Nick laughed. "But you didn't ride her out." He looked towards the balcony as McFadden signaled to continue. "Alright, who is next?"

Howdy took around next, but his performance fell short compared to Tye's.

Grant's turn followed, but he rode the worst yet. Rising from the ground, he gazed at Samuel. "I guess you'll have to ride her out so we can have jobs."

"Surely, he won't run us off if we don't finish her."

"That's the way I see it."

Samuel strode to the mare with the lariat in hand, roped her easily, then pulled her close. He met her frenzied state with composure and confidence. "Easy now, girl. I know this is tough, but you can handle it." He extended his hand, caressing her cheek. She responded by lifting her head, eyes widening with anticipation and her ears back, ready for whatever might come next. "We're going to do this now. So, give me a good ride, okay?"

Howdy worked his way to them to keep her calm. "I'll hold her steady while you mount."

"No, stay back. I think that's the problem with this one. Too many changes." Let me try alone.

"Are you sure?"

"Yes."

Howdy stepped back as Samuel assumed control of the reins, taking a moment to rub her neck. He extended his arm towards the saddle, positioned one foot in the stirrup, and hoisted himself up and down, allowing the mare to feel the weight. After several tries, he mounted her despite her whinnying and sidestepping. With a gentle touch and comforting words, he briefly calmed her before she plunged forward, propelling him into the air.

Samuel gripped the horn tightly and gave her ample reins to buck freely. After a long stretch, she shifted into a gallop, panting heavily, sweat dripping down her lathered coat.

"You got her, Samuel!" Howdy yelled.

"What a ride," Tye said.

Grant slapped him on the shoulder. "Yeah, after we broke her in for him."

"No, you didn't impact her at all," Nick said. "I witnessed ten men ride that mare, and none brought her to this point." She is the most hard-to-handle horse on this ranch."

Grant said nothing more, but in his mind, Nick was wrong.

"Alright, leave her and come with me. Someone will take care of her. Mr. McFadden will want to see all of you."

Nick stationed the men beside the porch, instructing them to wait on the benches.

Within moments, the sound of approaching footsteps echoed on the wooden floor. The rancher exited through the door and settled into a chair. "Men, you did well. But I have one more task. Call it a test. I want you to follow Nick to the other side of the barn."

Nick peered at his boss, arms folded. "Mr. McFadden?"

"Take them around to shoot for me, Nick. Gentlemen, you must possess gun skills to care for yourself. Bad hombres live in these parts, so I expect those I hire to at least be fair with their weapons."

Nick motioned for them and led the way. Behind the barn was a location where the ranch hands checked their weapons and practiced.

The foreman set up empty whiskey bottles along a beam of wood several feet off the ground.

"Ya'll know Samuel will take us all," Grant said.

"This ain't no contest," Howdy replied. "You are shooting for a job."

McFadden walked beside the barn. "So, why don't you go first?"

Howdy turned toward the target and pulled his weapon, firing five rounds, hitting them all except the sixth. "Thought I had them."

Tye stepped up next. "Guess I'll go now." He checked his weapon for bullets and turned and fired, hitting four out of six. "Better than I thought I'd do. I'm better with a rifle."

Grant peered at Samuel. "I know you'll beat us all, so I'll go next." He lifted his Colt from the holster and fired, shattering five of the six bottles. "I tied Howdy. Not bad."

The rancher nodded at Samuel. "Show me what you got, son."

Samuel's brow furrowed as he pondered the rancher's intentions for the exercise. If he shot up to his ability, it could impact how McFadden and his friends perceived him, but a poor outcome could cost them the jobs they had traveled all this way for.

He drew his Smith and Wesson Frontier .44-40 revolver and fired, blasting all six.

McFadden gave a half grin. "Alright, men. I've seen enough. Samuel, come over here. That is your name, right?"

"Yes, sir."

Samuel glanced at his friends as he walked toward the rancher, who led him inside the barn for privacy.

"Samuel, I need workers, bronc busters too, and your skills impressed me with how you handled the horse."

"My father taught me."

"I'd like to hire you as my main bronc buster. If you'd like, you can teach a few of my men some of those methods so long as we turn out horses for the Army."

"What about my friends?"

"They aren't all bad, but a dozen like them I can find."

"Mr. McFadden, we came all this way together for jobs. We read you were hiring bronc busters, and we all rode that way. Maybe because my friends went ahead of me, I could ride her out."

"Just maybe you are better than you give yourself credit."

"I *am* good with horses, but so are my friends. We all grew up on ranches. I'm not the only cowboy needing a job." Samuel turned and walked from the barn, waving for his friends to follow.

"Where are we going, Samuel?" Howdy asked.

"Away from here."

Howdy reached out for Samuel's arm and stopped him. "What's going on?"

Samuel ceased walking and stood, arms crossed. "The rancher wants me and no one else. I said no because we came here together."

"Are you crazy?"

"Maybe I am, but we are friends, aren't we? We rode all this way together, looking for jobs. I won't do it."

They marched toward their horses and mounted to leave.

"Wait! Don't leave," Nick called out from the barn.

Samuel reined up his horse.

"Hold up. Mr. McFadden changed his mind. Men, he'll hire all of you. We need you as bronc busters and for other jobs around this place."

Samuel peered at Nick. "Why is McFadden checking to see how we shoot?"

Nick gazed at McFadden a hundred feet away. "Keep this to yourself, but there's a chance of a range war over water. He was right about the need to shoot for protection."

The mention of a range war was unsettling. There was comfort, though, hearing that McFadden had no intention of hiring them to fight with gunfighters.

Samuel turned to the others. "This is up to you, men. Though I don't care about getting caught in someone else's fight. I'll leave it to you.

"We need these jobs," Howdy replied. "I like the idea of working for an outfit like this. I vote yes."

The other men nodded their approval.

Samuel turned to Nick. "Tell Mr. McFadden he has bronc busters."

"Good. I'll set you up in the bunkhouse." He pointed to a building a hundred yards away and guided them to it.

Chapter 15

Samuel and his friends settled in as ranch hands for JA McFadden. In the first week, they broke four horses for the rancher to sell to the Army.

Curley Dodd, the cook, called out, "Ya'll eating this morning? Cause I ain't cooking again."

"Well, you shouldn't had us wait so long," said Wash Seeley as they stepped inside to the table. "We have cattle to move, you know."

"Cattle can wait. You boys gonna eat this grub I made so I can get this mess cleaned up."

"Take a ride with me, Curley," Woodie Bosworth said. "Last time, Dusty and me found ourselves in a messy situation with cattle in a thicket. We both got cut something dreadful. I'll bet there's a cow giving birth in one of those thickets right now."

"They can definitely land themselves into some awkward fortuities," replied Wash.

"Fortuities?" Curly uttered. "I know you heard that somewhere else and bottled it up for this moment 'cause you don't know what it means."

"Sure I do."

"Bah!"

"It means there's a chance it could happen to any of them cows."

Woodie laughed. "Button it up, Wash. Everyone knows you've had no education."

Samuel reached for a biscuit. "What about a head count?"

"What?" Woodie asked.

"How many heads of cattle does McFadden own?"

"How many do you say, Wash, five to seven hundred?" questioned Woodie.

"Okay, now you want my expertise. Samuel, I'd say six hundred to be safe. But I suppose one day we should count them. Might surprise us all."

Nick Lambert stepped inside and hung his hat on the rack. 'Bout time, Curley. I'm starving."

"Nick, you got to ask the boss for a new cook stove if you want it on time. The old thing he has? It's broken. There are cracks all over, and don't feed air right."

"I'll ask, but don't expect much."

"Yeah, that's what I figured."

Nick sat at the end of the table and turned his plate up. "Men, we're heading out on a little trip today. Those men in the other bunkhouse will watch over the cattle while we're gone."

"What's the boss got planned this time?" Woodie asked.

"We're riding to Riverview."

"Riverview?" Wash said.

"Boss is tired of waiting, ain't he?" Woodie commented, nodding his head with a smile.

"It's not like that, Woodie. We're going to talk, that's all."

"If that's so, why is he carrying this bunch? Everyone at this table can handle a gun." He grinned and nodded. "Sounds to me like the boss intends to start his war."

"Woodie, stop that talk. McFadden is going there to negotiate."

"Nah, he wants to scare that woman into selling."

Samuel had heard talk of a budding range war since their arrival and hoped it wasn't true. They had come for bronc busting jobs, not to use their guns. If the rumors were true, it could mean the end of their jobs. "Woodie, let's leave it up to McFadden."

Woodie turned toward Samuel. "Fellows, I hope you got those shooters calibrated and oiled because today, you may need them."

"That's enough," Nick said. "Get your breakfast eaten and get saddled. McFadden is leaving in fifteen minutes."

* * *

Led by McFadden, twelve riders raised a dust cloud as they rode away.

Samuel watched McFadden rigid-faced, riding with a purpose as he led them. Was he planning to negotiate with acceptable terms, or was he intent on starting something?

Howdy spurred his mount in beside Samuel. "What do you think about range wars?"

"I hope it doesn't come."

"Yeah."

"We rode here for work, now this. I won't get into someone else's war against folks I don't even know. You boys can do what you want, but I'm leaving if it comes to a conflict."

"Samuel, you can't leave! You're the only reason the rest of us have jobs. McFadden didn't want us until you changed his mind. He'll run us off the moment you leave."

"I'm sorry. A gun war with strangers was not in my plans. We don't know these folks or why they want to kill each other. All we know is something is not right about the water."

"We still need jobs."

"Maybe it won't come to fighting."

Howdy said no more and sank into the pack beside Tye and Grant. They soon reached a farm trail where a large sign hung on posts that read RIVERVIEW.

* * *

Sheldon Bryant heard the sound of hooves beating and peered down the road. He bolted toward the porch and hurried inside. "Cora, McFadden, and his riders coming down the lane! Hurry now!"

Cora and Maggie reached for shotguns.

"Maggie, he may only be here to talk," Cora said. "So, don't overplay this."

"He's coming with guns, Momma. We can't take chances."

"Just let me do the talking." Cora opened the screen door and walked to the porch as McFadden and his riders lined across the front. The big man sat on his bay horse in the center of his men.

He peered at the ranch owner with a smile. "Good morning, Cora."

"It was."

"Cora, you know why I'm here."

"You're gonna try to bully me into selling again."

"I'm sorry you see it that way.

Woodie Bosworth spotted Sheldon a few feet away, his hand on his gun. He stretched his arm towards his holster and tugged at it.

Nick caught Woodie's maneuver. "Woodie, if you pull that hog leg, I'll kill you where you sit. We're here to talk. Nothing more."

Woodie's face contorted as he shoved his weapon into the holster.

McFadden dismounted and approached the porch as Maggie raised her shotgun at him.

Cora saw Maggie in her peripheral vision. "Put it down, Maggie. We're not starting a fight today."

"But, Momma."

"Put it down."

Maggie lowered the shotgun.

"Thank you, Cora," McFadden said. "You're right. I'm only here to talk. May I come inside and visit with you for a moment?"

Maggie glared at Cora. "You are not gonna bring him into our house, Momma?"

Cora considered the situation, remembering that her late husband, Stuart, would never agree to sell the ranch. Still, she knew McFadden was there, hoping to purchase it. "It's okay, Maggie. Just neighbors talking. Come on in, JA, but just you. I don't have refreshments for all your men."

"Sure, Cora."

McFadden advanced towards the porch, his eyes fixed on Maggie, who stood near the doorway, her gaze reminiscent of bees eager to attack.

"Come in, JA," Cora said. "We'll have some lemonade in the kitchen."

"Lemonade sounds delicious on a warm day like this."

Cora placed her shotgun in the corner and guided McFadden to the kitchen. Maggie trailed close behind, still clinging to the weapon.

"Maggie, pour some lemonade for us all."

Maggie drilled Cora with a deadly stare. "Where is Liza?"

"Liza's busy. Put down the shotgun and pour some refreshments. Now, please."

Fuming, Maggie placed the weapon against the wall behind the kitchen door and strolled toward the pitcher of lemon drink. She then poured it into glasses and put them on the table.

"Okay, Mr. McFadden. You wanted to talk."

"Oh, call me JA, Cora."

Cora disregarded the comment.

"I know this ranch means a lot to you and your family, Cora, though I fear it might overwhelm you going forward, especially after losing your man. A ranch this size takes a lot of work, and for a woman—well, it can't be easy. So, I've decided to up my offer to help you out."

McFadden pulled a piece of paper from a pocket containing a figure and laid it before her. "Right now, the cattle market is good. Beef prices are heading upward, but that may not always be the case. I can offer you this buyout price here and now. If the market falls, however, I'm afraid the price for a buyout would fade too."

Cora gazed at the impressive figure. With this sum, she could compensate the hands, pay her bank debts, and have enough to purchase a small dwelling suitable for her and her children.

Maggie watched from a few paces away as Cora sat silently. "Momma, you're not entertaining this, are you?"

"Maggie, I must think about you and Jeremiah and our future."

"Riverview *is* our future. This is our home. You know Father would *never* sell the ranch under any circumstances."

"Your Father isn't here, Maggie. I am."

"I wonder why?" Maggie needle-stared McFadden, seething as she exited the room.

Cora gazed at the rancher, amazed at the offer. "Look, JA, I'll need time to think this over. But I make no promises except that I will consider it."

"How long, Cora?"

"I can't say. Maybe a few weeks. I want to pray about it and speak with my children."

"Sure, and I'll not pressure you." McFadden stood and turned toward the doorway.

Like you haven't already pressured me, Cora thought. "I'll walk you out."

"No, I can find my way."

Cora watched as the big rancher stepped away from the kitchen. How could she refuse the offer? The future of her children may depend on it. I must pray more this week.

Chapter 16

Jesse and his friends arrived at Fort Gibson, and the soldiers waved them through the gate. Tight security was no longer necessary since most Indians lived on reservations. The one holdout was Geronimo. He refused to comply with the government's program.

Two privates sat mending leather bridles at the main office as they dismounted and approached the porch.

"May I help you?" said one soldier with a coarse beard and hat bent back in the front.

"We're looking for Colonel William Hazen. Someone told us he commanded the Fort."

"Not anymore. Colonel John Coppinger runs things now." He stood from his chair. "I'll get him for you."

As Jesse scanned the area, he noticed a man of Mexican descent approaching. A memory flashed in his mind of a tracker he once knew.

The man gazed at Jesse and grinned. "I know you, but I don't remember your name."

"Jesse Stalls."

"Yes, you rangered with Montgomery and Tom."

"Yes, I did for a while, and so did my friend." Jesse raised a hand toward Eli. "That's Eli Cole."

"I remember now."

"Sacho Ramirez," Eli uttered.

"Eli Cole. It's been a long time. Why are you here?"

"Looking for my son, Samuel," Jesse answered. "He and three friends rode this way looking for jobs at a ranch in Kansas, someplace near Clearwater."

"Clearwater?"

"Do you know where it is?"

"About one hundred eighty miles from here. Clearwater is west of Wichita. But you should see Montgomery and Tom first. The trail leads that way."

"Could you guide us there? I'll pay you."

Sacho rubbed his chin, considering the proposal. "Maybe. I must see the Colonel first. I finished job for Army, and if he has nothing more, I go with you."

Sacho strode toward the door, meeting the Colonel, making his way from inside.

The colonel turned their way, nodding, his gray beard resembling a goat matching his bushy brows. "Gentlemen, my name is Colonel John Coppinger. How can I assist you?

Jesse reached for his hand. "Glad to meet you, sir. I'm Jesse Stalls. I'm searching for my son, Samuel Stalls. He's riding with three cowboys, and I wondered if they may have traveled this way."

The colonel turned to the two privates, who now stood behind him. "Have you men seen this Samuel and his friends?"

The soldier who spoke to Jesse earlier said, "No, sir, not seen them."

"Mr. Stalls—"

"Please, just Jesse,"

"Jesse, I will need some time to ask around the fort. My Sergeant may know more about these men but is away, leading a troop on a training maneuver. Would be my pleasure if you gentlemen could stay the night? There is plenty of room in the old barracks. You may dine with me in two hours."

Jesse gazed at Eli, who shrugged, signifying it did not matter. "Sure, we're weary and hungry."

"Okay then. Return in two hours." He pointed to his privates. "One of you will show these gentlemen to the livery. The other, where they may wash up."

Sacho made his way towards the Colonel. "Sir, if you could be so gracious as to pay me, and if you have nothing else, these men need my services."

"I have nothing at this time, but stay in touch.

Sacho nodded.

"Come inside, and I'll get your pay."

Jesse and the other men found the barracks rudimentary.

"Well, Jesse, it ain't much, but beds are better than sleeping on the ground," Eli uttered.

"Been a while since they used them, but I'm glad the war is over."

"Which war? They still fight the Indians, don't they?"

"Most are on the reservations."

"I read that Geronimo and some of his warriors are not giving up," Eli said. "They want to keep their lands."

"They should surrender."

"You think they'll lose?"

"The government has more men than when General Custer fought Sitting Bull at Little Big Horn. Geronimo will lose."

Eli lay across the bed as Jesse washed in the basin the soldier had brought for them. "What do you think about them forcing the Indians to the reservations?"

"In my opinion, the government did them wrong. The land was theirs first, and our government took it away. The reservations won't provide enough for them. They should have access to buffalo, elk, and deer. Instead, the government supplies the Indians with flour and cornmeal., a little beef occasionally. That's not the life they know."

"I suppose. Guess they want to make them lazy and easy to control."

Jesse heard the knock on the door and grabbed a towel. He wiped his hands and opened it. "Hey, Sacho."

"I will ride with you," Sacho said.

"Okay, we'll ride to Montgomery and Tom's place as you suggested."

"Good. Been a long time for me. Are you hungry?"

"Sure am."

"Follow me."

∗ ∗ ∗

The Colonel's house was roomy and comfortable. Jesse settled on a sturdy wooden chair. Eli and Doc chose a wooden divan.

The door opened to the exterior. A tall man wearing a light gray suit entered the room. He had voluminous white hair and a matching mustache. He examined them briefly and said, "Hello, gentlemen. I'm Colonel William Phillips."

Jesse rose from his chair and walked to him. "Colonel, I'm Jesse Stalls. These are my friends, Eli Cole, Doc, and Sacho."

"Yes, Sacho, I know. Are you here to dine with Colonel Coppinger?"

"Yes."

"Good, then I assure you the meal will be excellent."

"Do you come often to the fort, Colonel?"

"Not as much as I once did. I took a job working for the personal advancement and protection of the Indians, particularly the Cherokee. I was their legal counsel."

"So, you don't work for the government now?"

"No, though Colonel Coppinger and I go way back." The colonel sat down.

"Colonel, what will they do about Geronimo?" asked Eli.

"You haven't heard?"

"I suppose not."

"That Geronimo is a tricky one. The Apache has always been difficult for us. But General Nelson Miles captured him in Arizona. They say the Indian had around one hundred and thirty warriors plus women and children with him. General Miles had him and the warriors captured once before, but Geronimo escaped with forty men. The word is, Miles, his men, and three thousand Mexicans have recaptured him."

"So, where is he now?" Eli asked.

"Close. He's at the Comanche and Kiowa reservation near Fort Sill. Geronimo is too old to fight the government now. He must have decided that fighting would bring harm to his warriors, women, and children."

"He defied them for a long time."

"Twenty years."

A door from the other side of the room opened, and a young soldier appeared. "Supper is ready. Will you follow me?"

"Yes, I'm starving," Eli said.

The room they entered held a spacious wooden table with chairs and a window on the right wall. On the opposite wall was a wooden buffet adorned with an array of food.

Above it hung two black and white photos of former American Presidents James Garfield and Grover Cleveland.

The soldier relayed the message that the Colonel would be there soon but requested that they wait to eat until after the Colonel's prayer. Afterward, they could proceed to the buffet for their food.

"This is a fine setting," Eli said. "I don't remember any of the headquarters in my army days being as nice."

Colonel Phillips stroked his mustache. Since the Indian wars, the government understood they must offer additional benefits to keep their leadership at the forts. So, with the closing of many of the garrisons came better funding for those remaining.

"I believe that," Jesse said. "I raised horses for the army but was told they no longer wanted them at Fort Smith."

"The army will still require horses, but only in certain areas."

"Sounds like what they told me."

"We won't need any here," said Colonel Coppinger, standing in the doorway. "There is an overflow of horses at the fort now. I expect they'll herd some away to another camp soon. Glad you gentlemen could join me." He sat in a chair at the end of the table. "Let's pray so you can gather some food."

Colonel Coppinger removed his hat. "Lord, we are grateful for this beautiful day. We are thankful you have cared for us and these men who have traveled. Thank you for watching over Jesse, his son, and his friends. Bless the food we are about to partake. Amen. Men, line up at the buffet and help yourselves."

After collecting food for their plates, they discussed which forts might need horses. Some spoke about the Indian wars of old. Colonel Coppinger told Jesse there had been no mention of Samuel and his friends coming to the fort.

"I'm sorry to hear that, though I'm not entirely surprised. Samuel's friends might stay clear of the forts and towns."

"Are they running from the law?" asked Colonel Phillips.

"I don't know, but I wonder if they influenced Samuel to leave home."

"Something changes when they run in groups; it always does."

"It's not so awful if you have them nearby to watch, but when they leave home on a long journey—"

"They must grow up, Jesse," replied Colonel Coppinger.

"I know, but it's difficult." Jesse remembered Samuel's love for shooting his gun. His biggest fear would be to learn that Samuel had gotten into a gunfight. "Thank you for the rooms. We'll head out first thing tomorrow."

"Figured you might. Be safe, and I hope you find your son."

"I appreciate that, sir." Jesse gazed at his men. "Well, we better grab some shut-eye, men. We can catch an early start."

Eli rose from his chair. "Not too early, I hope."

"Can't waste daylight."

"I knew you'd say that. I remember how Montgomery always hit the trail when it was still dark. You followed right in his footsteps."

"The cool air keeps your head clear."

"Maybe I don't need it too clear."

"Now, Eli, doesn't this place make you want to join the Army again?"

"Are you kidding, Jesse? I want nothing to do with Army life."

"You still have time to think about it."

"Don't need it."

Jesse snickered. Doc, too, afforded a slight grin as they entered the fort quarters.

Chapter 17

Howdy Millard struggled to maintain his grip on the saddle as the black mare bucked and thrashed inside the small corral. Despite his best efforts, the violent horse contorted and twisted his body like a sheet in the wind. Sweat poured down his face, his muscles straining as he fought to stay on top.

"You got her, Howdy," said Grant Boyd.

The cowboys cheered as Howdy held on to ride the most challenging of the day. Finally, the black mare twisted, catching Howdy unaware and tossing him to the ground. "I'll go again. I won't let her win, fellows."

"Now, Howdy, that was three times," Samuel said. "You'll be stove up tomorrow."

"That doesn't matter. Catch that mare for me."

Samuel tossed the rope over the black horse's head and drew her in.

Howdy inched closer, holding his arm downward, shielding the pain. "Why does bronc busting have to be so frustrating?"

"If you raise them as my pa does, you can bring them on slowly, but taking a green horse from the herd like this is the worst way."

"I get that, but how many times does it take to break one of your pa's horses?"

"Not long, and they don't throw you, hardly ever."

"One day, you'll have to show me."

"I will. Now get on the mare. If you can't break her this time, I will try."

"I got her, Samuel. Hold her steady."

Howdy set a foot in the stirrup and pulled himself up. "Get the rope. I got her."

The mare stood trembling and looking around the ring as Samuel retreated. Howdy spurred her, and she leaped forward, determined to bring him down again.

"You got this, Howdy man," Tye Morgan said. "Last time around."

They watched their friend's willpower win over the black as she calmed and found a gallop. Howdy then offered her the full reins. She took him several rounds inside the corral. He raised his hat, smiling at his friends.

"I knew you could," Samuel said.

"Yeah, this baby's mine," Howdy replied. "Now, you don't have to ride."

Samuel laughed, "I wasn't going to. Just wanted to push you a little."

"I had her. Grant gets the next."

Howdy slowed the mare and brought her to the fence. "Men, I think she's green broke and good for money. Let's unsaddle her." He dismounted and uncinched the saddle, and placed it on the fence. "Here you go, Grant. All yours."

Grant led her to the next corral and loosed the rope to find another.

"Good ride," Samuel said.

"Yeah, it was."

"Howdy, have you been thinking about what you're going to do if there's a range war?"

"There may not be a war."

"Oh, it's coming. You know it is."

"I'll take it one day at a time, Samuel. We're getting paid and so much better than Bartlett offered."

"McFadden doesn't pay enough for killing folks, though, and I think he will ask us to fight for him. You know that, right?"

"I hope not."

"Just seems like things are moving that way. So, remember, I won't fight against them."

"We're counting on you, Samuel. McFadden is counting on you because you're the best gun here."

"This is not my fight. And I can't see that woman selling out, so I'm leaving if McFadden demands any killing."

"But you're the only reason Tye, Grant, and me have jobs."

"McFadden knows now that you men can ride the broncs well. He'll keep you even if I leave."

"But we can't shoot like you. That's why he needs you."

"That's what I'm afraid of, Howdy, and I don't plan to get caught up in his fights."

"Why you——. Some friend you are." Howdy hit Samuel across the face with his fist, knocking him to the ground.

Samuel held his jaw and looked up, shaking his head. "I'm not fighting you either, Howdy. You're my friend."

"Maybe you should think about how you treat your friends."

Tye walked to the fence. "Samuel, I thought you could ride for me."

"You can ride, Tye. You don't need me."

Samuel rose and made his way to the bunkhouse, wondering if the time had come to depart. Perhaps his pa had been right about the gun, knowing it could mean trouble for those at the ranch who can shoot.

What was he doing in Kansas? Nothing had gone as planned. McFadden had surprised them by leading the cowboys to Riverside, though it had revealed that he was breaking broncs for a madman intent on claiming a neighbor's land.

He recalled a scripture in Proverbs he had once memorized. *He that is greedy of gain troubleth his own house; but he that hateth gifts shall live.*

His pa had told him never to be greedy for gain, no matter where life took him. At least he did not spend his money on whiskey like the other cowboys.

McFadden paid well, but how could he leave his friends? Would the rancher even allow him to go without a fight? How did he get into this mess?

He could sense his pa's anger for leaving home. With all the horses to break, Jesse needed Samuel's help to pay off the loan, but here he was in Kansas.

What had he done? What if his pa lost the ranch to the bank? He had created this outcome and now might have to turn against his friends. Still, he had not traveled all this way to engage in a senseless conflict. He must refuse to take the life of someone he didn't know.

Inside the bunkhouse was empty. Sitting on the bed, he remembered the Bible in his saddle bags. Retrieving it, he read for a time.

Maybe things would not be so bad if I had stayed close to the Lord. He lay the Bible on the bed and prayed until he knew God had heard him.

Chapter 18

Dust rolled through Clearwater as the townsfolk stirred about. Cora and several hands worked outside the general store, loading the wagon with supplies. Maggie stood beside them on the porch, hoping for time to visit the dress shop.

Cora walked from inside the general store. "Sheldon, how much more?"

"Three bags of corn and a bag of flour," Sheldon replied.

"When you finish here, take the wagon home and unload. Then, come back in a while and pick us up. Maggie and I are going to the dress shop. Take Jeremiah with you."

"Yes, ma'am."

The sound of hooves rumbled in the street as McFadden and his men rode up.

Sheldon saw the riders. "I suppose I need to hurry."

McFadden spotted Cora and reined his horse toward the general store.

"No, hold up, Sheldon," Cora said, watching the big rancher heading her way.

"Hello, Cora. Fancy seeing you here in town."

"Gotta get supplies, JA."

"Have you thought about my offer?" McFadden said, excitement brimming in his eyes. "I think it's fair."

"Yes, JA, I have, and spent considerable time praying about it."

"So, can you give me an answer?"

"I have to turn down your offer. My mind went back to Stuart and all the hours he spent working, clearing trees and stumps, putting up fences, and bringing in cattle to get started. Stuart would never sell to you or anyone else, nor should I. We'll continue to work and build Riverview so my children one day have a place they can live and work."

Samuel watched from his horse as McFadden looked on nearby, bearing a disappointed look, listening as the ranch lady turned him down.

Beside The Riverview owner stood a pretty young woman about Samuel's age with brown hair, wearing a light blue dress.

Maggie gazed at Samuel and offered a faint smile, then turned again to the confrontation between her Momma and McFadden.

Disappointed with Cora's response, the big rancher leaned forward in his saddle. "I'm not happy, Cora. The offer I made was more than enough. You should think about taking it."

"I can't, McFadden. I have my children to think about and my workers."

"We will take care of your workers."

"JA, how often do I say no before you understand? I don't want to sell Riverview!"

McFadden's gaze sharpened, and his mouth took a stiff slant. "Cora, I will have water for my cattle. I've given you sufficient time."

"I've told you that you can bring your cattle to my part of the river any time. There's plenty of water for us both."

"I can't trust that and have too much invested in my herd to lean on anyone's word."

"JA, did you come especially to taunt me? My family, my men, and I came to town for supplies, and now you ride in and ruin my day."

"Cora, I wouldn't have to be disrespectful if you accepted my offer. Now that you have turned me down, I'll remind you that accidents can happen on ranches. Stampedes occur, and lightning fires often start in fields."

"That's enough!" Sheldon said. "Cora has told you no, and that's final."

McFadden stared at the foreman. "Cora, do you always allow your foreman to butt into negotiations?"

"Sheldon has only repeated what I said."

McFadden scowled, offering a grunt. "Be careful, Cora." He reined his horse from the store, and his men turned to follow him.

Samuel held his eyes on the young woman, who again returned the gaze.

"Are you still going dress shopping, Cora?" asked Sheldon.

"Yes. I'm not letting that man change how I live. Get back here in about an hour."

* * *

Several of the dresses Cora saw were perfect.

The owner, Lolla Tate, brought another, a blue one with a lace collar. "Cora, here's one more. Someone left it outside the fitting room earlier."

"Yes, it's nice. Hang it there, and I'll look at it." Cora spun, searching for Maggie. *What is she looking at?* She hooked a dress on the rack and walked toward Maggie, who stared outside through the window.

Cora turned to look. A young cowboy stood outside the barbershop waiting for some of his friends. "That's one of McFadden's men, Maggie. Looks like one of those gunslingers folks say he's hired."

"He smiled at me. I don't think he's a gunman. How can a man so considerate be a killer?"

"Maggie, haven't you noticed how McFadden can put on thoughtfulness, but everyone knows you can't trust him?"

"But Momma, I don't have any friends."

"Don't you mean young men?"

Maggie turned to her, face reddened, "I don't have any girlfriends either. Living at the ranch keeps me from seeing those my age."

"I know, but we can't drive the wagon to town every day. Remember, Clearwater could not keep a teacher, or you'd have met more young men and women."

"And what about those living on the ranches? They have no friends either."

Cora understood the emptiness in Maggie's life. Her parents never allowed her to socialize with children her age. The work at the home ranch always came before education. She peered through the window once more at the gunman. "I'm sorry, Maggie. You'll meet the perfect young gentleman someday, but please forget those kinds of men. They will only bring you heartache. Did you try those dresses on?"

"I was going to, but—"

"Go on now. You need clothes."

Maggie turned from the window and picked up two dresses Lolla Tate had found for her. As Maggie walked toward the fitting room, Cora stared through the glass at the young men across the street, locating the one Maggie seemed drawn to. He wore a faded orange shirt and a leather vest and was clean-shaven. He stood with the other ranch hands with fresh haircuts, wearing a new Stetson hat, laughing and jibing with the others. The young man *was* nice-looking, but the gun on his hip concerned her most. Her daughter had no business having an interest in him.

She watched as McFadden rode by the barbershop, spouting orders. The young cowboys raced for their horses and mounted to follow him out of town.

Cora observed until the last of the dust settled. *That man better not cause us trouble. If so, he will see something he does not expect.*

Chapter 19

The gray horse reared as Samuel and his friends worked a rope over his head. Since hiring to work broncs, they had not seen such a strong-willed horse.

Howard tossed the lariat again, and it found the mark. "Someone put another on him."

"I got it," Tye said as he released the rope into the air, the hoop wrapping the neck of the gray.

"Pull him through the gate, and I'll saddle him," Samuel said.

As they worked to drag the belligerent horse into the corral, Nick jumped onto the fence. "Hey, Samuel, the boss wants to see you."

"Now?"

"Yeah, you better get up there."

Samuel dusted his hat against the side of his leg and walked through the gate. "I'll be back as soon as I can, Howdy."

Howdy and the other men watched as Samuel made his way to the ranch house.

"I wonder what that's about?" Grant asked.

"That's none of our business," Nick replied as he observed them wrestling with the horse. "Ya'll can work without Samuel for a while."

"No problem," Howdy said.

***

Knotty pine covered the walls and ceiling inside the ranch house. Samuel sat where the butler named Jose had suggested he wait for McFadden.

"You seem lost," came a voice from a hallway.

A young woman in a lacy gown with dark hair stood smiling. "My name is Jenny. I know all of my father's hands, and none are as pretty as you."

Samuel blushed. "You're the boss's daughter?"

"All my life, and that's a good name for him. Boss. He does boss folks around, even me."

Samuel searched for words. An unexpected meeting with the daughter of the man who hired him might cause a snag if mishandled, her wearing a nightgown. "I'm sorry, ma'am."

"Jenny, leave the young cowboy alone and get to your room. Don't you need to put on different clothes?"

Jenny turned to see her father coming down the hall behind her. "I suppose, Boss." She imparted a playful grin as she passed him and walked toward the stairway.

McFadden watched her for a moment before turning to the study. "Come in, Samuel. We'll talk."

Like the other areas of the ranch house, knotty pine decorated the study wall. A large desk sat by a window matching the wall of bookshelves filled with novels and other reading material.

The big man shuffled and sat in his desk chair. "Have a seat, Samuel."

A large chair sat in front of the desk. Samuel took a seat facing the rancher, wondering why they made him leave work.

"I'm sorry to pull you away from the broncs, Samuel. You know, it's great to have a good man like yourself working around the place. Nick tells me you are one of the hardest workers on the payroll."

"Thank you, I suppose. My pa raised me working hard."

"Yes, I'm sure he did. But listen, I brought you here for another reason. I guess you could say I'm saddened and disappointed that Cora did not accept my offer, and I need that water for the cows."

Samuel recalled the woman had told McFadden he could have all the water he needed for his cattle, so why the deception? Why did he not trust her word? Was there something about Cora Rivers he was unaware of? During their conversation at Clearwater, she seemed willing to work with the rancher, except for selling the ranch. "I understand, sir."

"Sometimes you must apply the right pressure so things turn your way. Often, you must dabble profoundly into the enemy's life to understand what hurts them and what turns their minds to think as you do."

Does he mean Cora Rivers?

"Samuel, you're a smart young man. When you first hired on, you sensed the importance of shooting firearms as part of my crew, right?"

Samuel recalled the day they rode in, the bronc riding, and how McFadden observed as they fired their weapons. Was it all for this moment? "I think so, sir."

"Every good ranch has a lead man, like Nick, who can distribute orders and assign the men their duties. But what if someone removed the lead man? What if an accident took

109

them out? If a ranch loses its leadership, it can fall into disarray." He paused, waiting for Samuel's response.

"Sir, are you asking me to murder Cora Rivers' foreman?"

"The man interfered with my conversation with Cora. But let's not use the word murder. What if Riverview's foreman somehow disappeared, or they had discovered him departed at Cora's place?"

"Sir, when my friends and I rode to your ranch, we came to find jobs. Bronc busting jobs. We never hired on to kill."

"Samuel, do you recall I told you we must protect ourselves and this ranch? Now, there is a threat to my cattle, so we must take drastic measures."

"I'm not a gunhand, sir, and neither are my friends. We'll shoot in self-defense but not for outright murder."

"But Samuel, I will offer a thousand dollars for this job. Taking out Cora's foreman might be all that is needed to change her mind. Don't you need some extra money?"

"That's a lot of money, but my parents did not raise me to avenge someone else's troubles, or even my own," Samuel remembered Grant mentioning the idea of cattle rustling, but even then, they never spoke of killing folks. "Maybe one of your other men would do the job for you. I'll bust your broncs, sir, but I won't kill for you."

McFadden drew a deep breath, mouth thinning, and rose from his chair. "Get back to work, and remember, you men are on thin ice."

As Samuel stood to leave, the rancher crossed his arms and turned, staring out the window.

The young cowboy left the ranch house through the foyer, pondering if he had caused him and his friends to lose their jobs.

Tye had mounted a buckskin mare when Samuel reached the corral.

Howdy spotted Samuel from inside the pen and rushed to him. "Samuel, what's going on?"

Samuel wondered if he should keep McFadden's request from his friends. After all, the rancher did not fire him. But these were his friends, and they had a right to know. "He wanted me to take out Cora Rivers' foreman."

"Murder him?"

"That's what he said."

"Are you going to?" Howdy asked.

"No."

Grant overheard them from a distance. "Did he offer money?"

"He said he'd pay me a thousand dollars."

"You turned him down, as good as you are with a gun?"

"Grant, I'm not a gunhand."

"But that's a thousand dollars!"

"Samuel is no killer," Howard said.

"That doesn't matter. I heard some of those other men talking, and they say there's not much law around here. McFadden gets by with what he wants. No lawman would ever come for you."

"I will not murder a man for McFadden," Samuel said.

"Do you think he'll offer that money to me?" Grant asked.

"Grant, have you ever killed a man?" Samuel asked.

"No, but it can't be all that hard. Have you?"

"No, I haven't, but my pa has. He said killing a man in a gunfight was the hardest thing he'd ever done. That man's death haunted Pa for years. I'm not sure he's over it yet."

Howard saw the foreman coming from the ranch house. "Heads up, men. Nick is coming to give orders."

Nick stepped up near them. "You men can't break horses huddle at the corral fence. So let's get to work. Samuel, the boss, wants to see you again."

Howdy jumped from the fence. "Good luck, Samuel."

Samuel did not believe in luck but knew God would be with him if he stood by his morals. He dropped from the fence and walked toward the ranch house.

GUNFIGHTER

Chapter 20

As the sun rose, a group of birds sang nearby, causing Samuel's horse, Sadie, to let out a whinny, waking him from slumber. Samuel shifted his head on the saddle, trying to catch a few more moments of rest as Sadie pawed the ground.

"Sadie, why can't you let me sleep?"

The mare, hearing Samuel was awake, pawed again.

"I suppose you want water. You better be glad I brought you a little grain from McFadden's. That much he owed me since shorting me on pay."

The young cowboy sat up on his blanket, questioning whether he should have done what McFadden asked. The money would have helped, and he would still have a job. But he remembered his Momma told him life was precious to God and that it was his place to decide when folks head for eternity.

"I feel lost out here, Sadie." He rose from the ground. "I'm not sure if anyone owns this property or if it's government land."

Sadie softly nickered when Samuel untied her and led her to the creek.

"What am I going to do, girl? I suppose there are other ranches around I could try. Or maybe I should ride to that ranch where Pa's ranger friends live. They might have work."

Sadie took in some water and raised her head.

"All I know is, I'm in Kansas and know very few people. McFadden shorted me on pay, but I have spent none from earlier paydays. Still, it won't last long."

He stood next to the mare, thinking about the day he left home. He nor his companions had prepared well for the journey to Kansas, and now he was alone.

His Pa was in a fit of anger, so it seemed like the right time. But peering around, stranded in an unfamiliar land with limited means, made him realize the foolishness of his decision.

After leading Sadie back to the trees, he gathered dry branches for the fire.

I better find food.

He pulled his rifle from the scabbard and turned into the woods. A light breeze stirred the leaves on the trees as he walked, searching for a game trail. A gray squirrel crossed his path, scampered up a tree, and bounced to the next. *Too bad.*

Not far away, a rabbit skipped across the trail. Samuel slowed his pace, minimizing the noise, his eyes peeled for movement. *Where did you run to?*

Pausing, he watched for the rabbit to advance from behind the briars. A motion soon caught his attention as the rabbit bounced again into the path. He lifted the rifle and aimed.

A shot rang out. Into his shoulder a bullet lodged, sending him crashing to the ground, the impact causing his rifle to deposit beneath a group of small samplings several feet away. *McFadden has sent someone for me.*

The sound of approaching footsteps set his heart racing, with the dense woods hindering his vision. Who was coming towards him?

The young cowboy searched for his rifle, but it had tumbled too far away, and his gunbelt lay beside his saddle at the camp. In excruciating pain and eager to defend himself, he strained to get up without success.

The sound of branches snapping grew louder, and he lay helpless and vulnerable. He supposed they would kill him now that he was defenseless.

He looked up as the noise of footsteps diminished to find a young woman standing over him, holding a rifle. He knew then McFadden had hired a woman to take him out.

Her piercing blue eyes glared at his vulnerability. He couldn't shake the familiar feeling as he gazed back at her face. Where had he seen her?

"You're on my land," she uttered.

"I...I...didn't—" Haziness fell over Samuel, clouding his judgment and vision. Something was wrong. *Was he dying?* Fear gripped him as he struggled for consciousness. And then everything went dark.

"I suppose you're gonna die," Maggie said. "Serves you right for being on our land. We can't have McFadden's men snooping around trying to kill my Momma. I hope you live, cowboy, but if you don't—I'm sorry."

The young woman turned and walked away, pausing when she reached her horse. "Shoot! If I don't do something for him, Momma will be angry." She untied her horse's reins and turned to lead it back to the cowboy.

She sighed as she gazed at him lying on the ground. "You are a beautiful man, and it's such a shame you work for a tyrant. I'll try to get you back to the ranch, though it could make things worse moving you."

After finding his horse, she ripped his shirt at the sleeve and wrapped a bandage she pulled from inside her saddlebags over the wound to slow the bleeding. *Maybe I can rouse you.*

"Hey, pardner, can you wake up?" She shook him forcefully. "Come on, wake up. I'm not strong enough to hoist you into the saddle."

Samuel's eyelids parted, and he stared at her, confused.

"Can you help me? Hold my hands and pull up."

Shaking and weak, Samuel reached for her hands.

"Hold there. I'll pull." With all of Maggie's strength, she heaved until he stood.

"Now comes the hard part. Take hold of the saddle horn and pull as I push."

His mind fixated on her, pondering what had happened. "You shot me."

Maggie peered into his face. "Um, I know this is tough, cowboy, but you can do it."

He reached for the saddle horn and tugged as she grasped his legs, lifting him to the seat. She put his feet in the stirrups to steady him. After tying him to the saddle and gathering his guns and belongings, she mounted and started for the ranch, leading Samuel's horse.

Chapter 21

Awooden cross hung on the wall, and a vase of flowers sat on the oak buffet as Samuel peered from the bed. *How did I get here?*

He turned to get up, but an odd surge of pain shot through his right shoulder, forcing him back to the soft bed. Something had happened, he recalled. *I was hunting. Someone shot me—a woman.*

He gazed at a doorway and spotted a young man about fifteen years old staring. "Wait," Samuel said as the boy turned and walked away.

I have to get up from this bed. He pushed off with his good arm until he sat on the edge, feet dangling from the single mattress.

"Hey you," came a voice. A woman with reddish brown hair stood watching from the doorway. "You be careful there. You might pull open that wound. Are you hungry?"

Samuel gazed at her with furrowed brows. "Some woman shot me. Was that you?"

The woman sighed and pursed her lips. "That was my daughter, Maggie. She caught you on our property and took it on herself to get you off."

"By shooting me?"

"I'm sorry. I'm afraid Maggie gets overzealous sometimes, but we are dealing with unwanted trouble around here, and even my men are on edge."

"I see."

"My daughter believes you work for a neighboring ranch owned by JA McFadden. Is she right?" Cora knew he did because she saw him with McFadden's men in town.

"I did, yes."

"Explain yourself, cowboy. Why you were on our land?"

"First off, I didn't know I was on your land. I thought maybe I was still on McFadden's property. I'm not from around here. Rode here a couple of months ago for a job busting broncs."

"Yeah, I hear McFadden's been hoarding the sales of horses to the army, though these days, ain't much. I figure he knows someone high up. But you still haven't told me what your business was here."

"He came here to kill you, Momma," Maggie said, standing behind Cora.

"Is that right, young man? Did you come to murder me?"

"No, ma'am. I no longer work for McFadden. The truth is, he asked me to do some things I refused to do. When I turned him down, he fired me."

Cora walked closer to the bed. "What things did he ask of you?"

"Ma'am, I'd rather not get into that. I *can* tell you that the man has no morals."

"I know that."

"Momma, what if he's lying and McFadden *has* sent him? What if he's telling us McFadden fired him so he can get close and kill you? That old man would love nothing more than to claim Riverview. I should have left him to die."

119

Cora peered into Samuel's eyes. "I don't think McFadden would send him to get shot. Son, are you being truthful about everything?"

"Yes, ma'am. My pa owns a ranch back in Arkansas, though not large like those around here. I told you why I came to Kansas."

"Okay, maybe I believe you, but I bet there's more reason than bronc busting *why* you left Arkansas—probably running from something. Do you have a name?"

"Samuel Stalls."

"I'm Cora Rivers, and this is my daughter, Maggie. I think you met my son Jeremiah, the shy one. I asked if you were hungry, but you wanted to talk about getting shot. Are you ready for food now?"

"Sure, I'm starving. Ma'am, thanks for doctoring my shoulder."

"That's the least we can do since we were the ones who put a bullet in you. Or my daughter Maggie was. She will help you to the table."

Maggie shot Cora a stern look. "Momma, why me?"

"Wasn't it you who shot Samuel?"

Maggie's chest rose as she took a deep breath and released it, stepping toward Samuel to put out her arms. "Grab hold, and I'll help you stand."

"Seems I remember you saying that once before."

"Yeah, almost left you there."

Samuel took her hands and stood. "I'm glad you didn't."

"I hope I don't live to regret it." She held to his arm.

"I'm shaky."

"You're weak, but you'll get better. Hold on, and we'll walk to the kitchen."

When they reached the kitchen, a Spanish woman helped Maggie to guide him to the table.

"Liza is our cook," Maggie said.

"I have some soup for you, sir, and some cornbread," Liza said."

"Do you have water? I'm parched."

"We tried to give you water when I got you to the ranch, but you were unconscious."

"How did you—"

"—lift you on a horse? I didn't. You helped me."

"Thank you."

Maggie sat in a chair beside Samuel as Liza set the food on the table. "I'm sorry I shot you. McFadden has threatened us lately. Momma is right that we are on edge, expecting almost anything from that man."

"He wanted me to kill your foreman."

"Sheldon? Why?"

"The way he put it, taking out someone who is a leader would hurt your mom. He thought his death might cause her to accept his offer. I heard most of what they said in Clearwater that day and how your Momma turned him down."

"You said McFadden let you go. So you turned him down and kept working for him?"

"I had already decided to leave him as soon as possible, but I needed the money. I don't know anyone in Kansas."

"I brought back both your guns. One a rifle, the other the kind those who kill wear."

Samuel took a drink of water and set down the glass. "I'm not a gunslinger. My gun is for protection."

In town, Maggie had seen the young cowboy, but she didn't realize he was the one on their land until after she shot him. Finding someone camped on their place had stirred a wave of anger with McFadden pressing on them. "Why don't you stay and work for us? We always need cowhands. You said you hired on to McFadden's to break horses. Well, we're about cattle mostly, but we have some horses. I'm sure Sheldon could use a good rider."

He took a few spoonfuls of soup. "Shouldn't you speak with your Momma first?"

"I will, but she'll agree." Maggie smiled, and Samuel saw how beautiful she was.

"I'll consider it."

"That's great. For now, you can stay in the bedroom while you heal."

He took several more bites and then put the spoon down. "Tell me more about Riverview."

"Sure," She told him about the cattle, the hands who worked at the ranch, and how her father had built Riverside before he died. Then she explained why she thought McFadden had her father killed.

As he listened, he soon realized Riverside was such a contrast to McFadden's ranch. Working at a place like this was a privilege.

After Samuel finished his meal, Maggie walked him to the porch. He peered around, and then they sat and talked for hours.

"I think maybe I should lie down a while," Samuel said.

"Sure. I've kept you out here too long."

She helped him from the chair. "You know, shooting you might be a good thing for Riverview."

"How do you figure?"

"Because we get a fine-looking, working cowboy and leave McFadden short of one."

They went inside and walked toward the bedroom so Samuel could rest.

"McFadden won't miss me."

"Well, we got you now. I'll speak with Momma, and if I have my way, we'll keep you around."

"I hope your Momma sees me as you do."

Maggie half grinned. "Me too."

Chapter 22

The rolling green hills reminded Jesse they were close to the ranch. Eli found the wagon road, and they took it north.

"I remember this area," Jesse said. "Montgomery and Tom's place is just ahead."

"Yeah, those large trees near the roadside, too," Eli replied.

Beyond the group of trees, cattle grazed in the field.

"Are you men ready to rest?" Jesse asked. "We're on Montgomery and Tom's land."

"I'm hungry," Doc said.

"I'll bet Samantha can still cook some fine food," Eli replied.

"I sure hope so."

As they came to the barn, they spotted two elderly cowboys struggling to put shoes on a horse. One man hammered the nail to the shoe, then raised and watched them go by.

"I see Monty got someone else to shoe those horses," Eli said.

Jesse peered around the area. "I wonder where he is."

The riders halted at the hitching rail beyond the barn and dismounted.

Doc bent over, stretching his back. "That last leg seemed long.

"My backside's numb," said Eli.

Sacho smiled. "You cowboys, weak. You need ride more."

Jesse spotted a man coming through a corral gate toward them. When he drew closer, Jesse realized it was Tom, but he seemed unsure about them.

"Who are you, and what do you want?" Tom asked.

"You don't remember us?" Jesse asked.

Tom took several more steps and smiled. "Oh, my goodness. Jesse Stalls, and there's Eli Cole. What are you men doing here?"

Jesse reached for his hand. "Rode this way, searching for someone. Where is Montgomery? He hasn't died, has he?"

"Now Jesse, you know Monty's too ornery to kick over. But I lost my Thelma."

"I'm so sorry, Tom. You folks were like family to me."

"Same here," Eli said.

"Tom, you know this other gentleman, I believe." Jesse pointed to Sacho.

Tom's eyes widened. "My tracker, Sacho. I suppose it's been fifteen years or so now." He reached and grabbed Sacho and hugged him. "This man saved my bottom side many times."

"We ran across Sacho at Fort Gibson," Jesse said.

"So, you're still tracking for the army."

"Not much these days, but Jesse bring me along," Sacho said.

Eli pointed to Doc. "This is my friend, Doc. We joined because we were both in the war. We came along to help Jesse."

"So what dangerous man are you chasing, Jesse?" Tom asked.

"My son Samuel and I hope he's not in trouble. He left home angry over a horse. Word has it, he and three of his friends came to Kansas to find work bronc riding at a place near Clearwater."

"Clearwater? That's a long way west from here."

"I know, but there was a chance Samuel came this way. So, we thought, why not come to see you folks? Now, where's Montgomery?"

"Monty and another one of the hands took the wagon to Humboldt for supplies. I expect them back within the hour."

"I remember that trip. I hope the road is better these days."

"Let's go inside, fellows. I'll bet Elizabeth doesn't know you're here."

Tom led the men inside the ranch house, then left them to search for Elizabeth. Moments later, he returned. "I don't know where she is."

"Would any of you like to clean up? I can take you to your rooms and show you where the water pump is."

"I sleep in barn," Sacho said. "Never good sleeping inside."

Tom laughed. "I remember. Jesse, I'll put you by yourself. Eli, you'll have to bunk with your friend."

Tom led them upstairs and pointed to a hand pump with a drain they had added in the hall.

"When you said water pump, I didn't understand," Jesse said.

"Well, there's no heated water, but right there—" He pointed to a wood cook stove at the other end. "We can fire that thing up and heat a few big pots when you're ready. Thelma and Elizabeth wanted it for our guests. Jesse, I believe they hoped you and Hanna would visit, and maybe Eli. I heard them talk about you maybe bringing your children."

"Sorry," Jesse said. "For sure, Hanna and I have been busy raising a family but have spent a lot of time building our ranch."

"I stayed in Texas for a while after I left here," Eli said.

"Oh, they understood. They just hoped."

"Tom, is that you upstairs?" came a voice from below.

"Elizabeth," Tom said. "Yes, I'm up here with some friends. Come on up."

Elizabeth rushed up the staircase with curiosity, and then she saw them. "Eli and Jesse. I can't believe it. I'm so glad you are here. Monty will be happy to see you both." She turned to the other man. "I don't know this gentleman."

"His name is Doc," Eli said. "Doc's a good friend of mine."

"I'm glad you're here. Montgomery will be thrilled. We don't get a lot of company out here on the plains."

"I tried to find you, Elizabeth," Tom said.

"I was in the woods on the other side of the pasture, picking blackberries. I'll head downstairs and help Samantha. We will start work on supper."

"Samantha still works for you?" Eli asked.

"Oh, yes. We couldn't do without Samantha." Elizabeth noticed Eli's eyes brighten and remembered his infatuation with Samantha before. "Eli, Samantha married Garcia several years ago."

He gazed at the floor. "I didn't know. Garcia is a good man, and I'm sure they are happy."

"Montgomery should be home soon, and he'll be hungry. Do any of you like blackberry cobbler?"

"Oh, yes, Mrs. Roe, it's been a long time since I've had me some of Samantha's cobbler," said Eli. "I bet it's still good."

"It is. We'll make two."

Elizabeth reached the bottom of the stairs, and the outside door slammed.

"Elizabeth, I saw several horses tied." Montgomery gazed around the room.

She pointed upstairs. "Jesse and Eli. They are here."

"Just now, in the barn hallway, I thought I saw Sacho, our old tracker."

"You did," Tom hollered from the top of the stairs. "Sacho will stay outdoors as usual."

"Get up there, Monty, and see them," Elizabeth said. "They are just cleaning off the dust before supper."

Montgomery met Jesse at the top of the stairs and hugged him. "Been a long while, Jesse."

"Yes, it has."

"Have you washed?"

"No, I'm waiting for Eli."

"If I remember right, that might be a long wait."

"I know."

"Come with me to the barn while they finish up. I want to show you a colt."

"Sure."

Jesse followed Montgomery outside to the barn.

"Ransom, aren't you and Wes about done with that gelding?" Montgomery said.

"We got one more shoe."

Montgomery shook his head as they walked inside.

"Those two are slow shoeing horses, aren't they?" Jesse commented.

"They're old. Shoeing doesn't get fast around here. I could use a hand catching up on that job."

Maybe I'll have time before leaving."

"When will that be, Jesse?"

"I don't know for sure. Maybe the day after tomorrow."

"Hmm. Come here and look this filly colt over. Black as an ace of spades but intelligent as ever. I call her Ebony. I've been leading her around for six months and am almost ready to set a saddle on her."

"You've taken up some of my training methods?"

"I saw how it worked when you were here. That's all we do here now."

"If she works out for you, I'd love to have a colt out of her, depending on who the father is."

"Do you remember old Buck?"

"Sure, that bay we broke before I left."

"Buck was the best cattle horse I ever owned. I don't ride him anymore because of his age, but he sired some fine stock. I kept a stud named Chance from him. He's worked out to be a fine stock horse as well. Chance will be the father."

"Would you allow me to buy the first yearling from her?"

"Sure, Jesse, but it may be two years before I breed her."

"Okay. Sounds like she's worth the wait."

"That first colt is yours after weaning. Now let's go inside and see how long until supper." They started walking toward the ranch house.

"If your men help, I'll take on that shoeing first thing tomorrow," Jesse said.

"That's a deal. Now, tell me why you're *really* here. You showing up with Eli, Sacho, and that other man says it's for something more important than shoeing horses."

"That's a long story," Jesse said. "I'll share it at supper time."

"Sounds good, Jesse. It's just good to have you here again."

Chapter 23

Nick waited two hours after the lamps went out inside the bunkhouse, making sure everyone was asleep. He eased from the bunk, slipped on his boots, and walked outside.

Through the darkness, he strolled until he reached the storage shed behind the main house. As he approached, he saw the faint light shining through the crack around the door and opened it. "Sorry, I'm late."

"I waited for you, cowboy," Jenny said, reaching out and kissing him. "I missed you."

"I missed you too. Those men stay awake, playing poker and oiling their saddles. Makes it hard to get away."

"You're here now, and we can have some fun."

"Not tonight, Jenny. I don't have long."

"Why not?"

"I gotta get up early. We're moving the large herd to water tomorrow, and they need me to ramrod things."

"This won't take long, Nick. Just for a little while."

"Please, Jenny. Can you wait?"

"If you're not willing to take care of my needs, maybe I should talk to another one of those cowboys, like that new man, Samuel."

"Samuel left us."

"When?"

"Several days ago. Your father asked him to kill one of Riverview's men, and he refused."

"Ugh, here we go again!"

"What do you mean?"

Jenny hesitated to share her father's experiences. Giving this story to Nick could backfire and affect her relationship with her father. However, if she and Nick were to become closer, she must learn to trust him. "I'm not sure I should say."

"Come on. I need to know what to expect."

Jenny gazed at the door. "Well, alright. In Texas, we had a cattle ranch. The ranch grew, and Father brought in more cattle and soon needed more water."

"So, he wanted more land to have more water?"

"Yes, in Texas, the rivers get low in the summer, and some turn so muddy the cattle have nothing to drink."

"So water was an excuse to buy up land?"

"That's what he wants with Riverside, isn't it, Nick?"

Nick nodded. "That's why he's trying out the new men with their weapons. He's looking for gunhands."

"That's my father. Something happened in Texas that he doesn't know I know. One of the hands told me the other big ranchers caught up with him in an alley."

"They beat him up?"

"Nothing like that, but they warned him they were onto his plan. They told him trouble was coming for him if he didn't stop buying up the small ranches. Those ranchers had cattle hands who could shoot guns well. I believe those threats changed Father. After that, I would see him sitting nervously at his desk, reviewing his books. I also remember that he sent the foreman to the telegraph office. He never explained why, but a few weeks later, a man showed up at the ranch. Even I knew what he came for, just looking at him and his gun." She paused. Her father would be so angry if he knew she had told Nick.

"So, what happened?"

"Maybe I shouldn't say more. Father will be upset if he finds out."

"Jenny, I won't tell him. You can't say what you already have without telling it all. I'm foreman here, and that's a reason for giving me the background so I can make the right decisions."

Perhaps she could use it to her advantage. "We moved and bought this land."

Nick could sense there was more. "What else? What happened before you came here?"

"Those ranchers, they pulled their workers away and formed an army. They came to the ranch, demanding we leave. Father said he wasn't going anywhere and brought out his gunhand. He made no difference. They shoved their way inside past our men, took our clothes and a few pieces of furniture—maybe enough to fill two wagons—and tossed it all on the ground and set the barn and the house on fire. They waited until the fire took over everything before leaving, though with a warning. They said they would hang Father if he didn't leave within the next two days. So Father loaded our things—what didn't burn—on a wagon and hired some of our men to drive the cattle north until he found this place."

"That's going to happen here, too. When it does, I'll have no job."

"Then let's leave, Nick."

"Leave and go where?"

"You'll find work somewhere. You need to get out from under my father, and I want to go with you."

Jenny had been a pleasant companion for Nick, but the idea of living together had never crossed his mind. He acknowledged her insight about her father's ways, admitting he had never worked for a rancher having such intense conflict with a neighboring rancher.

"Nick, Father's behavior has changed since that day in Texas, and we don't get along. He is cruel and cold-hearted towards me and others. My guess is he will find more gunfighters to do what he can't do."

"Yeah, to kill Cora Rivers to get her land cheap."

Jenny moved closer and wrapped her arms around Nick's body. "Let's leave before he starts a war."

Nick considered her words. Indeed, McFadden was bound for a range war. He debated leaving the next day, but paydays would vanish if he did. Still, how long could he give out the big rancher's orders, knowing they might lead to good men dying? He must wait until after payday.

What about Jenny? Was there genuine love between them, or was their moments together simply a good time? Taking her along would mean providing for her, and he knew McFadden would not support his daughter leaving.

"I got to wait until after payday. Nothing is certain, but I'll think it over. Goodnight, now kiss me."

"Goodnight?" Jenny frowned. "I need you, Nick."

"I told you I had to get up early."

"Tomorrow night, then?"

"Maybe." Nick turned to exit the shed.

"You better be here."

Chapter 24

Montgomery opened the corral gate, and in ran a feisty chestnut mare. He whirled the rope, creating a distinct swishing sound, forcing the mare around the pen. After multiple times, he halted the exercise. "Jesse, are you sure about this? She's spirited."

"I'll give her a go." Jesse dropped from the fence with a lariat in hand and tossed it over the chestnut's head. "Come here, girl. We're going to go easy on you today and get things going. Monty can take it from here."

He moved nearer and pulled her his way, assuring her his intentions were not harmful. He ran his hand gently over her coat. After a while, he slipped the lariat off her head and stepped away.

Eli, Doc, Garcia, Tom, and Montgomery sat watching Jesse as he twirled the lariat, forcing the mare around the pen.

"Jesse didn't train his horses this way," Doc said.

"That was because the buyer rushed him, and Jesse needed the money," Eli said. "But this is his favorite way. Just watch. Jesse has a way with horses like no one I've seen. He may stop here in a moment to see how she responds. If she doesn't do what he wants, he'll set her to running again."

"But how does this help when you have to saddle her?"

"He wants her trust. Once he gets her to that point, the saddle and bridle is a breeze."

After a long time, Jesse lowered the rope and walked to the center of the corral as the mare continued to gallop. When she saw he stood unmoving, she decelerated, panting to catch her breath, watching him as she came to a standstill.

The mare observed him momentarily and then, letting out a soft whinny, calmly ambled closer and stood behind him.

Jesse turned and rubbed her face and the side of her neck. "See, that wasn't so hard."

Montgomery dropped inside the corral and moved closer to them. "Do you think she'll remember this when you're gone?"

"She has to, Monty. If you're the one who plans to train her, she has to trust you. Be patient, and it will work."

Harry Dacota and Miguel Lopez rode in from the field and saw them at the corral.

Tom heard them ride up and turned.

"Tom, riders came through looking over the herd," Harry said.

"Are they still there?"

"They left but—"

"But what?"

The others had gathered, overhearing them.

"They are not cattlemen."

"Why do you say that?"

"The fancy rigs on their horses and fine outfits."

"Gunfighters?"

"They asked questions." Harry looked at Jesse. "They wanted to know how far to Clearwater. Said they were looking for jobs busting broncs at JA McFadden Ranch."

Jesse shook his head. "Samuel. I knew it was a terrible idea for him to come this way."

Tom turned to Jesse. "You don't know they want anything but jobs breaking horses. Don't let this get you down."

"Harry, did all of them look like gunfighters?" Montgomery asked.

"Maybe the other came along to support him."

"What about a name?" Tom asked. "Did he mention it?"

"He said his name was Jack Hagarty."

"Nah, never heard of him."

"Me either," Montgomery said.

"I have, and so has Doc," replied Eli. "When we were in San Antonio, Jack Hagarty killed a man in a gunfight. The fight was fair, but he was fast. I'm not sure I've seen another man this fast. He slipped that revolver from the holster so fast you almost missed it."

"Reckon a man like that would even look for bronc busting jobs?" Tom asked. "That's a little too much work for a man of his nature."

Montgomery walked to Jesse. "Have you heard anything else that might be happening in Clearwater? Maybe bad lawmen or cattle rustlers or even ranch wars?"

"All I know is what the sheriff in Booneville told me, and it was nothing like that. They were riding there for jobs."

As the others discussed the gunfighter, Jesse's mind whirled. Samuel was miles from familiar faces, save for the companions he journeyed with. If he had handled things differently, maybe his son wouldn't have ridden away. But now he had the opportunity to find and bring him home, and no one would stand in his way. *Lord, keep Samuel safe and guide me to him.*

Harry and Miguel rode away toward the herd. Eli and Doc mounted their horses and followed.

"Jesse, the man may have other things on his mind," Tom said. "Thought that bit about jobs at a ranch seems off for a man like that. Still, they could say it as a distraction to steal our cattle."

"Sure, Tom, but I have a bad feeling. Something's not right."

Montgomery heard what he said. "Jesse, you're stuck in what happened twenty years ago. You can't think this has to do with you."

"I read in the Bible that the father's sins can pass to the son."

"Jesse, you broke that chain when you gave your life to God."

"But don't you see? I'm the reason Samuel left. I should have heard him out, but I was intent on making money for the ranch. He rode away angry, and I knew he was. I should have ridden after him right then. If I had, I would not have to worry."

"Jesse, young men do what they want to do. You left your family farm looking for something better. Many young men do the same."

"That's what I mean. Samuel is following in my footsteps, and that scares me."

"Well, Samuel is growing up, and that comes with pain."

"All I know is my son might be in danger. Samuel is quick and accurate with a gun—better than I am. I had a challenging time getting him to stop practicing. Shooting a gun was like something that drove him, which scares me and still does. I'm concerned that if a man like Max Toliver came along, he might convince Samuel to fight him. Samuel is young and vulnerable."

"I remember another who was once young and vulnerable himself."

"Yes, and I remember my mistakes. I live with them every day. Samuel's life cannot turn out like mine. I'll do anything to stop it."

"I know you will."

"Well, the day is late, Monty, Tom. We will leave early tomorrow morning. I have to reach Samuel before anything happens that I'll regret."

Chapter 25

Rebecca brought a fresh cup of coffee to the porch and sat it on the small table.

Kendall reached for the hot cup. "Oh, that smells good. Thank you."

"You're welcome, uncle."

"Rebecca, your momma told me you write stories. What stories?"

"I wrote a fiction story about Pa and how he works the horses. The way I wrote it, no one will know it is about him. I wrote another about a gunfighter. Once, I overheard Pa talking about his past and thought that would make a good story."

"What did Jesse think about it?"

"He hasn't read it, and I'm afraid to show it to him. My story doesn't mention his name."

"I think he would read it with pleasure, Rebecca."

"Maybe I'll show it to him when he returns with Samuel."

"Yeah, that might be a while, depending on how far into Kansas those fellows went."

Hanna stepped from inside. "What are you telling Uncle Kendall, honey?"

"About some of my stories."

"Did you tell him about the pioneer women?"

"No, but I haven't written it yet."

"Tell him your idea. I think it's wonderful."

"Well, the thought of settlers heading west in their covered wagons and stopping for supplies intrigues me."

"Intrigues you? What a big word."

"That's not too big. Uncle, I can't help but think about the women who travel with those wagons and the challenges they must face. They help drive the teams. They cook, tend to the sick, watch children, and perform every job along the way. Their life on the wagon train must be overwhelming. I hope to interview them, one at a time, to gather enough information for my book."

"That's a great idea," Kendall said.

"I think so, too," Hanna replied. "Rebecca turns eighteen soon, and we'll give her more leeway to ride to town once this problem with Frank Bartlett is behind us."

Kendall lowered his chair from a leaning position. "Did you see that?"

"What?" Hanna asked.

"I thought I saw something move in the field."

"Might be a coyote or fox," Rebecca replied. "I see them a lot."

"Might be. He must have run behind the tall grass."

"I'm heading in, Kendall," Hanna said. "If you need anything, call out."

"Just keep the coffee going."

"Oh, we will," she said, smiling. "Rebecca, I need your help in here."

"Yes, Momma."

Kendall watched the field as the door closed. He couldn't shake the feeling that what he had just seen was not a fox or a coyote. *I wonder if that lawyer is up to no good.*

Kendall figured men like Bartlett would rather sit back and let their hired hands do the dirty work, especially when it meant breaking the law. The thought made Kendall wary of what lengths Bartlett would go to acquire a ranch that didn't belong to him.

He gazed to the left and saw two horses grazing in the open field and no other movement. His observation then shifted to the right of the barn, where there was a large patch of woods. Still, there was nothing else stirring.

Casting his gaze to the section behind the barn, he saw something green advance and then disappear behind a briar thicket. *I saw that. Who is it, and what are they up to?* He brought with him a spyglass he had purchased at a horse sale from a man needing money. As he raised it to his eye, he spotted someone wearing a green plaid shirt lurking behind a small tree. The intruder gazed towards the porch. Still, he was several hundred yards away.

Kendall rose from the chair and reached for his crutch. *I got to check this out.*

He stumbled down the porch steps, clutching his crutch in one hand and the rifle in the other. Walking to the barn would be slow, with one bad leg—but he must try.

A few months back, he recalled he had helped unload the extra hay his pa put in Jesse's barn. They worked it through the front door, but there was also a double set of doors near the back. *That's where I'll go.*

He reached the barn and opened one door back, slipping through quietly. Thankfully, the loose hay on the floor would minimize the sound of his dragging crutch. A crack between the boards on the backside of the barn was a place to watch. He peered through, searching for movement, but saw nothing. *He has to be here somewhere, hiding. What are you doing in Jesse's field?*

After a few minutes peering through the cracks, he reached to crack open a rear door. A pungent smell of smoke filled his nostrils. *No, not today.*

As Kendall shoved open the door, a man rose from the ground near the barn wall. Beside him, he saw a burning blaze.

The prowler gazed at Kendall's walking crutch from a few feet away and bore a grin.

Kendall held his balance on the one healthy leg and used his crutch to strike the intruder's chin. He watched as he fell to the ground. Then in one swift motion, Kendall chambered a bullet into his Winchester rifle. "Turn over."

The man lay on his belly as Kendall stomped out the fire. "Now get up and walk through that door, and don't think you'll overtake me just because of this crutch. I'll beat you with it and shoot your leg off. I know how a hurt leg feels. Now walk.

When they reached the porch, Kendall called out. Hanna and Laura stepped outside, figuring he wanted more coffee.

"Oh, Kendall, are you alright?" Laura asked.

"I'm fine. Caught this man trying to set Jesse's barn on fire."

"That's Barlett's man," Hanna said. "Do you remember at church? He's the man who wore the gray suit with the buggy and horse."

"Yeah, that's right. So what's Bartlett paying you to ruin another man's life?"

The man stared at Kendall but kept silent.

Kendall punched the crutch into his stomach. "You better tell me, mister."

The intruder rolled to the dirt and sucked for air, shaking his head. "He…he ain't paying me nothing. Do you remember those boys your family stood up to in Booneville some twenty years ago?"

"Yeah, Tolliver's brothers."

"Max Toliver. I'm Carlton Toliver's son, Jim. All Pa talked about until the day he died was how he and his brothers had the chance to get back at Jesse Stalls for killing Max. But Pa's brothers ran away from the fight before it was done."

"I suppose you came to get even."

"That's right."

"I don't know what your pa told you, but the truth is that day, they saw all the guns and knew they had no chance."

"They had a chance if they'd hung in there," Kendall said. "I was there."

"So, your name is Jim Tolliver?" Hanna asked.

"That's right."

"Maybe Bartlett didn't pay you, but he must have put you up to it."

"He offered the idea to get back at Jesse. He wanted to pay me, but I told him no reason for payment."

"At least we stopped him," Kendall said.

Jim Tolliver laughed. "You ain't stopped nothing. Bartlet has plenty planned for Jesse and his family."

Hanna reached and grabbed Jim by the hair. "What do you mean? Nothing better happen to my family!"

"May already have."

"Say it right now!"

"Barlett's got several men on the way to Kansas, but they ain't looking for Jesse."

Hanna's chest rose in rapid, uncontrollable heaves.

Laura saw this and ran to her. "Breathe, Hanna, slow, breathe."

When Hanna had caught her breath, she looked at Kendall. "Bartlett is after Samuel. We have to warn Jesse and Eli."

144

"We will. We'll take ole Jim here to the sheriff, and then you can send a telegraph."

"But I don't know where he is."

Laura reached her arm around Hanna. "We'll figure it out."

Chapter 26

Ellison McCarnnon roped the calf's neck while Andy McGrew heeled it. Sheldon reached for the branding iron and burned the brand into its hide.

"Let 'er go and grab another," Sheldon said.

Samuel twirled the rope from his horse and tossed it on the next calf, causing him to wince.

Sheldon saw his expression. "Samuel, you ain't ready for this, son."

"I have to earn my keep."

"I'll find you something else. You keep doing this, and you'll injure it for good."

Samuel knew Sheldon was right, but he held the calf until the others had it branded and released. He turned his horse around and lassoed another, only to realize the pain again. "Oh, man."

"Give it up, Samuel," Maggie shouted from the fence. "There's no need when we have these other men."

Reluctant to quit, Samuel followed her plea. "Maybe another week or so, I'll be ready."

"Sheldon, do you mind if I take Samuel to check on those calves?" Maggie asked.

The foreman raised from the firepit holding the branding iron. "That's a good idea. He's chomping at the bit for work, and *that's* something he can do."

Maggie opened the gate and let Samuel through as a stranger rode in near the porch and stopped.

She stared at him. "Who are you?"

The man tipped his hat. "The name's Lane Hansen, and I'm looking for work."

Hearing their voices, Sheldon raised to peer over the fence. "Boys, take this. I need to see about something."

"I'll get Momma," declared Maggie. "She will be the one who says whether we can use you. Get down from your horse and wait on the porch."

He smiled. "Oh, I'll just stay right here, ma'am."

"Suit yourself, mister, but call me Maggie."

"Yes, ma'am."

As Maggie turned toward the house, Samuel rode up beside the stranger. "How do you do? My name's Samuel."

Lane tipped his hat. "Samuel is it? But what's that last name?"

Samuel hesitated, pondering the request. "Stalls, Samuel Stalls."

"Stalls, you say. Are you kin to any of those over in Arkansas?"

Samuel leaned forward in the saddle with a slight grin. "Could be, this being such a small world."

Sheldon approached the hitching rail, spotting the gun on his hip and his attire, and knew he was inexperienced with cattle. "Is there something you need, mister?"

"I could use work. I rode here from Texas yesterday. A man has got to eat."

"I don't know if we can take on another man right now. Bunkhouse is getting crowded with cowhands."

"Mister, I don't need much."

147

"The name's Sheldon."

"Sheldon."

"Maggie told me you are looking for work," came a voice from the other side of the hitching rail.

Lane turned to find Cora standing with arms crossed. "That's right, ma'am. I suppose you are the one a good man needing work would speak with?"

"What can you do?"

"Well, I've done it all, herded cattle, helped calving Mommas bring 'em into the world." He turned in his saddle and pointed to the pen behind them. "Done some branding, and I can ride broncs if you need a man there."

Sheldon had it in his mind that this man's branding came from participation in cattle rustling. "Cora, may I speak with you on the porch?"

Irritated, Cora peered at Sheldon. She had grown tired of his interference in her ranch matters since Stuart's passing. The foreman had lately taken it upon himself to make judgment calls ahead of her decisions. She was determined to make him understand she was in charge. "Alright, Sheldon. Head that way."

When they reached the porch, Sheldon removed his hat. "Cora, we can always use a good hand around here, but I have a bad feeling about this one. Look at that gun on his hip. Any man can tell stories about what he can do, but I know cattlemen when I see them, and they don't dress like this or wear gun rigs. I'll bet that horse has worked very few cattle."

Cora knew one. Samuel wore a gun but was a decent cowboy. "You don't know what he can do until you see him work, Sheldon. You focus on what he wears and immediately jump to conclusions. Don't you think hiring him and finding out how he works is best—before judging him?"

"Maybe."

"And another thing. I run this ranch. I worked with Stuart for years and at my father's ranch. I am capable of running things and figuring out whom to hire. You leave the hiring to me and never question me again, especially when I've not even decided."

"So you'll hold off on him?"

She raised her hands to her hips and said, "I'm *going* to hire him and check him out." She then turned and walked toward the horses as Sheldon followed.

"Lane, I'll hire you on for a month, and we'll see what you can do. Be sure this is temporary, though."

A huge smile came over his face. "Thank you, ma'am. You won't regret it."

She turned to her foreman. "Sheldon, how can we get Lane started?"

"Maggie and Samuel are going to check on the calves. He can ride along with them."

"Good."

Samuel dismounted. "Maggie, I'll be right back."

Cora turned toward the porch and stopped. "Sheldon, when they return, show Lane the bunkhouse and where he'll sleep. After that, introduce him to old Jack." Peering again to the cowboy, she said, "Lane, Jack's our cook, and he can be temperamental, but he's a good cook."

"Yes, ma'am."

Samuel hurried from inside and mounted his horse.

Lane noticed he now wore a gun. "Are you expecting to find vermin, Samuel?"

"You never know."

Maggie led the two men away from the ranch house toward the south side pasture.

* * *

Seven cows with newborns grazed inside a small ravine as they came upon them.

"A cow and calf are missing from the bunch," Maggie said. "Sheldon said this morning that he counted eight. We have to find her."

Samuel peered across the broad field, thinking one had moved away from the others to graze. "Is there a creek or pond nearby?"

"Yes, see those trees." She pointed to the farthest end. "Just beyond that line is a creek. Maybe she's there." Maggie recalled mountain lions had before brought them trouble and hoped that wasn't the case for this cow and her calf.

Samuel nodded and turned his horse in behind hers as Lane followed.

Maggie didn't spot them when they reached the creek. "We should check both directions."

"I'll ride this way," Lane said, nodding toward upstream.

"Samuel, come with me," Maggie said. "Lane, watch out for mountain lions. We killed two big ones a few years back. They had killed some calves."

"Sure thing."

"If you find the cow and calf, give a signal. One shot in the air."

"Alright."

Maggie set her horse to a cattle trail and followed it for a good while. They came to a section of briars thick and scarcely passable. "Samuel, we can't take our horses through because it will scar them."

"Yeah, maybe we can go around." He turned his mount uphill, and Maggie trailed behind him as they searched for another way around toward the creek.

"What do you think about Lane?" Maggie asked.

"I don't think he's worked cattle before."

"You're thinking he's the same as yourself?"

"I know what you're thinking, but I worked cattle at my grandpa's place. Once, he needed a herd of cattle moved to the rails in Booneville. Pa, Uncle Kendall, and I helped him get them there. I also worked cattle at McFadden's while I was there, though I am better with horses. So yes, I can work cattle."

"Your job at McFadden's wasn't long?"

"A few months, but I can move on if you don't think I can do the job. Or maybe you're scared of the gun."

"I'm not, and I think you will do fine with cattle, but it's Momma that needs convincing."

"I don't think she cares for me, knowing I worked for McFadden. Probably still thinks I'm some sort of hired gunhand."

"Are you?"

"I came here with my friends for bronc busting jobs. Back home, we rode for extra money, but I've never hired my gun."

"You said you left McFadden's ranch because he wanted you to kill Sheldon."

"That's right."

"You turned that down, so that should be enough. After all, Momma hired Lane, whom we *both* know is not a cattleman."

Samuel saw movement in the corner of his eye. "Maggie, in the woods, look."

Maggie turned her horse and gazed through an opening to the opposite side of the creek. "There she is with her little one. She must have gotten water and then couldn't find the others."

"Hey, look. Wolves!"

Maggie reached for her rifle, aimed toward a wolf creeping close to the calf, and fired.

"Good shot."

"The other got away, so we better cross the creek and push her and the calf back with the rest. Then we'll drive them all closer to the ranch house."

They gathered the cow and calf and drove her through a shallow place in the creek back to the other side.

As they came out of the water, Lane rode up. "I heard the shot."

"Maggie killed a wolf," Samuel said.

"We're taking these momma cows closer to home," Maggie declared, urging her horse ahead of the men, pressing the cow and her young calf until they mixed with the others.

Lane pushed his horse in beside Samuel as they rode home. "Maggie's quite a woman, ain't she? Make a man a good wife—and pretty, too."

Samuel's head spun to stare. "I don't think you'll be sticking around long enough for matrimony?"

Turning with an impish smile, Lane said, "Well, that's the question, isn't it?"

Kicking his horse on, Samuel reined away from Lane to push a cow that had fallen behind the others.

As he rode behind the herd, Samuel wondered if Lane had come for another reason. Maybe McFadden hired him to complete the job he turned down. If so, he couldn't let that happen. He must keep his gun strapped on during his time at Riverview and protect Cora, her family, and ranch hands, however suspicious that made him appear.

Chapter 27

Liza Ruiz shooed everyone away from the dinner table so she could clean the dishes. Maggie volunteered to help, and Samuel joined in.

"Do not break the dishes," Liza said, looking at Samuel. "Cora get mad if you do."

"I'll be as careful as I can."

Maggie laughed.

"You don't think your Momma be angry? I've seen her. Once, I didn't get things cleaned up. I missed maybe three plates. She so mad at me the next day. If I had another job, I would have quit."

"Liza, you know you love Riverview and could never leave old Dolph. Why you two don't get married boggles the mind."

"None of your business about me and Dolphy."

"Oh, it's Dolphy now?"

Liza's face turned the color of red apples.

"What about you, Samuel?" Maggie asked. "Any girls back home?"

Samuel dried another plate and placed it on the table. "I took a few to the town dance, but never had one to call my girl."

"That's too bad. You're a fine-looking fellow."

"Glad you think that but what about my work?"

"You did okay with those Momma cows and their calves, and you can rope well enough, though your shoulder pained you a lot the other day."

"You mean the shoulder that took your bullet?"

Maggie bowed her head and shook it. "I said I was sorry."

Samuel smiled. "I'm only joshing you. I might have done the same in your situation."

"Somehow, I don't think you would. You're coolheaded, which makes it curious that you carry a gun."

"I told you, it's for protection. Pa hated when I practiced."

"Why?"

"Because he killed a man in a gunfight when he was younger. I think he doesn't want that to happen to me."

"I've heard it's a brief life."

"Well, I expect to live a long one. I only wish the boss lady thought more of me. Did you tell her I was no gunhand?"

"I mentioned it, but she said little. Now, that might mean she believed me, or it could mean she didn't."

"That's not much to hang my hat on."

"Look at it this way. Momma's still got you in one of our bedrooms."

"Now she does that, and I suppose that's revealing."

They finished the dishes, and after telling everyone good night, Samuel turned in.

"Samuel seems tired tonight," Cora said.

Maggie flopped down on the divan. "Yeah, he's trying to get back into the swing of things. But he did a great job with our cattle today. Momma, I'm a might bushed myself, so I think I might start toward bed."

"So, everyone's going to leave me here alone."

"I'm not tired yet, Momma," Jeremiah said.

"You never get tired, so you don't count."

"I don't count?"

"Oh, you know I love you."

"As long as I count," Jeremiah laughed.

"Stop laughing and let's play Chinese checkers."

"Yeah, sure."

* * *

Maggie hung a dress in the Victorian wardrobe her father brought for her from St. Louis. Afterward, she folded her clean riding clothes and stored them in a dresser drawer. Then she heard a noise from beyond the open bedroom door and turned her attention to it.

As she was about to close the door, she heard a voice coming from Samuel's room across the hall. Curious, she approached the doorway and listened. It sounded like someone was praying. *What an unusual man.*

She leaned in towards the door, her interest roused. The words he spoke she recognized from the Bible. It struck her as strange since few cowboys spoke of God or the Bible.

As he read, his demeanor shifted to something resembling a minister, a stark contrast to the gunfighter her momma had labeled him as. His genuineness appealed to her, even after she injured him. Intrigued by the young cowboy, she wanted to know more.

She raised her hand and gave the door a gentle tap as her heart raced, waiting for his response.

155

Samuel pulled open the door. "Hi, Maggie. Is something wrong?"

"May I come in?"

"Are you sure you should?"

"You can leave the door open."

"Come in."

The room was small, with a twin-sized bed occupying most of the space. They awkwardly perched themselves on the edge of the bed.

"This seems bizarre sitting here," Maggie said.

"Yes, it does."

"Um, I heard you reading the Bible."

"Did I disturb you?"

"Oh, no, I could hardly hear you with the door open to my room. But wanted to say you sounded like a preacher the way you read."

"A preacher?"

"I thought you were praying, but I listened closer and realized you were reading from the Bible."

"My Momma likes to read the Bible aloud. When she did, it seemed like God's word was so powerful."

"That's how it sounded to me. Momma takes us to Clearwater sometimes for church, though not since McFadden has stirred things. Minister Hartford reads with a firm voice like you. Growing up I had little schooling, so when I hear someone else read the Bible—"

"You didn't go to school?"

"Some, but with it being so far to town and ranch work taking priority, not enough. Momma tried to help Jeremiah and me as much as possible, but she had little learning herself."

"My momma should have been a school teacher. She taught me and my sister, Rebecca."

As Samuel spoke, Maggie realized there was much about him she didn't know, except that he was mild-mannered, the kind called by God to preach. "Are you sure you're not supposed to be a preacher?"

"Oh, that's doubtful." He could see in her eyes the inquisitiveness. "But I will ask God when I pray. I love reading the Bible, but speaking to others about spiritual things, I'm not so sure."

"I think you should try it. Well, I should leave you alone so you can read—and pray."

"Maggie, if you would like me to, I can help you with reading. Since you have some schooling, it shouldn't be hard to help you read better."

Maggie hesitated to respond. Compared to Samuel, her reading was like a first grader. "I don't know. I'm embarrassed for you to hear me read."

"You don't need to worry about me." He smiled. "After I leave, you may not ever see me again."

"I'll think about it, and I hope you don't leave. I can pray, too, you know, so that Momma will keep you."

"When do you want to start?"

"Start?"

"Reading school."

"You are determined."

"Well then?"

"Tomorrow after supper, we can read together, but not in the bedroom."

"Okay, after supper. You'll be reading well before you know it."

Maggie smiled as she closed his door. *He's a cute one.*

Chapter 28

Lim Rhodes and Coley Bage sat on the porch at the bunkhouse playing checkers as Sheldon rode in and tied his horse to the hitch rail near the ranch house. The other men sat inside, finishing breakfast and drinking coffee.

"Someone said Cora put our foreman in his place a few days back," said Coley.

"I heard the same thing," Lim replied. "I hope she doesn't get rid of him, though. I sure like old Sheldon."

"Yeah, Sheldon's a cowboy's cowboy."

They watched as the foreman walked from the ranch house to his horse.

"I wonder what he's planning for us today," questioned Lim.

"Something we ain't going to like."

"Yeah, I know."

Coley turned his eyes to the entrance lane. "What's that I hear?"

"Horses," Lim said, watching the foreman. "Sheldon hears it, too."

"I better tell the others."

As the men rushed from the bunkhouse, Sheldon met them on his horse. "Several of you men take cover in the barn. Some get behind the other buildings. Andy and Rush, you're with me at the house. Now hurry!"

Samuel and Maggie stood on the porch when the commotion started.

"My rifle is inside the door. Samuel, do you want a rifle?" Maggie asked.

"My sidearm will do."

Cora rushed from indoors, holding a shotgun, and watched as the riders lined up in front of her house.

Samuel leaned casually against the doorpost, counting as they positioned themselves. He tallied thirty men with guns on their hips and rifles across their saddles, aligned as an army destined for war.

McFadden spotted Samuel and sneered. "Didn't know you were in the habit of hiring turncoats, Cora."

Cora cast her eyes upon the big man. "JA, why have you come again?"

"I'm low on water, Cora. This drought is having a significant effect on the cattle. I got to have water."

"Oh, please give up on this crazy plan. You know I have my cattle operation and my men to support. So why would you think I'd sell to you?"

"You haven't heard my last offer." He reached for a piece of paper from his vest pocket.

"I don't want to see or hear about any new offers. I'm finished with these meetings, McFadden. Take your men and get off my property." She raised the shotgun and pointed it at him.

"Well, you are surely being trouble, Cora."

While the ranch owners conversed, Samuel observed the riders, noticing a man who didn't fit the mode of a working cowboy. The two guns on his hip latched down and how he sat his saddle confidently, a sure giveaway. No doubt that McFadden was about to instigate a war.

Howdy's eyes met Samuel's. He nodded, then looked away.

Samuel gazed to the end of the line and saw Grant and Tye. *Why didn't you fellows leave when I did?*

McFadden shifted in his saddle, having gotten nowhere with the cattle woman. "Trouble's coming for you, Cora. That's what I'll leave you with."

"Then you better hear this. I won't go down without a fight."

"It was bound to happen." He turned his horse and rode away as his riders followed.

"You pushed us to it!" Cora shouted, then gave her gun to Maggie. "I want to speak to our men, Sheldon. How many are in the field?"

"At least five," he replied.

"Tell them what I say. Gather around, men," Cora said.

She waited as they gathered from the barn and the second bunkhouse. "So the only ones left are those in the fields?"

Sheldon looked around at the men. "Yes, ma'am, that's it."

The ranch owner studied their faces, knowing they had concerns about McFadden's eagerness to take the land from her. "Men, I will not sugarcoat this. We have a fight coming. McFadden doesn't need water, as he claims. I have a copy of a map in my office that my husband Stuart got from the land commissioner, proving McFadden has one leg of the river running through his property. He claims he needs water, but the truth is that McFadden is a land grabber. With more land, he can add thousands of heads of cattle and push all the other ranchers out. That's the only thing that makes sense with him. Men, it's pure greed."

"Ma'am, I don't want to fight, but I will," said Ellison McCarnnon. "It's not right that one man owns everything around."

"McFadden is trying to steal it from you, Ms. Cora," said Dolph Coker. "That ain't right. I'll fight for you."

The others agreed they should help keep Cora's ranch from being taken over by McFadden.

"Alright, until things get better around here, I want everyone riding herd or moving cattle to ride in pairs, even if it's a small batch. Everybody has a partner. Do you hear what I'm saying, Sheldon?"

"Yes, ma'am. They ride in pairs," Sheldon replied.

"Make sure you men have your weapons with you, and if you need bullets, check with me. Carry a gun at all times to protect yourself. Alright, does everyone understand?" Cora asked.

They each nodded in agreement.

"One more thing. I want men watching the road coming in. Sheldon, have some of our men build a small shelter. Find a high-up place near the entrance so we see them coming and have some warning. Someone should be at that post around the clock. That means a few of you will sleep in the daytime. I want to rotate this job."

The cowboys grumbled and talked among themselves.

"I'm sorry, fellows, but we need a warning before McFadden gets within earshot. I don't trust him. Who knows what plan he will devise next? These changes are as much about your safety as mine."

"Ms. Cora," Samuel said, raising his hand. "At least one of those riders was a gunhand."

"Yes, ma'am," Sheldon said. "When I was gathering supplies yesterday, I heard a man talking about a gunfighter named Jack Hagarty, now working for McFadden."

"That's why you need your weapons," Cora said. "And please don't go up against him in a gunfight."

"How will we know what he looks like?" Dolph asked.

Cora turned to Samuel. "Can you explain it?"

Samuel nodded. "The man I saw wore a brown vest and hat and had a rough beard. He wears a polished gun on both hips. You'll know him if he tries to intimidate you into a fight."

"Sheldon, do you have anything to add?" Cora asked.

"No, ma'am, only that we've got to be vigilant. McFadden has threatened us for a while, but we can't give in to the likes of him. That's all I have."

"Okay, everyone, get back to work, and please be cautious."

Chapter 29

The next day, following breakfast, Samuel stepped into his room to put on his gun and grab his hat. He found Maggie speaking with Sheldon as he walked from the porch.

"Where'r you headed, cowboy?" Maggie asked.

Samuel turned to her. "Sheldon wants us to check on the yearlings in the southern pasture."

"I know. I thought we'd take the buckboard this time and check the fencing as we go. We should grab tools."

"But shouldn't we bring along a horse in case there are problems with those yearlings?"

"Sure, saddle yours and tie her at the back. I'll grab us a picnic basket to carry along."

Samuel gazed at her, confused. "Picnic basket?"

"Yes, I'm bringing lunch because we might be there longer than we hoped."

"Sounds good."

Moments later, Sheldon walked from the corral and spotted Samuel saddling his horse inside the barn. "I thought Maggie said the two of you were taking the buckboard."

Samuel pointed to the far end of the barn where a buckboard team stood ready and hitched. "She wanted to take a horse along in case we have trouble with those yearlings."

"Smart girl that Maggie. You ought to marry her."

"I thought you and Cora had me labeled as a gunfighter."

"Well, Maggie says you ain't, but I figure you're fast enough with that gun. Cora likes you, and I think you could protect her if something ever happened to me."

"I doubt he's that good," came a voice from inside a stable.

"Lane. Yeah, it don't matter any if he's fast or not. Maggie likes him."

Lane smiled. "Though I was thinking she's more partial to me."

"I never told you I like you, Lane," Maggie said, walking up behind them. "You keep those lies to yourself. Samuel, are you ready?"

"Yes, ma'am, and the buckboard, too."

"Tie your horse to the back."

Sheldon watched as they jumped into the wagon.

"We'll be back after lunch," Maggie said.

✱ ✱ ✱

They came to the large herd and worked their way down an old trail across a creek.

"I'll bet this creek gets high when it rains," Samuel said.

"I've seen it up three to four feet, though not so high that we can't cross on horses."

They rode along in the wagon quietly for another fifteen minutes.

"You're not a big talker, are you?" Maggie asked.

"Momma always said, if you're going to talk, it should be something worthwhile. She hates senseless babble."

"Sensible words to follow."

"So Maggie, how are you coming along on the homework?"

"I'm finished. I was going to give it to you tonight."

"Good. I have another reading assignment ready."

"I suppose it's from the Bible, too?"

"I don't have any other books with me."

"Momma has some. Maybe you could look those over. You might find something useful."

"I'll do that."

"Samuel, have you thought any more about what I said?"

"You mean you trying to make me into a preacher? Yeah, I thought about it, and I prayed about it too."

"Did you get an answer?"

"I think maybe I will pray more on that subject."

"At least you are praying. Samuel, I wondered, maybe Sunday, since we can't go to church, would you read the Bible to us?"

"Us?"

"Yeah, to me and Jeremiah and Momma. Of course, Sheldon always went to church with us. But he doesn't have to be there."

Samuel's eyes wandered the field where the cattle walked and grazed. He had read to his momma, but reading the Bible to strangers would seem odd. He wasn't sure if God had any plans for him in that regard, but maybe reading out loud for others is a way to determine what he should do with his life. "I suppose I can, but you should know this is not something I do."

"I know you can."

"I hope so."

Maggie raised and peered across the wide field, seeing several yearlings. "There they are."

"I see them. So, what is our job?"

"Not much. We count them and go back home."

"That's it?"

"Well, no. We're going to picnic for a while at the creek."

"So, that's what the blanket is for?"

Maggie laughed. "Well, you can't have a picnic without a blanket."

"No, you can't."

"Let's check on those yearlings, and then we'll find the creek."

As they came closer to the cattle, Maggie realized something was wrong. "There's some missing."

"How many should be here?"

"I don't remember, but this lot seems light." She peered at the fence on the opposite side of the cattle. "We got fence down."

"Pull closer and let's have a look."

"They broke the wire." She saw three strands lying on the ground. The lowest had not broken. "They knocked down the posts and jumped over."

"There they are in the woods." Samuel pointed to a wooded area thirty yards away on the other side of the fence. "Who owns that land?"

Maggie shook her head. "Who do you think?"

"You're kidding?"

"No, I'm not. That belongs to McFadden.

"I'll get my horse and bring them back through."

"Samuel, be careful. This might be a trap."

Samuel nodded as he mounted his horse and headed toward the opening. When he reached the four yearlings, he grabbed his lariat, whipped it around, and herded the cattle back toward the fence.

From out of nowhere, three riders approached, positioning their horses in front of the herd to halt Samuel's progression.

The lead cowboy glowered as he pulled up his mount in front of Samuel. "Cattle theft is a hanging offense, mister."

Samuel recognized McFadden's gunhand. "Hagarty, these are Riverview cows. Check the brands."

"You know my name. Well." He smiled, watching the young cowhand. "Brands make no difference if they're on McFadden land, partner."

"I'm not your partner."

"You're not anyone's partner," said Woodie Bosworth. "You're a traitor. He's the one McFadden sent to kill the foreman."

"Yeah, he ran out on us," Wash Seely replied.

Maggie noticed the riders from a distance, but the trees obstructed her view. She grabbed the rifle from her feet and chambered a bullet as she bounced to the ground. After slipping over the fence line, she slipped through the woods to make her way around in front, hoping no one spotted her.

"Oh, the man's no traitor, fellows," Hagarty said. "He's just a coward."

Samuel moved the lariat to his left hand, freeing up his right. "These are Riverview cows, and I'm taking them. But one more thing. You better not have cut that fence, or I'm coming after you."

Hagarty roared. "Do you know how many men McFadden has?"

"Yeah, about thirty. Out of all those, I bet only two can hold themselves with a gun."

Hagarty swallowed, realizing the young man didn't scare easily. *He couldn't be that good.*

"You ought to take him," Woodie uttered. "If he's the best Riverview has, McFadden can easily take that ranch."

Hagarty's mouth tightened, turning to Woodie. "Shut up. I'll do this my way."

"Yeah, sure."

Hagarty turned back to Samuel. "What's your name, mister?"

"Samuel Stalls."

"Mister, I've never heard of you, and I sure don't expect anything convincing from that gun." He peered at Samuel's sidearm.

Samuel realized that at any moment, he might die. Or he could send another man into eternity. *Lord, help me do the right thing.*

The three riders were in a perfect position for Maggie to shoot. She watched, listening to their conversation. Samuel held his ground. If she fired at the wrong time, his life might be in jeopardy. *Lord, we need you now.*

"Maybe. Maybe not," Samuel said. "Do you play cards, Hagarty?"

"Cards? Why do you ask?"

"I'm analyzing the situation. Since you don't know me, this is like a poker hand."

"How's that?"

"Because you don't know whether to hold or fold. Am I right?"

As Hagarty sat, his eyes drilling into the young cowhands, Samuel knew it was time.

A horse snorted. Woodie smiled, watching Samuel, anticipating something was about to happen.

Hagarty's hand lunged for his gun, but Samuel had his out, cocked, and aimed at him before he cleared the leather. The gunfighter halted, not a muscle moving, wondering why he wasn't already dead.

Staring at the gunfighter, Samuel said, "Holster it."

A look of fear came on Hagarty's face as he gently set the gun in its place.

"Now git."

"We better not go back empty-handed," said Woodie.

"Well, maybe you ought to stop him," Hagarty replied.

"There's three of us and one of him."

"There's two," Maggie yelled.

Woodie turned in his saddle and saw Maggie aiming a rifle at him. "Maybe we should give them back their cows."

"You took those cows," Maggie declared. "This was a deliberate act against a good neighbor."

Hagarty kicked his mount and turned him toward McFadden's ranch. "If you have a complaint, maybe you should see the ranch owner." He smiled as he passed by Samuel. "This ain't over, boy."

Woodie and Wash followed Hagarty.

Before they had gone far, Woodie pulled up, staring at Maggie. "My, you are pretty. Someday, I'm going to get my hands on you."

Samuel kicked Sadie, and she spun, running hard until she slammed into Woodie's horse, sending him to the ground.

Woodie pulled himself up. "You better watch your back, traitor."

Samuel nudged Sadie next to Woodie as he mounted. "Don't let me catch you anywhere near Maggie. She's off-limits."

Maggie watched as Woodie mounted and rode away. "Do you think threatening them will help?"

"I hope you don't want someone like Woodie Bosworth to get his hands on you."

Samuel rode and gathered the cattle, herding them to Riverview land through the fence.

"We should repair this, or they'll go back through," Maggie said.

"Do you still think I should preach?" Samuel asked.

Maggie remained quiet as she reached for the downed barbed wire.

Samuel hammered the staple into the one standing post as Maggie held the wire. "So, are we ready for a picnic?"

"Maybe we should return to the ranch."

"But Maggie, I'm hungry."

"That will have to wait."

Chapter 30

Hanna and Rebecca wrang out the last of the boiled clothes, rinsed them, loaded them into a basket, and carried them to the outside line to hang.

"Momma, can I ride to town and watch for wagons heading west?"

Hanna paused, considering how to answer her daughter, and turned to her. "I'm in favor of your writing. You know I am. Nothing would please me more than to watch you succeed as a writer."

"Then why can't I go to town? I won't be a problem."

"Rebecca, it's not you I worry about, but this Frank Bartlett business does concern me. The man is unpredictable. After he sent someone to burn the barn, we must be vigilant about everything."

"Why would he care about me?"

"Because you're our child. What if he saw you and sent his men to take you?"

"You mean, like kidnap me?"

"That can happen when evil men are determined," Hanna recalled how Mexicans had taken her as a young woman. Thankfully, the Rangers came that day, or Indians would have taken them from the Mexicans, and there was no telling where they might have ended up. "Sometimes it's done to gain something of value."

"Are you talking about the ranch?"

On another occasion, two men took Hanna and Audrey, her mother, to leverage Jesse into a gunfight. Fortunately, Jesse was able to rescue them from that incident. But she wondered if her past experiences made her hesitant to tackle practical viewpoints. "Rebecca, we need the ranch for our livelihood, but I can't see risking your life when I know that man could stoop to any level."

"I guess I understand."

"You have an entire life ahead of you. Someday, things will come together for your writing. I just know it."

"I hope so, Momma."

Hanna turned her ears toward the road. "I hear a wagon."

"I'll go see," Rebecca said.

"No. Finish hanging the clothes out. I will see who it is."

Hanna walked to the front of the house, where Kendall sat on the porch. "Who's that coming?"

"Well, it looks like Jasper and Molly have made their way here. I didn't think they'd come."

"Do you see the children?"

"No, they must not have brought them."

"Still, we'll have a crowded few days, but we'll make it."

Rebecca finished hanging out the clothes and climbed the steps onto the porch. "Is that Uncle Jasper and Aunt Molly?"

"Yes," Hanna said as she watched Jasper pull the team to a stop before them.

"We made it," Jasper said, peering at those standing.

"Get down and rest yourselves," Hanna said.

Laura came from inside when she heard the noise. "Kendall, you said they'd come. I didn't think Papa would let them."

"Yeah, I'd like to find out how Papa took their leaving," Kendall said.

Jasper stepped onto the porch and stretched. "That buckboard doesn't get any smoother."

"You are just getting old, brother," Kendall said.

Peering down at Kendall's leg, Jasper uttered, "I thought you'd have that casting off by now."

"Two weeks to go."

"I know you're ready to get back on a horse."

"I'm ready to do a lot of things. Lots of work waiting for me back home."

"Have you had any more problems here?" Jasper asked.

"So far, nothing, but any man that would send someone to burn down a barn can't be done."

"Your right. So, does Jesse have any broke horses in his place?"

"Yes, mine and Rebecca's are in the field," Hanna replied, overhearing them. "Use a little grain, and they'll come up."

"I'll start patrolling Jesse's place tomorrow morning, especially the fence lines," Jasper said. "Maybe when Emmet arrives, he can help, too."

"I thought Emmet was preaching," Laura said.

Jasper nodded. "He is, but said he'd preach the last sermon this Sunday and be done. The little church was having a revival. Since Emmet doesn't pastor anymore, he helps with revivals and camp meetings."

"I reckon we've all abandoned Papa," Kendall said. "How's he going to make it with us gone?"

"Papa said not to worry. He'd hire some of the neighbors to lend a hand when needed. I know our sister

173

Rachel and her husband Hershel have wired, saying they would visit for a few weeks. And Emmet's boy, Jared, is there to help, too."

"Maybe we can get over to Papa's before Rachel leaves," Hanna said. "I haven't seen her in a while."

"None of us have," Molly said. "Them living in Texas makes it hard for everyone."

"But she loves Hershel and gets to sing all she wants to at church," Hanna said.

Laura stood beside Kendall, listening to the conversation. "Hanna, I think we should get started on supper for this bunch."

"You're right. Molly, come in and help us. I picked vegetables from the garden. We're making a stew tonight with cornbread. I need someone to make pies for dessert."

"I hope it's a big pot because this bunch can eat. I can make the pies."

Jasper sat down beside Kendall. "So, you spoke to Emmet?"

"Yeah, Emmet came home last week for a few days. After Rebecca wrote and told us about the man you found behind the barn, he said he'd help. He could show up here any day, though he only has a small window before leaving to preach again."

"We'll take whatever help we can get," Kendall said.

"What about Jesse? Has Hanna heard from him recently?"

"Two days ago, she got a message that he was in Humboldt at that ranger's ranch."

"Montgomery Roe and Tom Hensley's ranch."

"Jesse said he was helping them at the ranch a few days, then riding on to a place called Clearwater."

"Clearwater? He thinks Samuel is there."

"I hope he doesn't run into more gunfighters. Kansas has a reputation for sprouting them."

"Yeah, I've heard that."

"Jasper, Hanna has coffee on the stove if you want some."

"Hmm. I think maybe I will." Jasper rose from the chair.

"All you have to do is tell them to keep your cup full. That's what I do."

"I don't think I'll be sitting on the porch much." Jasper opened the door and disappeared inside.

"I would trade you, brother. Yes, I would."

Chapter 31

Jesse and his men left Montgomery and Tom's ranch at daylight, knowing the ride would be long and difficult. The rain came down hard the first day, making for a wet and miserable ride.

"Keeps raining like this, Jesse, we won't find dry wood for a fire," Eli said.

"Maybe we can find an old lean-to, a cave, anything dry."

After several more miles, Doc spotted a ranch house.

"I see smoke coming from the chimney," Jesse said. "Maybe they will let us sleep in the barn overnight. Men ride close enough that they can see you but hold up at a distance. I'll ride closer and speak with them."

Two hounds barked as Jesse rode in near the farmhouse.

An elderly man came to the door bearing a shotgun. "Who are you?"

"Mister, we've been wet all day and wondered if we might dry a spell in your barn."

"You said we."

"Yes, sir, there's four of us. We'll cause you no trouble. We're riding to Clearwater to find my son."

"Clearwater? Eh, I suppose that will be fine."

"We'll build a fire outside and heat some beans."

"You got a pot?"

"A pot? Yes, we have a pot."

"One of you bring those beans inside and heat them on the stove. There should be a couple of empty stalls inside for your horses. You can dry them off with hay if you're pleased to. Watch out for that mule in the other stall. She's a picky one."

"Yes, sir. Thank you. I'll bring the pot in a while."

The man closed the door as Jesse waved the men forward.

When he reached the barn, Jesse dismounted, opened the large door, and guided them inside.

"This is better than a cave," Eli said. "Glad Doc spotted this place."

"Get your horses unsaddled, men, while I open some beans. The man at the house invited me to heat them inside."

"Did he seem tolerable, Jesse?" Eli asked.

"Yeah, maybe."

Doc took his and Eli's horses to a stable and tied them. "Eli, bring some hay, and I'll wipe them down."

Jesse removed his saddlebags and pulled out two cans of brown beans. With a hunting knife, he cut them open and poured them into the pot.

"I'll take care of your horse," Sacho said. "Warm the beans."

"Thanks, Sacho."

The rain had lightened as Jesse walked from the barn to the farmhouse, carrying the pot of cold beans. When he knocked, the door opened wide. A surly-faced woman stood staring.

"Hello, ma'am."

"Come in. Herb, he's here."

The older man walked from the bedroom. "The Lord has rained buckets and buckets on us."

"Yes, sir, he has," Jesse replied.

"Ruby, take his pot and put it on the stove. She'll heat it for you, and then you can take it out there for the rest of them."

Ruby reached and grabbed the pot from Jesse's hand, walked to the stove, and deposited it. "Won't take long for this to heat."

"Come sit down, feller," Herb said.

Jesse sat at the kitchen table and Herb beside him.

"I didn't catch your name," Herb said.

"Jesse."

"Jesse, you said you were on your way to Clearwater. What's your son doing there?"

"He and some friends came this way looking for ranch work near Clearwater. They heard there were jobs breaking horses there."

"They ain't no ranch work where you come from?"

"Sure, there is. My son got angry with me and rode off."

"There is a ranch in Clearwater that might be the one. I heard they need bronc busters. The owner is McFadden. My eldest boy lives between here and Clearwater. He sold McFadden a few cows earlier this year."

"If you don't mind me asking, what kind of man is McFadden?"

"I don't know. My son said nothing about him except that he got money for the cows. He drove the small herd to that ranch, the man paid him, and he left. Hey, mister, where you men from?"

"Booneville, Arkansas."

"That is a piece. Why would your son and his friends come all this way for ranch jobs?"

"I don't know the answer to that. You know how young men are. They think things are better in places that aren't home."

"Yes, for certain."

"Beans hot," Ruby disclosed.

Jesse peered at the elderly woman, sensing an eagerness to see him go. "I'm sure the men are hungry and waiting for them. Thank you for heating our food and allowing us a place from the weather. Rain or shine, tomorrow morning early, we'll pull out. We got a long way to go."

"I hope it's a might dryer on the morn," Herb said.

"Yes, me too." Jesse pulled open the door and left.

* * *

"I remember it raining like this in the war," Doc stated. "I was so cold I couldn't feel my feet. Sometimes, I think they are still stiff from those days."

"I know it," Eli said. "All us top shooters stayed in the woods one night. The Colonel got word that the Yanks were coming through the next morning. He said for us to find our places early. We hunkered down all night, and all night it rained."

"Did those Yanks come through?"

"Sure did, but we were so cold we could hardly pull the trigger. We lost a lot of men that day. The Yanks were warm, and us, as you said, stiff like a board."

"Did you fight in any wars, Sacho?" asked Doc.

"I was young and scout for General Houston."

"You must have been real young. The battle at Goliad was in 1835."

"Tengo quince años. Um, fifteen," Sacho said.

"You were just a child," Eli replied.

"Ah, yes."

"Who was a child?" Jesse asked, overhearing as he opened the door.

"Sacho. He was fifteen years old in the Texican war with Santa Ana."

"The Texas Revolution and President Antonio Lopez de Santa Anna," Sacho said.

"What did you do?" Jesse asked.

"Scout for General Sam Houston."

"I'm thankful you were on our side. Okay men, get some of these beans on your plates. We got to leave early tomorrow."

"You'll make coffee before we head out, right?" Eli asked.

"Sure, just before daylight."

"I don't reckon we'll catch up to those men with all this rain."

"Who knows, Eli? You'd think they would have to stop."

"You still haven't given us the plan."

"Well, I want to speak with my son and make sure he's safe from Hagarty. I can't allow him into a gunfight, Eli. Killing Max Toliver haunted me for years. I wasn't in a war like you fellows. Both his and the other man's deaths still bother me to this day."

"I understand, Jesse, more now than I did back when we ran cattle together."

"Yeah, riding the trail with Todd Garret was adventurous. We faced bad weather, snakes, and—"

"Mountain lions."

"Yeah, I'll never forget, but the memories of Fort Worth hit me the hardest. When they come, I stop to pray to clear my mind because that part is never a pretty picture."

Quiet set in, and the men soon found a place on the floor in the hay against their saddles for the night.

"Hey, Jesse."

"Yeah, Eli."

"I'm sorry you still suffer with those gunfights. I feel like it's my fault."

"No, Eli. That was all my doing. Don't you let that bother you, my friend. I made that choice. As I remember, you told me to stay out of it."

"Still, I'm sorry."

"Thanks." Jesse's mind returned to that day in the street at Fort Worth, picturing the eyes of Max Tolliver just before they drew. *Lord, watch over Samuel, please.*

Chapter 32

Samuel and Lane rode until they found the small creek.

"Those steers should be close to water, don't you think?" Samuel asked.

"Yeah, maybe," replied Lane. "Hey, noticed you and Maggie are pretty close these days. You should be glad."

"I should? Why?"

"Well, I have my eyes on Maggie, too, Samuel. So, I'm asking you to back off and let me have a chance at her. You seem a tad slow making points."

"All is well between Maggie and me. I'm helping her to learn how to read better."

"So, that's what they call it?"

"Just leave Maggie alone. The steers are in the creek." Samuel kicked his horse toward the creek and crossed. Sadie carried him beyond the steers before turning them back. "Lane, take the lead until we get them out of here."

"Got it."

Before they could get them headed in the right direction, the steers ran into a thicket and huddled.

"We can't let them stay in there," Samuel said. "That stuff will scar them and our horses."

He untied a whip that hung from his saddle and popped it once. The sound stunned the cows, and they hurriedly moved onto a trail.

"You got them now, Samuel," Lane said. "Say, where'd you learn to use one of those things?"

"I didn't. I saw it in town one day. I've been practicing behind the house. I almost caught my eye the first few times." He pointed to a small scar above his right eye.

"I see."

"Thought it might help training horses."

"I don't know about training horses, but it moved those steers. Have you tried with horses?"

"Not yet."

"Maybe you should."

"Sheldon doesn't seem to want me helping with horses. I suppose he still thinks I'm healing."

"Maybe you should ask him about it."

"Maybe I—"

A gunshot echoed off the canyon wall.

"That's not close," Lane said.

"Can you get these steers into the corral by yourself?"

"Yeah, sure."

"I'll head toward the rifle report. One of the men might need help."

"My bet is they shot at a deer."

"Maybe, but Sheldon said to be vigilant."

"Go on then and check it out. I'll get these to the corral."

Samuel pushed Sadie through the trees westward. They hurdled several logs along the ground and ran through two gulches before he saw the open range ahead. He reined the horse to a stop at the edge of the woods, watching for any sign. *They can't be far from here.*

Beyond a pine tree's sagging limbs hundreds of yards away, he saw a dark horse, its reins dangling. Pulling his gun, he took Sadie forward, scanning the trees as he rode along.

Beside the horse and wagon, Homer Vaughn lay on the ground. Samuel spotted the bullet hole in his chest. "McFadden."

* * *

Sheldon herded a cow and calf back into a group of cattle as Dolph Coker rode in beside him. "Dolph, did you get that other one?"

"Sure did. They are heading for water."

"I suppose we should drive these down there. I don't want cows at the river without riders."

Something caught Dolph's eye. "Hey, Sheld, what's Samuel doing in the wagon?"

"And with his horse tied behind it, pushing toward the ranch house."

"We better see why."

When they arrived, Cora and Maggie stood at the back of the buckboard, peering down at the body as several cowhands gathered beside them.

"Why would anyone hurt Homer?" Julian Stokes asked. "He was the easiest-going man I know."

Cora put her hands over her face and then turned to the men. "This is not Homer's fault, and we all know it's murder. Sheldon, leave Ellison in charge at the ranch and ride with me. Samuel, you and Maggie, come along with us. We're going to see Sheriff Gaynes. I want him to see what has happened. While there, Sheldon and I will have the undertaker prepare his body and bring him to the ranch for burial."

"Homer would like that," said Julian Stokes. "He has no family living, and all he knew of late was this ranch. He was a good friend of Stuart's before he died."

"I know he was Julian, and I will take care of him."

"Thank you, ma'am."

* * *

Cora climbed from the wagon once it came to a stop at the sheriff's office. People gathered around to view Homer's body.

"This man never hurt anyone, yet he lies here dead today because of JA McFadden. Murder, that's what it is," Cora uttered. "Homer was working on a fence, staying out of everyone's way, when a rifle shot took his life. I ask you, is McFadden the kind of people we need in these parts? A man who bullies folks into selling property we don't want to sell?

"A few weeks ago, McFadden rode into Riverview with thirty riders, offering to buy my land again. I've turned him down several times because my husband Stuart built that ranch from hard work. I will not sell."

She turned to see Sheriff Gaynes behind her. "Sheriff, you must stop this nonsense, or there will be war. McFadden will not stop killing until he owns every ranch in these parts. And then he will control Clearwater.

"Folks, I'm a Christian woman, but I don't believe the God in Heaven would want me and my family run over by powerful men like McFadden. If you don't want him controlling what you do in town, you must pressure this sheriff to do his duty. Sheriff Gaynes, if you can't take care of this with your men, then it's time you called in the Marshall."

Cora stepped behind the wagon. "Samuel, take Homer to the undertaker." She turned toward the porch where

Sheriff Gaynes stood watching. "You know this is McFadden's doing. What are you going to do?"

"Cora, do you have any proof that McFadden did this? How do I know one of your men didn't have a grudge against old Homer?"

"Sheriff, everyone in this county knows McFadden has set his eyes on my place. Even before Stuart died, that greedy rancher came wanting it. Because of what happened to Homer, I'm now convinced Stuart's death was by the hand of McFadden."

"You don't know that, Cora. That's just coincidental."

"And I don't believe in coincidences."

"I'm doing all the law will allow. But if I find proof, you can be sure I'll go after JA McFadden."

"You better, Sheriff, or he'll control everything in the county." Cora turned and walked away.

"Cora," came a voice from behind her.

She turned to see a middle-aged man in a dark suit. "Mayor Brisby. I didn't mean to stir things up."

"No, you haven't. I just want to say I believe you. We received a wire from a New York bank a few days ago looking for an endorsement. McFadden plans to build a bank here if he can get backing."

"What are you saying?"

"The city council looked the wire over and decided not to endorse him."

"I hope you know that could be a mistake."

"We'll not allow any rancher to regulate us. He does not own this town or the council."

"Are you prepared to see people die?"

Mayor Dan Brisby stared, speechless.

"McFadden already killed one of my men. I'm almost certain my husband died at the hands of him or his men. If things continue, they will kill more.

"What can the city council do?"

"Wire for the Marshall. Sheriff Gaynes seems to think he can handle McFadden. I know he can't. McFadden has hired gunfighters."

"I'll try to find him."

"And please don't give any endorsements for McFadden on anything. He is evil." She turned and walked from Brisby toward the undertaker.

Homer's body lay on the table as Cora entered Sal Freeman's place.

"I'm sorry for this," Sal said. "I'll make Homer look his best."

"Did you know him?" Cora asked.

"No, but Maggie told me his name."

"Will you bring Homer out to us?"

"Sure, I'll get done and ride him out tomorrow. I suppose you want to bury Homer on your place?"

"I do. I'll have some of the men dig a hole today. When you arrive, we'll have the funeral."

"Would you want me to say a word?"

"No," Maggie said. "Momma, Samuel can offer some scripture, and the men may have something to say."

"Maggie's right. We'll take care of that."

"Yes, ma'am. I should be there around mid-morning," Sal said.

"Thank you."

Cora and Maggie left the undertakers and started home.

Chapter 33

Jasper pushed his chair back. "Oh my, that was an excellent breakfast. Those are some mean cathead biscuits. Now I need to catch another hour or so of sleep."

"You don't have time for sleep," Emmet said. "We've got ground to cover."

"I know, and I'm glad you got here to help."

"Hanna, have you heard anything about Samuel?" Kendall asked.

"So far, Jesse doesn't know much, only that they think they rode toward Clearwater."

"That's a piece from Montgomery's ranch."

"I looked at a map in the telegraph office. If I read it correctly, it's about one hundred and sixty miles from the ranch."

"It feels like Jesse has been gone a year."

"No, only a few weeks," Molly said.

"Before long, you'll hear that he has found Samuel, and they've headed home," said Laura.

Laura's words brought her brief comfort. Still, Hanna knew they were far from home, and she worried something might happen to her son before Jesse found him. Not knowing was the worst thing she could imagine.

Rebecca had seen the sadness on Hanna's face. "Everything will be alright. God is with them. We've all been praying, and now we must walk by faith like Peter did when he got out of the boat."

Hanna smiled. "Thank you, dear. You understand how to encourage others. I hope someday you use this gift in your writing."

Emmet rose from the table. "If you folks will excuse us. Jasper and I have to saddle a couple of horses."

"Now, don't let Jasper fall asleep on that horse," Kendall said. "He might break his neck."

Jasper put on his hat. "I see the confidence y'all have in me."

"Oh, we do," Kendall replied, watching the two brothers walk out the door.

* * *

Jasper and Emmet rode from the ranch house toward the fields.

"You take the east pasture," Emmet said. "I'll ride west. The best thing that could happen is we find nothing going on."

"Sure thing, brother." Jasper reined the horse eastward. "Meet you on the backside."

Emmet proceeded towards the west fence line, maintaining an easygoing pace. He scanned his surroundings, keeping vigilant for any signs of danger.

He patted the side of the horse's neck with a hand, offering his approval. "Jesse has some fine horse stock, and buddy, you are one of them. Papa better watch out because I think Jesse is outdoing him."

Movement then captured his attention, and he stopped the horse. Two mares and a colt grazed in the field beside four deer. "I bet Jesse doesn't know he has this many deer on his place." After watching them for a moment, he nudged the horse forward.

***

Jasper rode along the east fence, humming a song. He peered across the open field and counted fifteen young colts grazing. "Beautiful. Jesse knows how to raise fine horses."

Something then caught his eye. He reined the mare to a stop. *Three men. Oh, no. They're cutting the fence.*

Hoping they didn't spot him, he turned the horse around and moved away. *I got to find Emmet.*

He rode until he thought he had put enough distance between himself and the trespassers. Taking advantage of a hill for cover, he urged the mare into a swift gallop. He knew Emmet would survey the other side of the field.

As he topped the next hill, Emmet spun with his horse and waved. "What are you doing over here?"

"We got trouble, brother. Three men have cut the fence straight across from here. Jesse has over a dozen young colts close to them."

"Probably thieves."

"Could it be that the lawyer sent them?"

"Could be," Emmet said. "Let's go."

Before they drew close, Jasper held up a hand. "How are we going to handle this? Two is no problem, but three—"

"Yeah, we need a plan. Ride back to where you saw them. Try to stay out of sight until you hear me."

"What are you going to do?"

"I don't know, Jasper, but I'll think of something."

190

"That's what worries me. Try not to get yourself killed. Momma and Papa would never let me live that down."

"Just get your rifle ready. You'll hear me."

Emmet soon found a place where he could see them. Two of the men were gathering Jesse's colts. *Jasper said he saw three. So where is the third? Cross that bridge—*

Jasper spotted them through a batch of trees and reined to a stop. The thieves rounded up the herd as he waited for Emmet, then they started for the opening.

Emmet cried out from across the pasture. "Hold it right there with those horses."

"Mister, it's not what you think," replied a cowboy wearing a brown hat and a plain blue shirt. "I'm friends with the man who owns them. Wanted us to take them to the train station and load them out."

"Oh, yeah. That's funny. I'm Jesse's brother, and he's not told me anything about that deal."

"But it's true. Maybe you should speak with him."

Emmet suspected the man already knew Jesse was in Kansas. "I hate to spoil your plans, but you can't have them until I hear from him."

The cowboy sat unresponsive, staring, and then reached for his gun, firing a round at Emmet and missing. Jasper responded, firing and taking down the cowboy.

The second cowboy threw his hands high. "You got me. Don't shoot."

Jasper rode from behind the trees, holding the Winchester until he reached the open place at the fence.

The third man sat on his horse, peering at them. "Mister, I ain't involved. I'm Jesse's neighbor. My name is Matt Fleener."

"So, what are you doing with these thieves?"

"They forced me to lead them to the back side of Jesse's place."

"You need to come with us to the sheriff's office and get this sorted."

"Sure, mister, whatever you say."

Chapter 34

Sheriff Glenn Moody strolled on the boardwalk and saw the riders as they entered the town. He approached them and watched as they tied their horses to the hitch rail in front of his office.

"What's going on, Jasper?"

"Brought you a present."

"Fleener, is that you?"

Matt Fleener nodded. "Not my fault, Sheriff."

"Got one alive and one dead. He tried his hand with a gun," Emmet said.

"Alright, but tell me what's going on."

Emmet pointed to the other cowboy. "They cut through Jesse's fence and went after his horses."

"Horse thieves?"

"Bartlett's men," Emmet said.

"How do you know?"

"He's right, Sheriff," Matt Fleener said. "These men came to my place and forced me with their guns to help them find the back fence. They as much as said they are Bartlett's men the way they talked about him, but I wasn't involved in this plot of theirs."

"We thought it best to bring Matt in to see you and get things cleared," Jasper said.

"Well, he sounds convincing to me."

"But Sheriff, as I told Emmet and Jasper, there's another one of Bartlett's men at my place holding my wife and daughter hostage," Matt said. "Do something."

"We can help with that, Sheriff," Jasper said.

Emmet nodded. "Sure, we could pose as those other two until we get close."

"Sheriff, you can't go in with guns blazing. I want my wife and son kept safe," replied Matt.

"We'll make sure we keep them safe," Sheriff Moody replied. "Let me get my horse. Emmet, lock that one in a cell. We'll drop the dead one off at the undertaker's as we leave."

* * *

Trees and bushes had grown up on one side of Matt's place, hiding their horses. The house sat thirty feet away with a rear door.

"There's no lock on that door," Matt said. "You can go in there."

"Sheriff, I'll get down low until I reach the other side," Jasper suggested. "Maybe I can gaze through a window."

"Yeah, that's good. Emmet, you take a peek from this side. Both of you, let me know what you see. I'll make my way to that back door."

Jasper nodded and then moved out, keeping low. Emmet followed him until they reached their designated locations.

Sheriff Moody followed behind until he reached the porch, then waited as Emmet removed his hat and peered through the windows.

Jasper hurried to the back after looking inside. "Sheriff, he's near the front door. If we enter that way, he will look to see if any of his friends have returned."

"That might work. Emmet, you go in by the front door. Open it slowly and try to get his attention. Watch out because he might shoot when he realizes you are not his buddies."

Emmet agreed. "I'll be ready."

"Jasper, distract him through the window on your side. I'm going to sneak in at the back. Hopefully, you men can get his attention long enough for me to make a move. I want to take him alive. Do you hear me?"

"Yes, sir," Jasper said.

Emmet nodded. "When I reach the front, I'll count about ten seconds, and then I'm going in." He started toward the front door.

Sheriff Moody eased open the back door that led into a bedroom. Wasting no time, he ambled toward the door to the living and kitchen, where a man in brown britches and a green shirt sat at the table, his gun holstered as he watched Matt's wife and daughter.

The kidnapper shifted his head when he saw the door move, leaning forward in his chair. "Berry, is that you?"

Emmet eased the door open.

When the kidnapper saw it wasn't his friend, he reached for his gun.

"Drop it now," said Sheriff Moody, coming in behind him.

The man stiffened, determining how to handle the situation.

"If you move to pull that hammer, I'll put a bullet in your back. So, it's best you drop it to the floor right now."

Raising his left hand, he dropped the gun.

"What's your name, son?"

195

"Randall Warring."

"Put your hands behind your back, Randall."

After Sheriff Moody had tied his hands, Emmet called Matt to come inside.

"Oh, Martha and Sally. I was so scared," Matt said, running to them.

"I didn't think anyone would come," Martha stated.

Jasper found the kidnapper's horse, and they put him on it.

Sheriff Moody walked over to Emmet before leaving. "Thank you for your help. Between him and that other one, maybe I can get one to testify against Bartlett. If so, I'll arrest the man, and there's a good chance he'll stand trial for all the havoc he's caused Jesse and others around Booneville."

"Well, I hate to see a good man arrested," Emmet said.

"I wouldn't call Bartlett a good man."

Emmet laughed as he walked toward his horse. "Jasper, are you ready to head to Jesse's?"

"Sheriff Moody doesn't need us?" Jasper asked.

"No, he can handle it. Hopefully, we'll head home soon."

"I like the sound of that, and I believe Kendall will, too."

"I'm not sure we should tell him yet."

Jasper chuckled. "Yeah, he might as well heal up on Jesse's porch because until that casting comes off, there's not much else he can do back home."

They turned their horses and rode away from Matt's place.

Chapter 35

Jesse reined his horse to the hitch rail and dismounted.

"Do you reckon this Sheriff will know anything about Samuel?" Eli asked.

"He'll know about the ranch we're looking for."

"Go on in. We'll sit and wait."

Jesse entered the office but saw no one. He turned and walked out. "No one inside."

"A man is coming this way. Might be him," Doc said.

They watched as a tall man strolled closer, wearing a tan hat and a gun on his hip.

"I see a badge."

"Are you the sheriff?" asked Jesse as the man kept walking toward them, seeing their guns.

"Yes, sir. Benjamin Gaynes is my name, and what might be yours?"

"Name's Jesse. I'm looking for the McFadden ranch. Can you point us to it?"

Sheriff Gaynes hesitated. "I don't know why McFadden needs more guns, and this time, hiring them in groups."

"No, you've got us wrong, Sheriff. We're not looking to work for him. I'm looking for my son, Samuel. We believe he came this way for a job breaking broncs."

"McFadden has hired several cowboys for various jobs, some for breaking broncs. You take the road out of town, heading west for about seven miles until you come to the river. Two roads come off the main road. Then you take the right one, about five miles from that juncture. What'd you say your son's name was?"

"Samuel. Samuel Stalls."

"Haven't heard of him, but that means little. I worry more about the gunhands McFadden hires. This may not mean much to you, but one they call Hagarty came in yesterday with two companions looking for that ranch."

"Sounds like this rancher is expecting trouble."

"More like going to make trouble. Mister, I'll warn you. Don't go looking for it because you'll likely find it."

"All I want to do is see if my son is there."

"Okay, ask and ride away. You might just get away from there with your life."

"Sheriff, if I find Samuel at that ranch, I'm taking him with me."

Gaynes looked at Jesse, shaking his head. "I was afraid you'd say that."

A gun cocked behind Jesse's head.

"Give me that gun," Sheriff Gaynes said. "I've got enough trouble around here without four more stirring the pot. Don't need gunhands mixing it with McFadden's crew. Joe put him in a cell. I'll get the others."

Moments later, Jesse watched Eli and Doc walk unarmed down the hallway as Sheriff Gaynes put them in a cell.

"Sorry, Jesse," Eli said. "We didn't see them coming up behind us."

"I know the feeling."

"Leave that one out," Sheriff Gaynes said, gazing at Sacho. "He's not a gunhand."

"Sacho's our tracker. He only came along to help us find the way."

"I'm letting him go free. The rest of you can hang in there until I'm sure there's no chance of you tangling with McFadden's bunch."

"Sheriff, we're not going to cause trouble," Jesse said.

"If you hadn't said that about taking your son, things might be different. Maybe you didn't come here to be McFadden gunhands, but you planning to run roughshod over him and his men don't sit right with me." Sheriff Gaynes turned through the doorway to his office and closed it behind him.

"This is bad, Eli," Jesse declared. "I should have been more aware of things.

"Maybe the sheriff is in with the rancher."

"I hope not."

* * *

A few hours later, one of the deputies brought them plates of food, and they ate. There was little else they could do.

Sheriff Gaynes came in as they finished. "Hope you enjoy the food. My wife cooked it for you. We don't often have this many in our jail."

"So us criminals are breaking your record," said Eli.

"I don't think you're criminals. I'm only protecting you."

"Sheriff, if we could find my son, we'd be on the way back toward Arkansas. Can you help with that?"

"Nope. McFadden's men would not want to see my face."

"What you're saying is you're scared of them," Eli said.

"Let me just say that things have gotten a little worrisome around these parts since the rancher started bringing in gunfighters."

"So, how are you with that gun, Sheriff?" Eli asked.

"I'm good for most, but men like Hagarty could pose a problem."

"We could take care of your problem for you."

"Oh, I'd love that, but I don't see it happening."

"Deputize us, Sheriff."

"Can't do it. I don't know enough about you."

Jesse walked to the cell bars. "Sheriff, we can't help you in here."

"Sorry. Gone too far. Folks already know you're in here. If I was to let you out, the city council might take my job."

Jesse turned and walked back to the cot. "Too bad, Sheriff. All your troubles could be gone."

Gaynes picked up the plates and walked toward the exit. "Sorry, fellows."

* * *

Several hours passed, and the town had grown quiet when a voice from outside the cell whispered. "Jesse. Jesse."

Jesse's eyes opened, and he reached and shook Eli, who lay on the cot beside him. "Did you hear that?"

"I'm sleeping."

"Jesse. Jesse," came the voice a second time.

"I heard that," Eli said as he rose and sat on the cot. "Someone's outside."

Jesse rose and walked to the window. "Who's there?"

"It's me, Sacho."

"Sacho, what are you doing?"

"Get you out. One man inside, and I think he sleeps."

Jesse knew how much trouble they'd be in if they escaped, though they'd given little reason for the arrest. The Sheriff had admitted it was for their safety, but would he let it go? The truth was that Sheriff Gaynes didn't want to pick up the pieces after a gun battle. Still, if they could find Samuel, they could head south and away from Gaynes' jurisdiction. "Alright, just be careful."

Sacho opened the door to the office. The young deputy leaned in his chair against the wall, sleeping. Sacho crept inside until he reached the desk. Pressing his rifle to the deputy's chest, he saw the young man's eyes open.

"Who are you?" the deputy asked.

"I'm one of them," Sacho said, pointing to the jail. "I came to get them out. Get up and get key to cell."

The deputy leaned forward until his chair came to the floor and stood. "Sheriff Gaynes ain't going to like this."

"Just hurry."

They walked to the cell, and the deputy opened it.

"Put him in here. Gag him and handcuff him," Jesse said.

Eli pulled a set of handcuffs from the wall and rushed into the cell.

"You don't have to do that. Just leave me here. No one would hear me call out anyway," said the deputy.

"Can't take a chance," Eli said as he snapped the cuffs and tied a bandana over the man's mouth. "Alright Sacho, shut the door and lock it."

They gathered their weapons and left, peering through the dark for anyone watching.

"The horses behind jail," Sacho said.

"You thought of everything," Jesse replied.

"You no time to stay. Must find son."

"Now, if we can find that ranch before the Sheriff brings a posse looking for us."

"Yeah, and it's dark," Eli commented.

"I can find," Sacho said. "That why you pay me."

"Now I'm glad you brought him, Jesse," Eli said, mounting his horse.

"I'm glad I brought all of you. But keep your heads when we get there. If that Sheriff is right about this rancher hiring gunfighters, anything is possible. I only want Samuel, and then we can leave."

* * *

Several hundred cattle grazed the field in the distance as they rode along the road to the ranch.

"This has to be it," Jesse said. "Seems the biggest spread around."

As they rode closer to the ranch house, three riders came near them, watching.

One dismounted and tied his horse to the hitching rail. "State your business."

"I'm hoping you can help me," Jesse said. "I'm looking for my son, Samuel Stalls. I was told he and a few of his friends rode here looking for jobs."

"What's your name?"

"Jesse Stalls."

"I'm Nick Lambert, the foreman. Let me get the boss." He turned and went inside.

"Jesse, I still can't believe Samuel would come here," Eli said.

"I couldn't believe he ran away, but he did."

The door opened, and a big man wearing a suit came out, followed by a man Jesse tagged as the gunhand the Sheriff told of.

"I'm JA McFadden, and I own this ranch. Samuel no longer works for me. The boy wasn't one for taking orders." He sighed and nodded. "I suspect you knew that, you having the same last name. How are you kin?"

"I'm his father."

"You're Jesse Stalls?"

"That's right."

Hagarty stepped closer to the edge of the porch. "He's that Jesse Stalls that killed a man in Fort Worth—a man called Max Tolliver. He was one of the fastest guns around. I believe this man killed another named Wesley Parsons."

"Mister, that's all in the past."

McFadden held up his hand. "Hold up there, Hagarty. Let me speak to the man. I'm looking for men who can handle a gun. You men seem experienced—the kind I need around here. I'm paying good money. Why don't you put your horses in the stable? They look like they could use some relief. Come and work for me."

"I'm sorry, Mr. McFadden, but my priority is finding Samuel. Would you know which way he went when he left?"

"I don't," McFadden looked at his men. "Any of you know where Samuel went?"

The men shook their heads.

"Jesse Stalls, if Samuel *is* around. I'll find him for you," Jack Hagarty said. "I got plans for him."

"Why would my son interest you, Hagarty?"

Hagarty smiled. "Do you know a man named Bartlett?"

"I think you know I do. What does Bartlett have to do with any of this?"

"It seems a brother of Max Tolliver has a son who wants revenge for what you did to Max. He offered me good money to take out your son—and you—if the opportunity arose. You coming here played right into my plans."

Eli kicked his horse forward. "If you try to oppose Jesse or his son, Samuel, you'll have to contend with me."

Hagarty and two of McFadden's men drew their weapons and aimed them at Jesse and Eli.

As the conversation lingered, Nick slipped from the porch unnoticed, mounted his horse, and rode away.

"That can be arranged," Hagarty said.

"Put those weapons away!" McFadden cried. "We're not fighting on this porch. Can't you see these men didn't come for a fight? Holster it, Hagarty. You're on *my* dollar."

Hagarty's face tightened as he shoved the gun into its place.

"Mr. Stalls, I apologize for these men," McFadden said. "They are good men, but we have a situation keeping us on edge. That's all it is."

"We understand. Thanks for your help. We'll ride on now and try to find my boy."

"We'll have a good day."

Jesse turned his horse, and the others followed as they rode away.

"Jesse, where do we look now?" Eli asked as they neared the main road.

"I don't know. I was hoping we were near the end of this journey."

"Hey, Jesse. Rider coming behind us fast," said Sacho.

They reined their horses to a stop and turned to face him.

"I'm glad you weren't gone," Nick said.

"What's going on, Mr. Lambert?" Jesse asked.

"Call me Nick. I couldn't say anything before, but I wanted you to know that we saw Samuel at Riverview."

"Where is Riverview, and what do you mean you saw my son there?" Jesse asked.

"You'll learn more about it if you stay around. McFadden wants Riverview and has ridden there with heavy gun power a few times to scare Cora Rivers into selling. The last time we rode there, Samuel was on the porch, standing. He must be working for Cora now."

"Nick, it sounds like your boss is about to start a war."

"Yes, and that concerns me. I don't want any part of it. McFadden is cold and menacing, and I don't trust him."

"Then why don't you come away with us?"

Nick thought of Jenny and their plans to leave together. "I can't go yet, but I plan to leave soon."

"Don't wait too long. From the few things we heard, trouble is coming soon, and you don't want to be around when it does."

Nick nodded in agreement. "I'm working on it." Then he explained how to get to Riverview.

"Thanks for the information. We'll ride on now."

"I'll see you. Maybe sooner than you think."

Chapter 36

Maggie put on her riding clothes and walked to the kitchen. "Momma, I'm going to take Samuel to the north pond to look for strays. Sheldon said the other men were busy."

"Why do you always want Samuel to ride with you?" Cora asked.

"Momma, I like Samuel."

"I worry he brings trouble for you."

"I think he should be a preacher."

"He reads the Bible well, but that doesn't make him a preacher."

"How many other cowhands do you hear or see reading the Bible? Samuel is praying about what God wants for him, and I am, too."

"But Maggie, why would Samuel wear that gun if he had no intentions as a gunfighter?"

"For protection. I'm glad he had it on when Hagarty and those other men tried to steal our cattle."

"You said Samuel pulled his gun fast enough to stop the gunfighter in his tracks. That should tell you something, Maggie."

"Samuel is no gunfighter. He said he's never hired his guns and wouldn't. Did you know he comes from a Bible-believing family?"

Cora paused. She knew Maggie was in love with Samuel, and she would never convince her he was wrong for her. "I hope you're right, dear. Men who wear guns scare me."

"He only put it on after Lane arrived, and you *know* he should wear it now."

"Maybe you're right. Just be careful, please."

"Momma, I know you're trying to look out for me. Believe me, I'm praying and know I'm right about Samuel." Maggie reached and hugged Cora.

"What was that for?"

"Because I love you."

"I love you too, dear."

Maggie left to go outside and walked toward the barn. She found Samuel assisting Sheldon with a colt and watched them for a while.

"Easy fellow, I got you," Samuel said as he led the colt with the lariat.

The colt pulled against him, but Samuel drew him closer as he spoke to him and rubbed the side of his neck. "So, he's had no training?"

"You're the first," Sheldon said. "What do you think you can do with him?"

"Won't be fast to get him there, but he has a calm nature, which tells me he's worth a try."

"Well, you've been bugging me to get started with horses. I want to see what you can do with this one."

"Today?"

Sheldon turned and saw Maggie watching them. "I believe Maggie has plans this morning."

"A few rounds, then I'll help Maggie." Samuel tugged the rope and started the colt walking around the corral.

Lane Hansen scaled the fence beside Maggie. "I can't figure out what someone as nice as you needs with a man like Samuel. He may be great at training the horses, but I bet he falls short satisfying a woman."

"You've got me all figured out, have you?"

"Well, I *would* like to know you better, Maggie." He pulled her closer and reached around her waist, overpowering her resistance. Then he stretched to kiss her, but Samuel caught his move and leaped onto the fence, sending a punch to his face and knocking Lane to the ground.

Sheldon ran through a gate and met Lane getting up from the ground. "Pack up your things. You're leaving."

"Well, now, if I remember right, you have no authority to fire me."

"I do!" Cora called out, walking up behind him. "I saw the whole thing. You overstepped your place here, son. I want you off my ranch in five minutes."

Lane smiled, "I'll do that. Just so you know, Hagarty's not done with you yet." He dusted his britches off with his hat and walked toward the bunkhouse, slamming the door. Moments later, he came out and walked to his horse with his things, grinning as everyone watched. Then he mounted up and rode away.

Cora shook her head, peering down the road. "Did Lane just admit that Hagarty was the one who killed Homer?"

"Could be, but I don't think that's what he meant," Sheldon said.

"What if Lane was working for McFadden?" She peered across the fence at Samuel. "Didn't you say McFadden wanted you to kill Sheldon?"

Everyone stared at him. "I would never have done that. I knew I was leaving before he asked me to do it," Samuel replied.

"Maybe Lane was your replacement," Sheldon said.

"I only know he wasn't working for McFadden when I was there."

Maggie watched as the last of the cowboy's dust filled the air. "Lane mentioned Hagarty. He must have ridden in here when the gunfighter did, or at least he knew of Hagarty from somewhere."

"That don't even make sense," Sheldon said. "Two of the better gunfighters working together? That's hard to figure."

"We don't know that they aren't, but what if Lane was the one who killed Homer?"

"We can't know that," Cora said. "I won't blame him without evidence."

"There was no evidence in Stuart's death either," Sheldon said. "That seems to be the mark of men dying at the hands of McFadden."

"Maybe so, Sheldon, but God will have the last say in the matter."

"Let's talk about this later," Maggie said. "Riders are coming this way, and I don't know them."

Sheldon turned to look down the road. "Men, get your guns."

"Maggie quick. Run, get the shotguns," Cora cried.

"No, leave it," Samuel uttered as he peered from inside the corral. "They're not here to fight."

* * *

Jesse kept his eyes on the people as they rode in but didn't see Samuel. He reined his horse to a stop, and the others followed suit. "May I ask who is in charge here?"

"I am," Cora said. "I'm the owner of Riverview."

Jesse dismounted. "I'm looking for my son, and I was told he may work here."

"You're looking for Samuel, I presume."

"How did you know?"

"I'm right here, Pa," Samuel said at the corral fence.

Jesse peered beyond the wooden planked fence and saw him. Weeks of riding and searching were over. "You have no idea what we've been through."

Samuel stepped through the corral gate. "Everything is fine, so why are you here, Pa?"

"I came to find you. Your momma wouldn't rest until I hit the trail tracking you down."

Samuel stood speechless, staring at his pa. Then he spotted the others who came along.

"Samuel, we'll be inside while you talk," Cora said, and shooed the hands away, then walked to the house with Maggie.

"But *you* didn't want to come find me?" Samuel said. "That was Momma's idea."

"That's not what I said."

"I wish you'd have listened to me."

"I'm listening."

Samuel turned toward the porch. Jesse followed and sat beside him on the swing as Eli and the other men dismounted.

"That was a long journey, and I'm glad we found you."

"I'm doing fine, Pa."

"Your momma doesn't know that and expects me to bring you home."

"I can't leave. Cora needs me here."

"Did she hire you on?"

"Uh-huh. Lots of going on around here."

"You're not talking about caring for cattle."

"Some, yes."

"Range war?"

"Hasn't come to that yet, but one man has died."

"Maybe we can stick around for a while."

Samuel jerked his head to Jesse. "Why would you do that? You'd put your life in danger for people you don't know?"

"Nothing is settled yet. I've got to wire your Momma and speak with these men, and I can't predict what Eli and those other men will decide."

"Is that the same Eli you talked about, the one you rode with on the cattle trail?"

"The same."

"I remember you said he was better than you with a gun."

"That's right, he is, but those days are long behind us both. He may not want to get involved in something requiring killing, though I could speak with them."

Maggie stepped to the front door, hesitant to disturb them.

Samuel turned when he heard her. "Maggie, it's okay. Come on."

She stepped toward the swing where they sat.

"Pa, this is Maggie, Cora's daughter."

"It's very nice to meet you, Maggie," Jesse said.

"We're glad to have you, Mr. Stalls."

"Please call me Jesse."

"Certainly. I wanted to say that Momma would like you and your men to come inside for refreshments. She and Liza, our cook, will offer a meal in about an hour. You can eat with us. Until supper, you can sit inside and relax and have some lemonade. I will have one of the hands unsaddle your horses and give them water."

211

"Thank you," Jesse said as he stood and waved at Eli. "Come inside, all of you."

Eli, Doc, and Sacho walked toward the porch.

"So, is this the end of the line, Jesse?" Eli asked. "You found Samuel." He smiled, peering at Samuel standing beside his pa.

Jesse shrugged. "Yes, we did, but we need to talk."

Chapter 37

As they sat eating, Cora detailed their struggles with McFadden's persistent attempts to purchase the ranch and her concern about his hired guns.

"Men like McFadden are driven by evil," Jesse said. "I've faced a similar circumstance, though not on a large scale like here. There's a lawyer in Booneville desperate for my land. I found out he grew up on the land I purchased. In his mind, it belongs to him."

"How is that going while you are gone?" Cora asked.

"My brother Kendall is watching over things. But I received a wire saying my two other brothers, Jasper and Emmet, had shown up to help. They thwarted an attempt to burn down the barn and another to steal my young colts."

"That's terrible," Maggie said.

"But my wife had a wire waiting for us at Clearwater saying with the testimony of two of Bartlett's men, the sheriff has arrested him."

"That's great news, right?"

Samuel half-listened, his thoughts divided between their conversation and Maggie's question of whether God had intended for him to preach. "May I be excused, Ms. Rivers? I have some work to catch up on."

"Sheldon can have someone else do it while you visit with your pa."

"I'll have time later. I'm the one behind on my work."

"Okay, then," Cora said as Samuel left the room. She turned to the others. "Your son is a fine worker. You should be proud of him."

"I am, except for the gun."

"My father never used that type of weapon, only a shotgun. He was very gifted at farming and ranching—and still is. As a child, I wanted to follow in his footsteps. I watched every move he made, how he turned the cattle with his horse, the work he did in the stables. Sometimes, I overheard him talking to Momma about money for the ranch. I was always learning from him. If Papa whispered something about ranching, I wanted to hear it because no one around knew it any better than he did. Maybe Samuel has heard so much about his pa and wants to be like him— and that gun is a huge part.

"I bought him a gun so he could protect himself. Not once did I encourage him to use it for gunfights. From the earliest days of practicing, I spoke to him about using it properly."

"Never can tell what drives young men to do what they do," Eli said. "I was stubborn when I was his age. I ran away and joined the war. I'd change a lot of things from my younger years if I had it to do over again."

Jesse stared out the window. Could he have done better raising Samuel? He had worked at steering him away from gunfights. Hanna gave much of her time instilling the Bible in their children. Had none of that mattered? "Cora, this was a wonderful meal. If you don't mind, I need a bit of fresh air."

"Sure. I know how you feel. Liza cooks well, and it isn't easy to stop. I'll meet with you men later on the porch. If you find Sheldon, he will see you have beds."

"Thank you." Jesse stepped toward the door and went outside.

* * *

Maggie exited the room behind Samuel. Concerned, she trailed him to the barn and found him saddling his horse. "What has Sheldon got you doing?"

"I'm just checking on the cows, the ones where McFadden's bunch cut the fence."

"Do you need me to go along?"

"I'll be fine. See you in a while."

Samuel mounted Sadie and set off towards the southern pasture. Soon, he saw Andy McGrew and Rush Quick keeping an eye on the herd nearest the ranch house. Andy gave a friendly wave as he passed by.

After topping a hill, he came to a creek. *That looks like a perfect place to think.* He brought Sadie to a halt beneath an oak tree and dismounted and then let the horse graze freely. Spotting a sizable rock by the creek, he took his Bible from the saddlebags and settled beside the water.

With his gaze fixed on the sky, he prayed, "Dear Lord, I'm only a lowly cowhand, nothing more. I'm committed to reading the Bible because Momma taught me that your word is the law and is important. I guess I want to say that I'm troubled by Maggie's suggestion about whether I should become a preacher. Surely, it would be hard to do, but if that's what you want, I require your instructions for the path ahead."

He opened the Bible to 1 Peter and began reading at chapter four. When he reached verses ten and eleven, he read them aloud. "As every man hath received the gift, even so minister the same one to another, as good stewards of the manifold grace of God. If any man speaks, let him speak as the oracles of God; if any man minister, let him do it as of the ability which God giveth."

He reread a portion of it. *Even so minister the same one to another as good stewards of the manifold grace of God.*

"Lord, is that like a calling? That's such a difficult thing because I'm not sure I'm ready to preach."

He gazed at the next section. "Does preaching your word make a man a good steward? Helping people find their way to God seems a challenge. Lord, how can I preach *and* help Cora's ranch? A rancher is targeting them and will surely kill them unless something changes."

He bowed and prayed for a long while, listening for God's voice yet hearing nothing.

He pulled his Smith and Wesson Frontier .44-40 revolver from the holster and examined it. He had honed his shooting skills since the day he acquired it. In his mind, the gun gave him practical confidence—something to hold on to.

Then, the memories of his pa and the men he killed flooded his mind. Jesse had once revealed that he often felt isolated. He had often distanced himself from his family, hoping to draw trouble away from them. The burden of taking lives—that constant reminder of his past actions—weighed heavily on his conscience.

"Lord, someone must stop Hagarty, or McFadden will surely kill Cora and take over her ranch."

The Lord then reminded him of his pa's presence at Riverview. "Father, I can't ask them to risk their lives. Pa has to make it home to Momma and Rebecca."

Frustrated, he stood and paced alongside the creek as the water rushed, cascading over the rocks and fallen logs. He paused and watched a hawk soar overhead. Then it swooped, caught a small hare with its claws, and flew away.

"Lord, you saw the hawk as he captured the young rabbit. McFadden and his gunfighters are like that hawk. Cora and her children are the rabbit. Death for them is at the door. Please do not allow this. Maybe you *are* calling me to preach. But at this moment, will you intervene in this trouble that has found my friends?"

Immediately, he felt God impress upon him to convince his pa to stay until the dispute ends. His friends could move on unless they chose to help.

No matter what, McFadden must never take ownership of Riverview, or his cattle operation would expand until he controls the whole territory.

"God, I will preach for you if you will help Cora and her children. Yes, I'll go home and see Momma, then tend to your business."

Remembering a paper he put in the Bible, he walked back to the rock. Days before, he had noticed it tacked outside the mercantile in Clearwater. There was no time, so he took it down and folded it for later but never got the chance inside the bunkhouse to read it. Pulling it out, he read.

WAGON TRAIL FORMING. COME JOIN THE WESTWARD TRAIL WITH OTHER CURIOUS TRAVELERS ON A JOURNEY TO THE NEW WORLD.

He could see Maggie's face as he reread the words. Would she ever leave her momma's ranch? Did she love him enough to go westward with him? Could she commit to marrying a man caught between a gun and committing to preaching God's word? There was only one way to find out.

Chapter 38

J A McFadden sat gazing at his men as they strained to get on the bronc. Wash Seely held to the rope as Tye Morgan pulled himself up.

"Let him go," Tye said. The pale gray horse reared and lunged forward, nearly tossing him. Still holding to the saddle horn, Tye bounded into the air as the gray bucked him high.

McFadden noticed Nick standing on the sides of the fence, watching. "Nick, come over here."

Nick dropped to the ground and walked to the porch where McFadden sat with a glass of tea in his hand. "Yeah, boss. What's up?"

"What do you have Hagarty and Lane doing?"

"Nothing, since they don't take orders. Said so the first day they came."

"Well, have them come to the office. I've got something for them. Come along so you'll know what's happening."

"Yes, sir, I'll fetch 'em. I'm sure they are in the bunkhouse playing poker."

Jack Hagarty took the cushioned seat beside the desk, and Lane sat down in another at the front as Nick stood nearby.

"Men, I'm ready to move forward with my plan," McFadden declared. "Our water is at the bottom. I got to have more. Since Cora won't sell to me, it's time for the next phase of my plan. Good job, Lane, taking out one of Cora's men, but we must do more. So here's what I want."

McFadden spent the next thirty minutes going over his plans.

When they had finished, Hagarty walked to McFadden's bourbon table and helped himself. "You don't mind a little celebration, Mr. McFadden, do you?"

McFadden was stingy with his drink but knew it best not to antagonize those with the means to end the dispute with Cora Rivers. "No problem. You other men help."

Nick put on his hat. "I'm good, boss. I've got work to do, so I'll pass."

"You're not passing up good whiskey, are you, Nick?" Hagarty questioned.

"I don't have time for pleasure drinking," Nick replied as he walked out the door.

Lane laughed. "His loss."

Nick mounted his horse and rode toward the entrance. Mr. Stalls was right. If I don't move on now, they could blame me for McFadden's dirty deeds.

Chapter 39

Clearwater buzzed with folks shopping and gathering supplies. A stage pulled by four sweaty horses drove into town, tossing dust high into the air, and halted at the freight office. Four passengers stepped down as several of the townfolk met them. One young man wearing a light gray suit and bolo hat holding a leather satchel peered around as if searching for someone.

"You might be looking for us," said Jack Hagarty. "Is your name Dorse?"

The young man looked at Hagarty curiously. "I was expecting someone else."

"You were expecting the boss, JA McFadden," said Lane Hansen.

"Yes. Mr. McFadden was to meet me here in Clearwater."

"We represent Mr. McFadden, so I'm afraid we'll have to do," Hagarty replied. "McFadden has a ranch to run. What's your name again?"

"Jimmy Dorse."

"Well, Jimmy, Lane here will take you to the ranch in the buggy. I have other business to attend to."

"Sure, that's fine," Jimmy said as he turned to follow Lane. Then he stopped. "Wait, I need my bag, please."

"That's not my job. Just grab it and follow me."

Jimmy peered at the cowboy, confused as he turned to walk away.

Lim Rhodes and Codey Bage stepped from the saloon, bumping into Lane as he passed.

"Hey, watch it there, fellow," Codey said.

"You watch it," Lane replied.

"Hey Lim, you know who that is?"

"No, who?"

"That's Lane Hensen. Don't you remember? Cora fired him a few days back."

"Guess I hadn't heard."

"What does it matter?" Lane said. "I got another job the same day."

"And who would hire you after bullying Maggie?

"Well, I'm working for McFadden now."

"I bet *he's* not so proud he hired you," Lim said.

Codey laughed. "That's right because I don't remember you offering Cora much work. McFadden got himself a dud."

The two men cackled louder.

"Are you finished?" Lane asked. "Get yourself ready." He gazed hard at Lim. "You're going to pull that hog leg. Get out in the street."

"Wait a minute," said Jimmy. "Stop this right now." He pushed his way between them.

Lane reached for his gun and hit Jimmy over the head, and he fell. "Don't ever get in my way. You're not in St. Louis anymore." Turning again to Lim, he said. "Now, get in the street."

"Mr. Lim ain't no gunfighter," Codey said.

Lim Rhodes walked into the street with boldness. "Don't worry about me, Codey. I got him."

Lane took his place twenty steps from him, staring at the young cowboy. "No one makes fun of me, son."

"I ain't your son, mister."

Lane forced everything out of his mind as he peered at the cowboy.

Lim never wanted to take on a man like Lane in a gunfight, but he couldn't run away either. His hand trembled as it hovered above the cold metal gun, hoping he remembered to replace the bullets he had used to fend off the wolf the day before.

Lane smirked as he stared, and Lim thought he would go for his gun. So he pulled his—only he was too slow. Lane's bullet found Lim's chest in a split second.

"I'm sorry, Codey. I think he killed me." Lim's gun released from his hand and pounded into the dirt.

"No!" Codey cried. "You rotten murderer." Codey reached for his weapon, though too late. Two bullets left Lane's gun, finding their places in Codey's stomach and heart.

"Jimmy Dorse walked to Lane. Did you have to kill them?"

"I thought you came here for the proper story?" Lane asked.

"Yeah, Lane, did you have to kill them?" Hagarty said as he walked closer, grinning.

"Well, I did," Lane said. "Someone has to get things going, or else the boss's cattle will run out of water."

Hagarty roared. But Jimmy stood shaking his head, wondering what kind of country he came to.

Lane hopped into the buggy alongside Jimmy. Hagarty mounted his horse, and they left town, headed toward McFadden's ranch.

Sheriff Gaynes ran from the other end of the street, but Lane and Hagarty were gone. He turned to his deputy, Joe Fields, "Get my horse. Cora Rivers ain't going to take this well."

PREACHER

Chapter 40

J asper drove the horse behind Jesse's young colts, herding them to a new area. When he had completed the task, he turned toward the ranch house.

Kendall sat outside, watching as Jasper rode up near the porch. "How's those colts doing?"

"They look great, but I wonder if it may be time to start working them. But you would know more about this stuff than me."

"Yeah, I got a look at them when they came by, and you're right. Jesse needs to get back here and get on this stuff."

"Kendall, I'm going to ride to town and find out if Sheriff Moody has actually arrested Bartlett."

"You don't think he would?"

"I'm sure he'll try, but Bartlett's a lawyer, and I don't trust him."

"Then hitch a team," Kendall uttered. "I'd like to go with you."

"Go where?" Hanna asked, stepping outside.

"Booneville," Kendall replied. "Jasper is concerned whether Sheriff Moody will follow through and arrest Bartlett."

"I've had my worries about it, too."

"Let's all go, then," Kendall said.

"No, if both of you are going, maybe I should stay behind and keep an eye out," Jasper said.

Kendall stood holding to the porch rail. "Might not be a bad idea to leave someone here until we know something."

"You mean until we see Bartlett in jail," Hanna said. "I'll tell the women."

* * *

"Momma, can we go to Sally Fae's Dress Shop?" Rebecca asked as they drew closer to town.

Hanna gazed down the street at the three covered wagons. "Wouldn't you rather talk to some pioneer women?"

Rebecca turned to see the wagons aligned in the street. "I would, Momma."

"That's fine, but wait until we check with Sheriff Moody."

"Alright."

They reached the sheriff's office, and Kendall stopped the team. "Let's not get too scattered until we learn something."

Hanna stepped down at the back. "We'll go in with you."

Rebecca followed Hanna. Laura walked along with Kendall as he strolled with his crutch.

Sheriff Moody sat at his desk, cleaning a rifle when they entered. "Hello, folks. I bet I know why you're here."

"I know you do," Hanna said. "Is Bartlett in one of those cells?"

"You know, he tried to sneak out of town before we brought him in, but my deputy got word from a neighbor he was packing things in a wagon. Bartlett knew I was coming for him."

"So he's back there?" Kendall asked.

"Yep, and he'll stay there until Judge Perkins comes through, which could be another month."

"Maybe Jesse will be back by then," Hanna said.

"Jesse better be back if the trial starts because I don't know how it'll go without him."

Hanna shook her head. "Bartlett can't get out, Sheriff. He'll start after us again."

Sheriff Moody stood up. "I'm just saying the trial will go much better if Jesse is here to testify, being it is his land."

"But most of the trouble happened under our watch," Kendall said.

"And may not be over yet."

"What do you mean?"

"Kendall, Bartlett still has a lot of hands on his payroll. Two of the meanest were in here visiting him this morning."

"So, you think they might still cause trouble?"

"I would watch my back if I were you. All Bartlett has to do is eliminate a few witnesses, and he goes free."

"That's not fair, Sheriff. We've done nothing wrong," Hanna said.

"I know, and I'd love to offer protection, but I can't spend all my time at your place."

"Bartlett knows that, too," Kendall replied.

"Bartlett's a smart man when it comes to dealings with the law, so be careful."

Hanna made her way out of the sheriff's office and stood beside the wagon. "I wish Jesse was back."

"Momma, maybe we should let Pa know," Rebecca said.

"No, because Jesse can't stop his search for this. We'll deal with Bartlett."

Kendall walked to the wagon and grabbed hold of it. "What are you thinking, Hanna?"

"More men."

"Gunfighters?"

"Maybe," Hanna said. "At least those who can hold their own. I'll hire them long enough to see Bartlett go to trial."

"Or until Jesse returns with his men."

Hanna turned, facing the sheriff's office. "I want to talk to Moody again." She hurried inside and shut the door.

"Did I forget something, Hanna?" Sheriff Moody asked.

"Um, I just want to know if any good men around here might want a job and can use a gun if needed."

"More guns? I wish you wouldn't."

"Sheriff, you said it yourself. You can't spend all your time at our place. I don't trust Bartlett, and from what you told us, the possibility of conflict still exists. I can't let him get the upper hand while Jesse is gone."

Sheriff Moody leaned back in the chair. "Around town, there are men who think they are gunhands, but you can't trust any of them. They could be on Bartlett's payroll, though I did see a group of men come riding in from a cattle trail. I believe there were four or five riding together. You may know one of 'em. His name's Billy Cantrell, and he's from these parts."

"He and Jesse rode a cattle trail together years ago. Billy is Laura's brother."

"That's right, Hanna. Wasn't that the cattle trail that ended in Fort Worth?"

"Yeah, Jesse still has nightmares about Fort Worth."

"I'm sorry to hear that. It was a long time ago."

"Where are these men staying, Sheriff?"

"At the old Cantrell place. I don't think anyone lives there now. Billy comes in on occasion and stays until his next batch of cattle is ready for market."

"Thank you, Sheriff. I'll tell the others." She walked toward the door.

"Hanna, please be careful. I don't trust Bartlett either."

"You just make sure he doesn't escape." Hanna nodded and stepped from the office.

The rest sat in the wagon as Hanna strolled their way.

"So, did you find out anything?" Kendall asked.

"Take us to the Cantrell place."

"My family's place?" Laura asked.

"Yes, Sheriff Moody said Billy was there."

"I can't believe he hasn't written to me."

"Well, you can ask him when we get there," Kendall said.

"Believe me, I will."

✳ ✳ ✳

Billy nailed a plank to the fence inside the corral. He looked up when he heard a wagon drawing near. Wiping the sweat from his forehead with a sleeve, he returned his hat to his head.

Laura spotted her brother and was the first to hurry to the ground.

"Oh, boy," Billy said. "Hi, Laura."

"Billy Cantrell, I hardly see you, and here you are, working away at the old place. The only reason I know is Sheriff Moody informed us."

"I'm sorry, Laura. I don't get home enough to take care of things."

"You sure don't," Laura said, standing with her arms crossed. "Come here and hug me."

Billy reached his arms around his sister as she cried. "I'm sorry, sis. It seems there's one herd of cattle after another to move."

Kendall walked up, leaning on his crutch. "How long before you drive the next herd?"

"Maybe two, three weeks or could be longer. This one's mine, so I have some time to work around the place on a few things."

"How many men with you, Billy?" Hanna asked.

"I have four excellent hands with me. Why?"

"I could sure use your help."

"What's going on, Hanna? And where's Jesse? I was hoping to see him."

"Jesse's in Kansas, gone after Samuel, our son."

"I saw your son when we crossed through the Oklahoma territory."

"You saw Samuel?"

"Yes. Samuel and three of his friends came by our campfire. They were wet to the bone from the river that was up when they came through. The young men ate a meal and stayed the night, and we parted the next morning. They said they were headed to Kansas. So Jesse's gone after him?"

"That's right."

"What do you need our help with?"

Hanna told Billy about Samuel leaving upset and the problems Bartlett had given Jesse over the land.

"Yeah, Hanna, we can help as long as I'm not driving a herd of cattle. I can't stay around for long, though."

"I understand, and I'll pay you for the time you're here."

"No pay. Just feed us. Jesse is my friend, and I would feel terrible if something happened to one of you. This will give me more time with Laura and Kendall."

"Thank you, Billy."

"I hope sleeping in the barn suits you. I'm all out of beds. Jasper and Molly are also at our place."

"Me and the boys don't know what a proper bed is, so no problem there."

"We'll head home, then, Billy. Come when you can."

"A couple of the men rode to town for supplies. We'll be over as soon as they get back."

Hanna and the others loaded into the wagon and started for home.

Chapter 41

After they had finished the dishes, Liza Ruiz chased Samuel and Maggie out of the kitchen. "Lunch is over. Don't you both have work to do? If you don't, the others are on the porch."

"I suppose we should visit," Maggie said. "Your pa may head back soon."

"He can't go yet."

"I thought you would leave with him since that's why he came."

"Not yet." Samuel hurried to the front porch, where a conversation was underway.

Eli and Doc sat on the porch floor, their legs dangling over the sides. Jesse, Cora, and Sheldon sat on the chairs and the swing.

"So, you've only raised a few horses?" Jesse asked.

"That's right. When Stuart was alive, he felt we couldn't do both justice and thought cattle was best because the army needed meat. With Fort Gibson soon to shut down, they won't be accepting horses, but I hope the Army keeps needing meat, though we can sell to stockbrokers who may not give us a great price. I'd love to raise horses to help diversify if I knew I could sell them."

"What about Fort Leavenworth? I hear they are in full operation. I know that's a might further, but it might be an opportunity for you."

"I heard Fort Leavenworth was staying open to assist those traveling west on the Santa Fe."

"That's what I heard."

Jesse turned when he saw Samuel and Maggie. "Samuel, are you ready to head home tomorrow?"

"Pa, I need to speak with you about that. Can you walk with me?"

Jesse got up from the chair and followed Samuel. "Must be important if you need privacy."

Samuel led Jesse to the corral fence. "Have you spoken with those other men about staying?"

"They want to go home, and I do too. What's on your mind?"

"I didn't want you to get riled in front of folks when I tell you I'm not leaving, at least not for a while."

"Samuel, I rode for days and days to find you. I've missed a lot of training horses at the ranch, not to mention that Kendall and your Momma had to deal with other pressing issues."

"I'm sorry for that, but you should have stayed home if those horses were so important."

Jesse paused, shaking his head. "Samuel, that's not what I meant, though you left me in a terrible spot without warning."

Samuel scratched in the dirt with the toe of his boot. "I know I did, Pa. I thought about how hard it might have been for you to ready those horses by yourself, and I'm sorry."

"Thankfully, Eli and Doc came along and helped. But Samuel, I wish I'd considered your feelings instead of losing my temper. I'm sorry, too. Now, I know you have concerns for Riverview. Is that your reason for wanting to stay, or does it involve Maggie?"

"Riverview is in trouble, and Cora needs my help. You've heard about McFadden and how he wants to buy her ranch. With those gunfighters he's hired, there's a chance he will succeed."

Jesse had hoped not to get involved, but what should he do if his son did not leave with them? "Samuel, range wars usually work themselves out. Why do you feel you need to get tangled in this?"

"I'm involved because I work for Cora. I can't leave her to deal with this without at least lending a hand."

"Samuel, I told you what happened to me in Fort Worth. I was eager to help a friend, and I'm paying for that kindness today."

"Pa, what if you were gone and someone demanded you sell your place, and they were persistent?"

Jesse had yet to tell him how bad things were back home. "I was going to tell you when I had the chance. Even after I paid off the loan, Bartlett has caused trouble at the ranch."

"But why?"

"Bartlett lived there as a child and wants it back. He pushed the banker to force closer on the loan."

"I'm sorry, Pa. This is all my fault."

"No, no, Samuel. Bartlett is the only one at fault. There's nothing to worry about. Kendall, Jasper, and Emmet are there watching over things. Last I heard, Sheriff Moody was about to arrest Bartlett."

"Then you should understand what Cora is dealing with."

The sound of riders caused them to turn.

"Do you know them?" Jesse asked.

"I don't."

"Strap your weapon on."

Samuel hurried into the house as Cora and Maggie reached for their shotguns.

When Samuel returned to the porch, Cora stood with the others, watching as the riders came near the porch. "That's Sheriff Gaynes."

"Cora, how are you?" Sheriff Gaynes said.

"We're doing fine. What brings you, Sheriff?"

"I never enjoy being the bearer of bad news. You've lost two men to a gunfighter named Lane Hansen."

Cora turned to Sheldon. "Do we have men in town?"

"Yes. Codey Bage and Lim Rhodes took the wagon in for supplies, but they should have already returned."

"Well, I'm afraid they won't be coming back, at least breathing," Gaynes replied."

"What happened, Sheriff?" Cora asked.

"I only know from a couple of bystanders that those two came out of the saloon and ran into Hansen. I figure they were full of whiskey, what started it. But who knows when it comes to gunfighters?" He paused, not caring to share the rest.

"Go on, Sheriff. Tell it all."

"Hansen became upset when they bumped into him on the boardwalk. Then those boys said things about him not wanting to work and how you fired him. That seemed to stir the pot, and Hanson took offense. He incited Lim into the fight. After Lane shot Lim, Cody pulled his weapon, but the gunfighter was too much. I'm sorry, Cora. Their bodies are at the coroner's, getting sized for caskets."

"Sheriff, that makes three dead by the hand of McFadden. When are you going to stop this madness?"

"Cora, that was a fair fight. Lim pulled his weapon first, according to witnesses."

"And what about Homer? He was doing nothing but fixing fence when they assassinated him in cold blood."

"I wish there was something I could do."

"The law's not working, Sheriff. Do you have any idea what's coming?"

"I think so, but there's little I can do."

"Sheriff, I'm going to find men who can shoot, and more men will die."

Sheriff Gaynes had noticed Eli and Doc standing in front of the porch on one side. On the other side, Jesse and Samuel waited with Sacho. He figured it was Sacho who helped them escape his jail. "I hoped you men had moved on. Never expected to find you at Riverview."

Jesse stepped forward. "I told you, Sheriff, I was looking for my son."

"Well, now that you've found him, you should ride on to Arkansas. As you just heard, we don't need more trouble. We have our own."

"Sheriff, you heard Ms. Rivers say she would find more men who can shoot. I can't speak for these men, but since my son works for this woman, I think I'll stick around."

"We're with you, Jesse," Eli said.

Doc and Sacho nodded.

"Sheriff, all you have to do is lock up McFadden, and all this goes away."

"You know it's not that simple. I sent word to the territorial marshall as you had asked. The wire I received said he was in Missouri, taking care of criminals. So, we're on our own in Clearwater. I have two deputies, and neither can shoot well."

Cora stepped closer. "Sheriff, I'm riding to McFadden's to warn him. Can't sit back and watch him kill us off. So from now on, you should know I will take out anyone who comes on my land trying to kill my men."

"Be careful, Cora. I don't want to see the coroner working on a casket for you." He turned his horse and rode away with his deputy.

Cora stood watching down the lane as the dust settled. "Well, that was enlightening. Seems we are on our own."

"No, you're not, Cora," Jesse said.

"Did you mean what you said?"

"Yes, we'll help, but I have to send a wire to my wife to let her know."

"Thank you so much." She walked toward the porch. "I'll have Liza make us some fresh coffee."

Jesse watched as Cora walked inside, then turned to Samuel. "Maybe while we wait, you can read the Bible to us. Cora said you were great at reading, though I'm not surprised since your momma was the one who taught you."

"Alright."

"Son, much about you has changed."

"More than you know. Let's get some coffee."

Chapter 42

Branding day arrived, and Jesse decided he and his men should watch for trouble while the rancher's hands worked. He and Eli rode alongside each other to the branding area.

"Eli, Cora has a lot on her right now. I don't enjoy getting involved in someone else's trouble, but what if it was me? Maybe we should stick around for a while. What do you think?"

"Sure. I sort of like Cora."

Jesse grinned. "Yeah, I saw you watching her. Riverview is a real nice place for a man to live out his days."

"You trying to get rid of me, Jesse?"

"No, only to say that life brings changes, and we should be ready to step into them."

"The thing is, Jesse, I have to know the changes are for me. I'm not sure about it right now."

"Well, I noticed how Cora looks at you."

"Maybe, or she's just being nice."

"If you'd pursue her a little more, you'd find out if she's only being nice."

"Alright, since you think I should pursue her, I think I'll ride back to the ranch house and watch out for trouble."

"Trouble, huh?"

Eli grinned, kicked his horse, and headed away from the herd as Jesse continued toward the firepit.

Sheldon looked up and saw him. "Jesse, you men don't have to get into the branding. You are guests of Cora's."

"We're here for whatever you need."

"Then I would appreciate it if you'd watch out for the men. We're not asking for trouble, but we know it could come."

"I will. Eli headed back to watch at the—. Who's that riding in?"

"That's Andy McGrew. Oh, Lord, Tollie Mefferd's with him, and he looks hurt."

Andy rode to the firepit and reined up the horses. "They shot across the river, Sheldon. How we gonna water cattle if we can't get them to the river safely?"

"Take Tollie to the ranch house and find Cora. She needs to get the doctor to remove the bullet."

"Yes, sir, I was heading there."

"Sheldon, I'll go with him and bring back Eli," Jesse said. "We'll find out if those ambushers are still around."

"Good."

* * *

Eli sat in a rocker on the porch beside Cora when he heard the horses. "What's up with this?"

"Someone's hurt," Cora said.

She met them at the fence and saw that Tollie had a bullet in his shoulder. "Who'll hitch a wagon for me? This man needs a doctor."

Jack Keeton heard her. "Well, cooking ain't the only thing I do. I'll hitch it for you."

Jesse rode in beside them. "Eli, ride with me. We've got to check out the watering hole where this man was shot."

Maggie ran out of the house when she saw Tollie leaning over in his saddle. "What's happened?"

"McFadden's men shot across the river," Cora replied.

"Where is Samuel?"

"He's branding calves with Sheldon," Jesse said.

"Thank you, Lord. Momma, what are we going to do about this? McFadden will keep on killing until all of us are dead!"

"No, dear," Cora replied. "These men are going to help us. Honey, go with Jack and me to take Tollie to the doctor."

"But Momma, shouldn't I help here?"

"No, Maggie. This is not the time. I need your help. We'll pick up Lim and Coley's bodies while we're in town." She turned to Eli. "You men, be careful. McFadden is a hard man and doesn't care about anyone but himself."

Eli mounted his horse. "Yes, ma'am. We'll get to the bottom of what's happening at the river. Hang in there. This will be over soon." He turned his horse and rode away.

Jesse followed beside him. "Why did you tell her that?"

"Because it has to end. People can't live like this, always wondering if a shooter is around the corner targeting one of them."

"You sound like you've seen the future, but we don't know what's coming or what it will take to shut down the trouble."

"Yeah, we do. We know what we have to do."

"Or we only cause Cora more harm."

"I only wish I could get inside that fat man's house one night for a little while. I'd scare him so bad he'd never want another piece of property."

"Those gunhands of his don't sleep much, you know."

Eli turned to his friend as they came closer to the herd. "McFadden better not give me a chance."

Jesse grinned as Eli pushed on in front of him. "Nothing like a man falling in love to put a fire in his belly."

Soon, they reached the branding camp.

Samuel had returned from rounding up cattle. "I'm going with you."

Jesse shook his head. "Samuel, maybe you should help Sheldon with the calves. We can handle this."

"They have plenty of help. I need to do this."

Jesse smiled, watching Samuel step up to help Cora with her troubles, showing some maturity.

Doc and Sacho mounted and followed along toward the river.

Sheldon watched as they topped the hill. "I hope they know what they're doing."

"At least they are doing something," Dolph Coker replied. "All we're doing is riding around gettin' picked off."

"Hmm."

* * *

The five men reached the river and rode in behind the trees and the brush for cover until they reached a lofty position.

"Hold up here," Jesse said. "We have a good view."

"Jesse, did you bring your spyglass along?" Eli asked.

Jesse dug into his saddlebags until he found the tattered metal lens and handed it to Eli.

Eli peered through the lens. "Yep, I see four men hiding behind trees." He walked toward his horse and pulled free his rifle. "I can pick them off easily from here."

"Wound them," Jesse declared.

"Wound them? But we're still rangers and have the law on our side. We gotta protect this ranch from McFadden."

"If we start killing, we're no better than they are. Didn't you once tell me your commanding officer in the war became weary of killing good men and asked your people to wound them?"

"But the war was almost over."

"Samuel has friends who rode with him to McFadden's."

"They made their choice, Jesse."

"Men like McFadden put fear in others to get what they want. My bet is those boys regret what they've done. Besides, we can't be the ones to escalate a range war. Cora wouldn't want that."

Samuel listened as his pa gave the order to wound the enemy. Remembering what Jesse had faced before, he knew he must speak. "Pa's right. Maybe they killed some of our men, but we don't have to be the same as them. If we can injure them, and it stops them from keeping our cattle from water, then I agree with Pa."

"They might return," Eli said.

"I know the risk, but we must try," Jesse declared.

Eli turned, gazing at Samuel. He knew the younger Jesse would not mess around with these folks. Samuel's presence had turned Jesse's thinking. Then he recalled not long before he first rode with the cattle drive he had hired with the railroad assigned to stop Indians from destroying the tracks. The men he worked alongside chose to kill, but he had wounded the Indians because it was the right thing to do. "Alright, let's do this together, or they will run to their horses."

"Doc, will you and Sacho shoot with us?" Jesse asked.

"I can barely see that far," Doc replied.

He turned to Sacho. "What about you?"

"Yeah, I can see, but I cannot shoot. Why you think I'm a tracker?"

Jesse smiled as he took hold of his Winchester and pulled it from his saddle.

"I'll take the two on the far end," Eli declared. "Someone count it off."

"I guess I can count," Doc said.

They spread across the ridge, aiming their weapons.

Eli nodded he was ready.

Jesse and Samuel did the same.

"I'll count to three," Doc said. "Okay, one, two, three."

Shots rang out across the river. The men on the other side yelled out and returned fire. Jesse caught one that grazed his arm.

Eli shot the bootleg of one and then turned to another, catching him in the backside as he ran into the woods.

Samuel knocked the rifle out of one man's hand. With his other hand, the cowboy reached for a gun from his holster, but Samuel sent a second bullet that caught flesh and bone.

Then Jesse hurriedly mounted his horse and led them toward the river. McFadden's hands feared for their lives when they spotted the horses coming.

"Tell McFadden there'll be no more executing good men, or he'll not like what's next," Jesse yelled. "You men are alive because we kept you alive to send a message. Tell that rancher this is a warning. Stop pushing for Cora's ranch! Her place is not for sale. You tell him what I said."

Samuel sat staring at the wounded. One was a friend.

"I'll tell him, mister," said Grant Boyd. "But nothing is gonna stop the big man from taking Riverview."

"Grant, what are you men still doing here?" Samuel asked. "What McFadden's planning is wrong. Too many men have already died over this crazy war of his."

"At least we aren't traitors."

"McFadden is evil, Grant! Can't you see that? Leave him now."

"You just better watch it, Samuel. What I hear is Hagarty wants you badly."

Jesse turned his horse toward Grant. "You tell McFadden if he still thinks pursuing this endeavor is in his best interest, tell him he'll never have enough gunfighters that I can't make his life miserable."

"Who do I say is sending the message?"

"Jesse Stalls, Samuel's father." Jesse turned his horse away from the river, and the others followed him.

Grant peered at the riders as they rode away.

"Grant, who is Jesse Stalls?" Archie Dolton asked.

"One of the fastest guns ever."

"So, what are you saying?"

"What I'm saying is McFadden's got big trouble."

"Hagarty can take care of him. Can't he?"

"Maybe."

Chapter 43

Jesse and the other men returned to the ranch, waiting to report to Cora. Soon, the ranch woman, Maggie, and Jack returned with Tollie bandaged along with the caskets of the dead.

Sheldon and those men who were branding sat on the porch of the bunkhouse as Cora drove near. "We finished with the branding. I sent three men to watch the river from a distance to see if McFadden's men return.

Cora blew out a deep breath. "I wish we had a sheriff who would deal with this. Sheldon, while Julian takes the buckboard to the barn, call up as many as you can."

Then she walked toward the porch where Jesse and Eli waited. "Jesse, I know this is not your fight. But if your men will ride with us, I want to visit our unfriendly neighbor."

"You're going to pick a fight," Jesse assumed.

"Don't plan to, but I am going to warn McFadden and make a show of strength."

"Maybe that will work. Just make sure your men know we don't want to get into a shoot-out in the open."

"They'll do what I say if they want to keep their jobs."

Sheldon led two saddled horses from the barn. "Ride this bay, Cora." Then he walked to Jesse. "I hope your men can control themselves."

Jesse watched as one of the hands helped Cora to mount the tall horse. "My friends and I are never eager to hurt anyone unless the situation turns or they fire first."

"I just don't want to see Cora get hurt. She's not only my boss, she's a close friend."

"I don't want to see her hurt, but remember, we didn't start this fight."

Sheldon reached out for his horse's reins. "No, McFadden did."

After everyone had mounted, Cora led the men toward McFadden's ranch.

* * *

As they trotted along in a group, Jesse eased beside Samuel. "Are you sure about sticking it out with Cora and Riverview? This all could get nasty."

"I'm sure Pa, and I want your help, but you don't have to stay."

"Of course, we're staying.

"Then maybe this is a good time to tell you something."

"Oh, yeah."

"Maggie and I are real close."

"I figured as much."

"You did?"

"That's not hard to see, son. When Tollie got shot, Maggie asked about you. I also saw how you two worked together around Riverview."

"I'm thinking of asking for her hand in marriage."

"Oh, you two *are* that serious." Jesse grinned. "Maybe getting shot by a woman is a new way to court a man."

"That was an accident."

"Yeah, maybe. So you spent time at Riverview and became good friends."

"Something like that."

"Your momma will like her."

"I hope so." Samuel looked down as he rode along.

"Is there something you are not telling me?" Jesse asked.

"I think maybe God has called me to preach."

Jesse was speechless.

"Are you not going to say anything?" Samuel asked.

"Um, I was thinking how your momma will enjoy having a preacher in the family. She taught you the Bible well, so I know you'd make a great preacher, but Samuel, that gun and preaching won't mix."

"That's my dilemma."

"A mighty big dilemma. If you mean business with God, you must leave the gun behind."

"I'm still praying about it."

"Praying's a good place to start."

* * *

Those watching over McFadden's cattle turned their horses in behind Cora's group as they made their way to the big ranch house.

The sound of hooves brought Hagarty and Lane from inside. They took their places beside the doorway, awaiting their boss's exit.

Soon, McFadden pushed open the screen door onto the porch, offering a huge smile. "Ah, Cora. Did you come expecting another offer? If you did, I'm all out."

"Forget your offers. I came to declare you as a murderer, McFadden. I knew you wanted my land badly, but

I never thought you'd stoop so low and kill three of my men just for land."

"Now, wait a minute, Cora. I have killed no one."

"Your men have, and you are responsible."

"Cora, the gunfight was deemed a fair fight, according to the sheriff. I heard about your other man, but I promise that wasn't us."

"And I suppose it wasn't your men down at the river shooting across, stopping my cattle from getting to water."

McFadden's smile faded. "Now you listen here. My cattle need watering, and I will fight for it."

"There's plenty of water for you, JA. I've seen the map."

"Oh, you mean the maps your husband got from the land office? Cora, you know as well as I do your husband had them drawn to falsely show that one of the river's branches lay on my property—but there is no branch."

"You're lying."

"No, I'm not."

"Forget the water, McFadden. I will protect my people."

"How are you gonna do that, Cora?"

"The rancher lady has plenty of help," Jesse said.

McFadden turned toward him. "Yeah, I remember you came looking for your son, and I see you've found him."

"Samuel is no problem, sir," Hagarty said. "I told you he's mine."

McFadden turned to Hagarty. "And what about these other men?"

Hagarty smiled. "Ah, we can give it a go."

"We can take them, Mr. McFadden," Lane said as he walked closer.

"Do either of you know who this man is?"

Hagarty shrugged.

"I sent a few wires for info on him. He's Samuel's father, Jesse Stalls, of course. He is also a famous gunfighter," McFadden responded. "He killed Max Tolliver a few years back. Jack Horn thought he wanted him but walked away without a fight. The other man is his friend, Eli Cole. I hear he's faster with a gun than Jesse."

Hagarty's grin shrank. "Well, the famous ones have to go down sometimes."

"McFadden, I don't want to fight you, but I won't sit back and let you pick us off," Cora declared. "If any of your men come onto my property, we will meet them with force."

"Cora, it's not personal, and I don't care to fight, either, but I have a cattle business to run."

"JA, you are a greedy man going after more than you deserve. I will pray for you."

"I wouldn't waste my time praying. Why didn't you accept my offer, Cora? We'd have avoided all of this."

"Why can't *you* accept mine? I don't want to sell! So, come on my property again, and trouble will find you. JA, I expect you to warn your men that I am no longer playing." Cora turned her horse and led the others away.

McFadden watched as they rode from the ranch house. "We'll see about that."

Chapter 44

After making his rounds through one side of town, Sheriff Gaynes stepped into his office and hung his hat on the rack. Deputy Willis Hobbs walked from the jail cell area and sat down.

"Did you get those floors cleaned, Willis?"

"Yes, sir. You know, those drunks can surely make a mess."

"Nothing we can do about them but lock 'em up."

"At one time, it was a fine town."

"How would you know? You're only a youngster."

"Well, I hear my grand say it was. He said the town was so quiet you got a little nervous."

"Those days are gone."

"Is there gonna be a war, Sheriff? I heard some of those men from McFadden's ranch saying that trouble is coming."

"I thought it was already here. Didn't you hear about those men getting shot at Riverview?"

"Yeah, Sheriff, but nobody knows who did it."

"I know, but these things often show themselves in time. Did you get done with your work back there?"

"Yes, sir. What else you got for me?"

"Find Shep. I sent him to make rounds across the street. My guess is he's at the saloon talking to one of those gals."

"Alrighty, I'll find him." Willis opened the door to leave, but halted, peering outside.

"What's the holdup, son?"

"You better come look, Sheriff."

Gaynes rose from his chair and strolled to the door. Outside, five of McFadden's men and the big rancher dismounted. "I wonder what he wants?"

A buckboard pulled up near McFadden, and he shouted orders for supplies. Then he turned toward the sheriff's office.

"He's coming here," Gaynes said.

"Looks upset, Sheriff."

"McFadden always looks upset."

McFadden reached the porch and stepped beneath the overhang. "Sheriff, we got business to discuss. May I come in?"

"Sure, Mr. McFadden. Come in and have a seat," Sheriff Gaynes replied.

McFadden stepped through first, strolled to the sheriff's seat, and sat down.

Gaynes peered down at him with disdain. *Who does he think he is?*

"You might not want your deputy hearing what I have to say. Send him away and any others you have around the cells."

Gaynes gazed at Willis and nodded. "Leave us. Find Shep and keep him away until I come get you both."

"But Sheriff—"

"Do it."

Willis opened the door, pausing, watching the gunhands waiting patiently for their boss. Finally, he stepped through the doorway and closed it.

"You will do well, Sheriff Gaynes. Your men listen to you—although somewhat sluggish.

"They're good men."

"I'm here to make a proposition."

"Proposition?" *Bribery, maybe?*

"I think you know I want Riverview Ranch. I've got to have more water."

"I've heard about the problems you're causing. We know a man was assassinated on Cora's land."

"I assured Cora that my men did not kill him. Maybe Cora has other troubles—something to do with those gunfighters at her place."

"You can't be one worried about gunfighters. Look at all those at your ranch."

"Just hired hands, Sheriff. They all have jobs to do."

Gaynes leaned on the desk, tiring of the rancher. "What did you come here for, McFadden?"

"I told you. A proposition. Sit down."

Gaynes sat across from the rancher. "What proposition?"

"There may be some things coming down the pike, and you can make some money if you turn the other way when these things occur."

"If you're talking about more men getting shot, I can't help you."

"Now, Sheriff, you should be very careful with hasty decisions. I wouldn't want any danger to come your way. There's a sizeable reward awaiting if you work with me."

"You mean bribe money? That's not why I took this job, McFadden."

"Call it a contribution."

"That's still a bribe."

"You hear me good, lawman. From now on, I run things around here. If you don't comply, removing you isn't out of the question. I have men who would love to take over for a dead sheriff."

Gaynes knew how dangerous McFadden was and had his family to think about, but how could he go against everything he believed? He had sworn an oath to uphold the law and protect the town. Was that possible in McFadden's world? "I'll have to think about it. I didn't take an oath to become a lawman and then turn my head. So, give me some time."

McFadden rose from the chair. "Not too much time, I hope. I heard you have a wife and a child. Is that right?"

Gaynes nodded.

"You wouldn't want to see trouble for them, would you? Making wrong decisions can lead to accidents, and who's saying the next one won't be you or your family? I heard of a town down in Texas. A rancher faced an uncertain state and made an offering to the sheriff. That sheriff refused the offer, believing the law was on his side. Later that day, his house caught fire and burned to the ground. No one died, but the sheriff got the message. He quit the job and moved his family away."

Gaynes was fuming inside, but knew better than to reveal it. The rancher's threat was convincing enough. "I heard you, McFadden."

"I'll be back in a few days, Sheriff. I want your answer when I return."

McFadden made his way to the door and opened it. Two men stood outside, guarding the doorway. "Make the right decision, Sheriff." Then he walked toward his men, who watched from the hitch rail.

Gaynes leaned against the desk, pondering the rancher's request. If he did what McFadden suggested, he could never be in law enforcement again. What about his wife and child? Could he protect them without submitting to the crazy rancher's demands? Maybe it was time to get more aggressive toward this evil. "I must inform Cora and her men."

Chapter 45

Ellison McCarnnon and Julian Stokes rode to the porch of the ranch house, where Cora and some of Jesse's men waited with her, drinking coffee.

Cora rose when she saw them and walked to the hitch rail. "Any trouble last night?"

"No, ma'am," replied Ellison. "Heard some coyotes during the early morning, but that's it."

"Good. Get some breakfast, then a few hours of sleep. We'll keep this going for a while."

"Yes, ma'am."

Ellison and Julian rode away and tied their mounts at the barn, where Sheldon had the saddles removed.

Cora returned to the porch as Jesse came up. "My men can help with the night watch."

"I'd rather your men keep an eye out over the place. You're better with weapons than my men."

"Someone's coming, folks," Eli said.

"That's the Sheriff," Cora said. "I hope McFadden's men haven't shot another one of mine."

"Sheldon has most of them working the herd today," Jesse said.

"I hope with all that's gone on, you have time with your son."

"Cora, God is going to see you through this. I don't know how, but after praying last night, I'm confident he has this."

"Thank you for sharing, Jesse. I suppose this trouble has shaken my faith. Pray that I keep my hope through it."

"You better see what Sheriff Gaynes has to say."

"Yes."

* * *

Sheldon's answer to avoid McFadden's men at the river was to move the cattle from the north field to the southern pond. The water supply would not sustain the entire herd for long, though with so much friction in the air, the foreman felt it was best.

By the time Samuel reached the north field, the herd was nowhere around. He made his way to the nearby creek and dismounted.

After tying Sadie to a small sapling, Samuel walked to the water and threw a few smooth stones, watching them skip across. He then spotted a log on a graveled section. Removing his gun belt, he laid it on top and kneeled against it.

"Father, I don't know what to do. Cora is facing a dire situation not of her making. I need to know if your intention in bringing me here was to help address the issue.

"Hagarty is a fast gun who threatens Cora and her family. Maybe I am not quick enough to take him down, but someone needs to stop him. Asking Pa to intervene would burden him, and I don't want that. He has lived twenty years without being pursued by other men.

"And Lord, how can I become a preacher if I kill a man in a gunfight? But I see no other way to protect Cora and her family."

He picked up another rock and remembered a scripture passage when David defeated Goliath with a smooth stone. The stone was David's weapon of choice, and the Lord had given him the strength to defeat the giant that day. "God, give me the strength if it comes to a fight. I am nothing without you."

When he raised his head, a gray wolf stood ten feet away, staring. The wolf snarled, revealing his front teeth and fangs. Samuel sensed his eagerness to pounce.

"Easy, fellow. I'm not here to hurt you. Leave me alone, and I'll leave you alone."

The wolf's growl intensified at Samuel's voice, stepping closer, head lowered.

Samuel gazed to his right, where his weapon lay on the log, leather belt wrapped around the gun and holster. Reaching it was risky. "Friend, I'm not going to hurt you. Now I'm getting up from the ground." He raised a knee to a half-squatting position, and the wolf snarled louder.

As he lifted to his feet, the wolf started toward him. "Wait!" He raised his hands to the air as if surrendering, and the wolf stopped in his tracks three feet away.

Samuel pointed at the gray wolf. "I resist you, in the name of the Lord!" After a brief pause, he cried, "Leave now!"

The predator broke off growling, turned, and ran away.

Samuel sighed and reached for his gun as he heard a voice behind him say, "Keep your weapon buckled until he is gone."

Turning, he spotted Maggie standing thirty feet away, eyes wide at what she had witnessed.

"Maggie, I didn't know you were here."

"I didn't know you kept company with wolves."

"You saw that, huh?"

"Some of it. Why did he stop coming for you?"

"I rebuked him."

"I heard, but still."

"Momma taught us to resist evil. I sensed an evil spirit when the wolf growled, though no fault of the wolf. The Bible says the devil comes as a roaring lion. I suppose this time as a wolf."

"He ran toward you, and your gun was too far away. I would have run to my horse for a rifle had I not been frozen stiff. Were you scared?"

"At first, but I realized it was the devil's attempt to distract me from the fight ahead."

"I've been wanting to speak with you about that."

"Oh, yeah?"

"Samuel, don't go against Hagarty or Lane. Please!"

"What if I can't avoid it?"

"Try hard. You know you are called to be a preacher, but how can you stand before people and preach against murder if you kill a man?"

"Maggie, you put me in a difficult position. I can't stand by and let those gunfighters continue to kill people, especially your mom and you or Jeremiah."

"I love you, Samuel, and I don't want you to have this over you the rest of your life."

"Well, it's one thing to kill a man in cold blood, but quite a different matter to kill him in defense of others or yourself."

"Maybe so, but there's still the taking of life. When people do this, they never recover from it. Sometimes killing a man can haunt a person."

His mom had told him about Jesse and his many dreams and nightmares because of killing a man. He didn't want that to happen but had to do the right thing. "But I can't let you or your family die because of McFadden.

"We can take care of ourselves."

"I have to be sure."

"Then I have to do this. I know we have only spoken a little of marriage, but if you go against these men, I will not marry you."

"Maggie, please don't lock me down. I can't be bound when they come."

"Just the same. That's my request."

Samuel kicked the dirt as he turned toward the creek. "Is that what you came to say?"

Maggie folded her arms, sighing. "I love you, Samuel. No matter how this turns out, just know I love you." She turned and walked toward her horse.

That was her ultimatum, he thought. Kill the gunfighters who come to kill Cora and her family and lose any chance of marrying Maggie.

"God, this is hard, much harder than I first imagined. How can I leave them unprotected?" He knew his pa would step up if needed, but how could he let him face another gunfighter? "Oh God, please guide me."

Chapter 46

Jasper and Kendall loaded the feed into the buckboard.

"I thought Emmet would get more work in before he left," said Jasper.

"You know those preachers. Just seems they always skirt the hard stuff. At least he's not eating with us."

"Did you see him eating chicken? Wow! He put a lot of that bird away."

"And it wasn't one bird, Jasper. Hanna killed three."

"Emmet must have eaten two of them himself."

"I figure that's about right."

"That's the last bag. Did you get the flour?" Jasper asked.

"Yes, tossed it on first. I hope Hanna doesn't mind that I bought some peaches."

"If she does, we'll buy them. Peaches are a pleasant change from beans and cornbread."

Kendall laughed and stepped into the driver's seat. "And chicken. We're going to run her out of chickens."

"Hey, you're getting around on that leg without a crutch now. Maybe it's time we went home."

Kendall popped the reins to signal the horses to move out. "Yeah, that casting gone helps, but I can't leave until I know Jesse's place is safe."

"Things are getting better."

"Jasper, if you and Molly need to head home, now is a good time with Billy and his men helping."

"Thought about that, but I couldn't face myself if I left and something happened."

"Well, nothing has happened in over a week. Maybe Bartlett figures if he does anything, it might hinder his defense."

"Let's hope so."

"When we get unloaded, I think I'll take a knap."

"There are a lot of other things we can help Jesse with."

"Kendall, I'm tired. I got up at daybreak and rode the fence lines."

"I'll help you tomorrow."

Gunfire sounded before the buckboard reached the crossroad to Jesse's ranch. A bullet ricocheted off the wagon.

"I guess we didn't wish strong enough," Kendall said as he slapped the reins to the horses, urging them to a faster gait.

Jasper cocked the Winchester and spun around when he spotted three riders coming in behind them, firing once, missing the first riders. "Ain't easy shooting from a bouncing wagon."

"Doesn't matter. Just keep firing. You might get lucky. They don't know you're grappling."

"I kinda think they do," Jasper said, then fired another round.

They came to the fenced entrance and pushed the team on through as the riders gained ground behind them.

Kendall spotted their womenfolk on the porch and Billy's men at the barn.

"When I pull beside the house, jump down and get those women inside."

"What are you going to do?"

"Something crazy, probably. I'll use the wagon as cover and hope Billy can send them on their way. Just make sure our women are safe."

The wagon halted as dust rose behind them, helping their cover.

Jasper dropped to the ground and ran toward the steps. Laura and Hanna fired rifles at the riders.

"Get up here, Jasper," Hanna said.

"Get inside, ladies. Don't take chances in the open."

"But we have to return fire."

"Billy and his men are giving it to them. Get inside before you—."

A bullet came fast, hitting Hanna in the leg.

"Laura, take her inside. Give me that rifle," Jasper said.

Laura grabbed Hanna around the waist and walked with her through the door.

Taking Laura's rifle with him, Jasper ran to the wagon for cover. Kendall hunkered behind, shooting at the riders.

"They don't give up," Kendall said. "But there goes one."

One of the riders took a bullet and fell to the ground. The other two fired toward the barn. A man with a dark beard pulled a rifle from his saddle and fired twice, hitting Billy once in the shoulder.

Kendall raised his rifle and fired, the bullet catching the bearded one in the chest, and he fell from his horse, dead.

The third rider turned to depart, but Jasper fired, placing a bullet in the man's abdomen. He fell, floundering on the ground in pain.

Billy raised and walked from the barn. "Are there any more of them?"

"We only saw three," Jasper said.

"Are the women folk alright?"

"Hanna took a bullet in the leg, I believe. Laura helped her inside."

"You better check on them, Jasper."

"Come with me and get that shoulder tended to."

"Oh, this is nothing," Billy replied. "My man, Jake, can pull the bullet."

"Alright, I'll check on Hanna."

Jasper and Kendall went inside and found Laura wrapping Hanna's leg.

"I can't get the bullet out," Laura declared.

"Billy has a man who knows how. I'll get him," Jasper said.

Hanna raised from the pillow. "Yes, get him. I don't want to lose my leg."

"You're a long way from losing that leg. I'll be back."

∗ ∗ ∗

Billy sat on a hay bale as his man dug into his shoulder. Grimacing, Billy turned to look when he heard Jasper. "How is she?"

"She's hurting but could use some help with the bullet."

Jake looked up from working on Billy. "I'll help her."

"Where did you learn how to do this?"

"I was a doctor before the war. I felt so little like going into business when the war ended. Been with Billy for a while now."

"Yeah, we've seen our share of bullets, ain't we?" Billy commented.

Jake pulled against Billy's shoulder. "Yep, and here's yours." He held it up for them to see.

"Such a small thing to cause so much pain," Billy said.

Jake reached into a saddlebag, pulled out a piece of cloth, and tore it into pieces. He wrapped Billy's shoulder and made him a sling.

"I suppose you expect me to wear this contraption?"

"I know you're tough, Billy, but tomorrow, you won't be able to move that arm for the pain."

Billy reached with his good arm and jerked away the sling. "Then you can strap me tomorrow. "I'm fine right now."

Jake shook his head and raised, turning to Jasper. "Let's go look at the woman."

"Billy's tougher and a bit more rigid than I remembered," Jasper commented as they walked toward the house.

"Yeah, cattle drives sear a man's mind, and you become hardened."

"What was Billy meaning when he said you've had your share of bullets?"

"Indians. We've run into them so much over the years. I think all of us have taken bullets."

"Then it's good Billy has a doctor along."

"They ain't got much. I still have nightmares about that war."

"I'm sorry."

They reached the porch and went inside.

When Jake reached Hanna, he unwrapped the wound and looked it over. "I know I should know your name, Mrs. Stalls, but I've forgotten."

"Hanna."

"Hanna, this is going to hurt."

"I know. I removed a bullet once."

"You did?"

"Yes, Jesse shot an Indian who came into our camp. I had Jesse take him to our wagon and removed it."

"Then you know about the pain."

"I'll try to be like that Indian. He hardly showed his pain."

"No, Hanna. You don't need to do that." He turned to Laura. "Bring some boiled water and a small towel for her to bite down on."

"Hanna, Jake will get the bullet out," Kendall said. "You follow his instructions."

Hanna nodded.

"Momma, you should tell Pa when you send the next telegram," Rebecca suggested.

"No, Jesse can't know, or he'll ride away. He has to stay until he finds Samuel and brings him home. I don't want anything to distract him."

Laura returned with the water.

"I'm going to clean the wound. Then, after I extract the bullet, I'll clean some more. Put the cloth in your mouth to protect your teeth and bite down on it."

Jake looked up at Kendall and Laura. "Hold her down. Here goes."

Hanna moaned as Jake dug into the leg wound.

"The bullets deep. Hold on."

Jake dug deeper, and Hanna groaned, biting down hard, her eyes widening. He soon pulled free the lead bullet and laid it on a table beside the bed.

Hanna relaxed, allowing the towel to fall from her mouth as she fell asleep.

"What's wrong?" Laura asked.

"That's the body's way of responding to the pain. She'll rest now."

Kendall turned to Jake. "I'm glad you were here. Thank you."

"Yes, thank you," Laura said.

"Well, I better check on Billy. He's stubborn and won't follow doctors' orders."

"I'll walk along with you," Kendall uttered. "I want to thank Billy."

"He didn't mind, and his sister's here."

"Still, I should thank him."

"I'm coming too," Laura said.

"Good idea."

Chapter 47

Kendall gazed across the breakfast table as they finished eating. "I think Laura and I should head home. A week has passed since Bartlett sent his men for another attempt. I've got so much work to catch up on, and now that the doc has removed the casting, I can get to it. Unless you think we should stay on, Hanna?"

"No, you're right. You folks have been so wonderful to help. I know we can never repay for the time you spent here."

"I think Kendall is right. I spoke to the sheriff yesterday," Jasper said. "He told me after our shoot-out with Bartlet's men that the rest pulled out. Said Bartlett can't pay enough from jail. So, unless we don't need to stay, Molly and I will also head home.

"Hanna is wounded, Jasper," Molly informed.

"We'll be alright," Rebecca said. "I'll be here for Momma."

"We could stay a little longer, just in case," Kendall said.

"No need," Jasper replied. "Billy said he and his men would stick around another week or more."

"Oh, no," Rebecca said.

"What's wrong, honey?" Hanna asked.

"If Billy and his men stay, I will have to cook for them."

Laughter burst through the room.

"Don't worry about that. I'll show you what to do. This is a great time for you to learn more because one day a man will come along you like, and you better know something about cooking."

"Momma!"

"Everything will be alright, dear."

"I'll see Billy before we load up," Kendall said. "He might know something about folks needing trained horses. I've got several back home I want to get to."

"Papa will be glad we're coming home," Jasper responded.

"I know. Can't you just imagine his list of projects?"

"Don't remind me."

Two of Billy's men were playing cards outside the barn when the brothers walked up. "I thought you folks were heading back home?" Billy asked, leaning against the fence.

"We are," Kendall said. "How's the shoulder?"

"I can't lift my arm at all. Jake said it could take a couple of months. Did you know he wants to move my shoulder next week, even if it hurts?"

"Seems that would hinder healing."

"He said he read in some book that doctors are experimenting with it. They call it therapy. I call it stupidity, and I told him so."

"I was always told to follow the doctor's orders because they know best."

Billy turned, peering at Jake. "Jake's been out of practice for years. The only thing he's done is bullets and a few cuts."

"I'm sure glad he was here," Jasper said. "Hanna might have bled to death if we had taken the wagon to town."

"Yeah, next time, I might just bleed out. Just not sure I want to go through all that pain the Doctor Jake plans for me."

Jake rose from the bale of hay. "You'll try it if you want motion in that shoulder. I've removed many bullets from shoulders in the war. Those men can't use their arms. This method has to help."

"Maybe it's worth a try."

"Billy, I have a question before we leave out. Have you run across places that might need trained horses?" Kendall asked.

"The army is dwindling at most forts, but Fort Worth and St. Louis might work for you. I also heard New Orleans was good for sales, though it is a long trail. If you really need to move horses, though, you might try Montana. Cattlemen show up in droves and always need broken cattle mounts."

"Long way to Montana."

"Yes, but you can take the train part of the way now."

"Hmm. A man might want to take a trip and find clients beforehand."

"Sounds like something that might interest Jesse," Jasper said.

"Jesse raises fine horses," Billy said. "I wish we could stay around until he returns, but I have a cattle drive that needs to be moved soon. There's one horse of Jesse's I'd love to own."

"Are you staying another week?" Kendall asked.

"Yes, I already promised Jasper, but we got to ride out in a week, headed for Kansas. Do you think that lawyer will send more men this way?"

"If Bartlett has more, the sheriff knows little about it. The others left town," Jasper said. "The chances seem small."

"Well, since we've got time, we'll stay a week," Billy said. "You men have been here longer and have lives to get to."

"Thanks for all your help, Billy," Kendall said. "You men made the difference."

"Just glad to help."

"Jasper, I suppose it is time to load up."

"Yes, it is."

They turned and walked toward the porch.

* * *

Hanna sat on the porch watching Jasper, Molly, Kendall, and Laura load their wagons. The time spent with them had its trials, but being in their presence was enjoyable, if only for a short while. The one thing that could have topped it was if Jesse could have joined them.

Laura and Molly had become like sisters to her, and their departure would produce a significant void. However, while they awaited Jesse and Samuel's arrival, she would teach Rebecca much about cooking.

Kendall smiled as he walked onto the porch. "Hanna, I tried to turn that seat into a better sitting place. You can take over for me."

"I'll do my best."

"I don't think it will take long for you to get back on your feet. At least you have no broken bones."

"Tell that to my leg. The pain today is excruciating."

"I know, but you'll feel better a few days from now."

"Hanna, I will miss you," Laura said. She reached down to hug her.

"I will miss you too."

Jasper and Molly walked closer.

"Hanna, we hate to leave you, but you know how it is," Jasper said. "I have several furniture orders to get out."

"We've enjoyed having everyone."

"I figured you'd be glad to get us gone," Molly said.

"Not at all."

Molly reached down to hug Hanna. "Thank you for the hospitality."

"I will miss you, Molly."

"I will miss you and Rebecca, too. She's growing up fast."

"She wants to be a writer."

"Yes, I read one of her stories. She will be wonderful."

"Well, folks, it's time we pull out," Jasper said.

"Jasper, tell Emmet I am very thankful he came to help."

"I sure will, Hanna."

They climbed into the wagons and started down the lane. Billy and his men stood near the barn and waved as it rolled away.

"Well, Rebecca, it looks like it's time to start lunch," Hanna said.

"Already?"

"I'm afraid so."

"I'll be glad when you are on your feet. Momma."

Hanna grinned. "Don't count on that happening soon."

"Oh, Momma."

Chapter 48

Clearwater's Deputy Willis Hobbs stepped into the Sheriff's office. "Sheriff, three men just rode into town looking for the McFadden place. All of them with guns tied down."

"So, they look to be gunfighters, is what you're saying?"

"Yes, sir. What are we going to do?"

"I spotted two yesterday. Seems McFadden is out for a war."

"I thought it had already started," Willis said.

"Maybe, but it could get worse. Are those men still in town?"

"They went into the saloon."

Sheriff Gaynes opened the gun cabinet and reached in for a shotgun. "Take this Greener with you. Let's take a walk to the saloon."

"You're going against them?"

"Just wanting to set the rules, Willis." He reached for a second shotgun and shells. "Load it."

When they had prepared the weapons, Sheriff Gaynes and Deputy Hobbs started towards the saloon. Townsfolk backed away when they noticed the shotguns.

Gaynes pushed open the saloon doors and stepped inside. There was no missing the ones Willis had referred to. They leaned confidently on the bar, drinking their whisky and beer.

Patrons observed and made room when they realized the Sheriff was looking at the newcomers.

"You three at the bar drinking. I need a word," said Sheriff Gaynes.

The cowboys turned and grinned when they saw him.

"What can we do for you, Sheriff?" said one gunman, wearing a black hat and vest.

"I hear you're looking for the McFadden place."

"That's right, Sheriff."

"State your business there."

The man shrugged. "Not too much, Sheriff. We're looking for jobs, not that it's any of your concern."

"Around these parts, I make it my concern."

"I suppose that's part of your job, Sheriff, but you have no need to worry. Seems that ranch needs men who can break a few broncs."

"Mister, I don't see bronc busting in any of you. What I see are the kind of men who come looking to pull their weapons."

"Sheriff, we only wear them to protect ourselves."

"What are your names?"

"I'm Brody Marks." He pointed toward the man beside him. "This here is Reno Boyd. The man at the end is James Spears."

"Mr. Marks, can you assure me I'll not see any of you in gunfights in my town?"

"Well, like I said, we're only here for the work."

"Yeah, broncs, I remember. Let's keep it that way."

Brody smiled, exposing a dimple. "Yes, sir, Sheriff. We're not here to cause trouble. Just came to calm a few wild horses."

Sheriff Gaynes turned and exited the saloon. From outside, he could hear the cowboys whooping loudly.

"Broncs, my foot," Gaynes said.

"You did what you could, Sheriff," said Willis Hobbs. "They've broken no laws, so there's not much we can do."

"I know that, but I'd like to put them in jail. As sure as I do, McFadden will ride in with his army and take them."

"This is a dangerous situation, Sheriff."

"Yes, but I don't have to give in."

"Give in to what?" Willis asked as they entered the Sheriff's Office.

"Never mind. What I am going to do is side with Cora Rivers in this thing. She's in the right and doesn't deserve what McFadden's trying to do."

"But Sheriff, by now, McFadden must have forty men. Half may be gunhands."

"Cora also has gunhands working for her, if they stick around."

"Um, Sheriff, remember those men we had in our jail?"

"The ones looking for the man's son?"

"That's the one. I was talking to my friend Seth at the mercantile. He said there is a story about a man with the name Jesse Stalls. Seems he killed a man in a gunfight about twenty years ago."

"He's sure it's the same man?"

"Not one hundred percent."

"I wonder how he lasted this long? Most gunhands I've heard of are dead a year or two after their first kill."

"I don't know, Sheriff."

"I think I'll search my papers for those men at the saloon."

"There might be one," Willis said as he stared out the window.

"If I find anything, I'll bring them in before they reach McFadden's. The arrest would be easier."

"Sir, it's too late," Willis said.

"Why?"

"They're riding out now."

"Oh, this war is gonna be bad, and lots of people will die. If only the army could get here."

"Maybe they will, Sheriff. We should wire for them."

"I already have, but it will take weeks for them to plan something."

Chapter 49

Woodie Bosworth and Howdy Millard herded the cattle and calves into the corral.

Foreman Nick Lambert observed their work. "Woodie, how many more calves to brand?"

"Maybe forty or fifty."

"We've got to get this done today."

"We could use some help," Woodie said.

Nick turned, watching several of McFadden's men sitting on the front porch, each a gunhand hired to take control of Riverview Ranch. "I'll see what I can do. Where's Benson?"

"He's running line."

"Then I'll find Wilburn. He's watching the south herd."

"Alright."

Nick mounted his horse and rode until he came to the pasture and spotted Wilburn. He called out as he slowed his mount. "I need you at the ranch house to help with branding."

"Sure." Wilburn turned his horse to leave and then stopped. "Hey Nick, I don't like this idea of going against Riverview. That ain't right."

"And many of us agree with you."

"Is there anything we can do about it?"

"Quit."

"I thought about it, but I need a payday."

"We are all the same."

"Well, I better get to the branding area." Wilburn kicked his horse into a gait and left.

Nick agreed with Wilburn. This war will only get worse since McFadden hired more gunfighters.

He turned his horse and headed back to the ranch behind the elderly cowboy. As he drew near the ranch, he saw three riders coming in. *More gunhands.* There was nothing he could do except maybe quit. He wondered if Cora Rivers might hire him. Maybe he should speak with Jenny before leaving.

* * *

Jenny had received Nick's message to meet him in the shed after everyone went to sleep. She waited inside with an oil lamp burning as he entered.

"Haven't I warned you about the lamp, Jenny? Everyone will see it," Nick complained.

"I don't care."

"I do." Nick hoped Jenny and he could make a go of it away from her father, but he didn't want others knowing.

Jenny drew closer and kissed him passionately. "You know I love you, right?"

"Yes, and I love you."

"Will you spend some time with me tonight?"

"Jenny, I have something to say."

She stared curiously, wondering if something terrible was coming. "What do you mean?"

"You mentioned leaving before. Well, I've decided that now is the time."

"Then I'm leaving with you."

"What about your inheritance?"

"I don't care about that. I'll be old when that happens if it ever does. I just want to get away from Father. When are you thinking about leaving?"

"Tonight."

"Tonight? I can't leave tonight. I don't have anything ready."

"We're going light. You can carry only a few things if you want to get away."

"I suppose."

"Can you ready a small bag and meet me at the barn in an hour?"

"You really mean it."

"Yes, I do."

"But where will we go?"

"I thought I'd check with Cora Rivers and see if she might hire me."

Jenny smiled. "That would infuriate my father for sure. But will Cora Rivers hire you? And what about me? I can't stay in some dirty bunkhouse."

"We'll know more when we get there. She will either hire me or not, and I can't see Cora putting you in the bunkhouse with the men."

"I hope she pays you well. That's all we'll have, Nick."

"We'll have each other. Samuel is there, and Maggie. We'll have some friends."

"Nick, what if your leaving causes other men to leave my father?"

"Jenny, it's their choice, but I hope you're right. If they came to Riverview, that might help even things."

Jenny peered downward.

"Are you alright?"

"I just thought about what might happen to my father. I told you how close it came for us in Texas, didn't I?"

"Yes."

"I will be sad if he dies in some war over water, but he's brought it on himself."

"I'm sorry, Jenny." Nick reached and wiped the tears from her eyes. "Let's get ready to leave. The least we can do is save our lives and help others."

"I'll get my things." She kissed him again and ran out the door with the oil lamp as Nick walked toward the barn to saddle their horses.

Thirty minutes had passed when Jenny came through the door carrying a brown suitcase.

Nick gazed up at her. "Did anyone spot you?"

"I don't think so. Nick, what will my father do when they realize we are both gone?"

"I'm sure they will look for *you*."

"I hope he doesn't make a huge deal about it. Maybe I should leave a note."

"That's not necessary. We'll deal with whatever happens."

Nick tied Jenny's suitcase onto the bay mare and turned toward her. "We're doing this, and no one will stop us."

"I'm happy we're leaving."

Nick helped her mount the bay. "I know you've had your struggles, and I hope things get better wherever life takes us."

"I know it will. Get on your horse, Nick, and let's leave before someone sees us."

Riverview was lively when Nick and Jenny arrived. They watched as two cowboys escorted them to the porch. Others waited after noticing.

From the barn, Samuel saw Nick dismount and walked to him. "Nick, what are you doing here?"

Nick turned when he heard the voice he recognized. "Samuel, how are you?"

"I'm doing fine, but I didn't expect to see your face."

"I quit McFadden."

Samuel gazed at Jenny, still mounted. "You brought us trouble."

"I hope not."

Jesse walked to meet them. "You finally left that place."

"Yes, sir, I did."

Maggie and Cora hurried from inside the ranch house when they heard folks talking.

Cora peered at them as she neared, wondering who they were. "What's your name?"

"Nick Lambert, ma'am. I know you from the few times I saw you in town."

"You work for McFadden?"

"Not anymore, because I don't like what he's doing to you."

"We advised Nick to leave as we rode away from McFadden's ranch," Jesse disclosed.

Cora looked Nick and Jenny over. "Leaving took you a spell."

"Yes, ma'am. I held on because of Jenny, but we've both had enough."

"She work for McFadden, too?"

Nick sighed. "No, ma'am. Jenny is McFadden's daughter."

"Oh, dear Lord. This ain't right bringing her here."

Jenny dismounted and walked toward them. "Please don't send us away. *You* know how terrible my father is, and he's the same to me. I can't go back to him, no matter what."

Cora pondered the situation for a moment. "Nick, I suppose you're looking for a job?"

"Yes, ma'am."

"What can you do?"

"Anything to do with cattle and horses. I was McFadden's foreman."

"Already have a foreman, but I can hire you as a regular hand."

"That's fine and thank you."

Cora shook her head, peering at Sheldon. "McFadden will be boiling with anger, losing not only a daughter but his foreman."

"Yes, ma'am, he might."

"We should prepare. Listen up, everyone. McFadden could come riding in here at any time. Sheldon, get everyone in for now. Make sure the men at the gate know to fire two shots in plenty of time for a warning."

"I'll get on it."

"Jesse, I'm thankful you haven't left us, but again, this is not your fight. You don't have to stay."

"Yes, ma'am, I do. Samuel is here. The men and I realize the difficulty you face, and we can't leave you to fight gunhands on your own."

"Then maybe you men can help me figure out a plan."

"We can try."

"Let's go inside. Ask Eli, Samuel, and your other men to come as well. Sheldon, you come too because you will need to inform the men."

"Yes, ma'am," Sheldon said.

"Maggie, see if you can locate a place for Jenny to stay in the house. Nick, we'll find an empty bed for you in one of the bunkhouses later."

Nick nodded and led their horse into the barn as the others marched toward the ranch house.

Chapter 50

Tollie Mefford sat on the bunkhouse porch, watching the other cowhands prepare to leave. "Ya'll moving cattle to the river today, Dolph?"

"Yep, sorry you got shot. You just sit here and heal up. When I get time, I'll play cards with you."

"Yeah, gonna tire of this porch."

"You'll get paid. Cora won't let you down."

Sheldon strolled to the bunkhouse porch. "Where's Nick Lambert?"

"He's in the other bunkhouse," Dolph replied.

Samuel and Nick were talking as Sheldon opened the door to the second sleeping quarters. "Hey fellows, I need both of you with us today."

"Are you expecting trouble?" Samuel asked.

"With McFadden, there's always a chance for trouble," Nick commented.

"I'd just like to get our cows to water this morning," Sheldon said.

"Our horses are saddled," Samuel said.

"Good. Heading out in about five minutes."

"I wonder if we should ask your pa to go along?" Nick asked as they strolled toward their horses.

"I don't see why. A few days ago, we gave those boys something to think about."

"Yeah, but this is McFadden. You can never tell about him."

"Nick, we'll have plenty of gunhands along. I think we'll be fine."

"I hope so."

When Sheldon had gathered the ranch hands, they rode out to locate the herd.

* * *

Sitting across from Jesse and Eli, Cora took a sip of coffee as the hands rode out. "I'd like to hire more men to help with the cattle, but good men are hard to find in these parts."

"I'd help you if I could," Eli said.

"I know you would, but we need you around here. Maybe Nick will work out."

"He seems competent."

Maggie heard them and came outside. "Momma, I wonder if there are men at Rolling Green or Hayesville?"

"Maggie, I don't have the time to ride and find out. McFadden's holding us down here."

"This will soon be over," Eli said.

"I need it to be. I'm tired of sitting on pins and needles, waiting for him to do something stupid."

Jesse grinned. "None of what McFadden has done is stupid to him. In his mind, it all makes sense."

"I guess he doesn't even notice the people he hurt."

"Cora, men like him are full of evil," Jesse said. "Darkness drives what they do. I learned long ago that a flesh man exists in each of us. If you feed that man, he will grow stronger. According to Ephesians, the prince of the power of the air, the devil, works in the children of disobedience, gives life to the lust of the flesh, and fulfills the desires of the flesh and mind. We were born with a nature of the children of wrath. Only when we serve God do we overcome this nature."

"Jesse, what does that mean?" Cora asked.

"Well, to me, it means that unless we allow God's grace to save us from that old man, there's no telling how far sin will take us. The evidence this is true is McFadden."

"Beyond what I want to go," Maggie said.

"I see why Samuel has preacher inclinations," Cora said.

"No, that comes from his momma. Hanna reads the Bible all the time. I read it, but not like her. She taught Samuel and Rebecca to read from the Bible."

"She certainly has made an impact on Samuel. I don't know your daughter, so I can't comment."

"You'd like her. She's hoping to write true stories about pioneer women and their lives as they travel west."

"I would love to read them."

"Me too," Maggie said.

Eli raised in his chair and walked to the edge of the porch.

"What is it, Eli?" Jesse asked.

"I hear gunfire."

Jesse turned to Cora. "They were only taking cattle for water, right?"

"Yes."

"We better ride and see what's up," Eli said.

Cora rose from her chair. "Maggie and I are going with you."

* * *

The gunfire grew louder as they rode closer to the river.

"Stop here," Eli said. "Jesse, why don't you ride closer and see what's happening? I'll watch the women until you return with a report."

Jesse nodded and kicked his horse forward. When he topped the hill, he saw cattle in the river stirred by the gunfire. Some had crossed over, and McFadden's men were herding them away. He searched for Samuel, who had dismounted with several of Cora's men. As shots rang from both sides, Jesse turned and rode to find Eli.

After explaining what he saw, Jesse and the others rode to the top of the hill and dismounted.

"Let's spread out along here," Eli said.

"That's a long shot, Eli," Jesse said.

"How can we get closer?"

Jesse spotted a jag in the terrain beside the river north of where the fighting occurred. "Not we. I'll go." He pointed to the section of the river. "Cover me when I cross. Distract McFadden's men."

"I hope our men don't take you for one of theirs," Eli said.

"I do, too."

Jesse kicked his horse and rode down the other side until he reached the trees and rode to the water. As he approached the river, he noticed McFadden's men returning after herding away Cora's cattle.

Shots rang behind him as Eli and the women gave him a chance. He pulled his rifle from the horse, urging it on. When he had reached the other side, he dismounted and moved his horse to a second jag of the river bank for safety.

Wading in the water, he found a tree blown down by a storm, offering cover at the edge. He spotted two riders returning from herding the cattle and took his aim, hitting one in the shoulder and the other in the neck. The second went down.

Using a tree for cover, one man raised his rifle to aim at Cora and Maggie. Jesse sent a bullet that found the man's arm. He turned to see Jesse but took another shot in the chest.

One of McFadden's men called out, "Let's go men. There are too many of them."

The riders ran for their horses, and the shooting ceased.

Jesse mounted his horse and joined Cora's other men as they gathered the herd, moving them away from the river.

Cora rode up beside them. "Jesse, did they take some of my cattle?"

"Yes, ma'am, but I don't know how many."

She turned to one of her hands. "Dolph, how many cows did we lose?"

"About fifteen or sixteen, maybe."

"The law has got to do something about this."

"Ma'am, the law won't go against all those guns."

"They got to try. I want my cattle back."

"You got other things to worry about," Dolph said.

"What things?"

"Three men took bullets. One will be okay, but Andy is on the bank bleeding and may not make it. Sheldon didn't."

"Oh, no, Sheldon's dead?"

"Yes, ma'am."

Cora sighed and looked away. "Dolph, pull a couple of men and take Andy and Sheldon back. We'll get Andy to Dr. Hosner before we lose him, too."

"How about having Mr. Stalls and his men go along? You might need help in town, ma'am."

"You want Samuel here?"

"Yeah, we need a few good hands with this herd."

Cora turned to Jesse. "Do you mind?"

"Not at all. I'll get Eli, and we'll take Andy back with you. Sorry about your foreman."

"McFadden has to pay for this." She turned and rode toward the injured cowboy.

Chapter 51

Cora paced the porch outside Dr. Hosner's office as Jesse and the others waited with her.

"Cora, maybe you should speak to the sheriff. We can wait here," Eli said.

"No, he's my man. I'll make sure he's okay, then have a conversation with the sheriff. Men, McFadden *will* hand over my cattle."

"Someday, he will pay for his evil deeds," Jesse said.

"I do not wish recompense on any man, but this one has caused much harm. If he would get his heart right and be the kind of neighbor, every rancher hoped for when he came."

"That's not impossible, but greed has a way of penetrating and distorting a man inside."

"I know."

The door swung open, and Dr. Hosner stepped out.

Cora turned to him. "Is Andy going to make it?"

The doctor said, "Right now, it is touch and go with your man. The bullet was deep, and he lost a lot of blood before you got him here. My assistant and I will keep watch over him through the night. If he holds out, he stands a good chance of making it."

"Thank you, Dr. Hosner. Either myself or one of my men will ride in tomorrow to check."

Hosner nodded. "Tell me what happened, Cora. Is this McFadden's doing again?"

"I'm afraid so."

"The law should do something about that man."

"Doctor, Sheriff Gaynes, and his deputies can't do much. McFadden has too many guns."

"He should call in the army. They're not fighting Indian wars these days."

"Going that way now, and I'll ask. Are you ready, men?"

Eli nodded, and they followed behind Cora toward the sheriff's office.

* * *

"What else do you want me to do?" Shep Parvey said as he walked from the jail area with a broom in his hand.

"Well, I don't know," said Sheriff Gaynes. "Sit over there and be quiet. I want to drink my coffee and read through these new wanted posters."

Shep peered casually out the window as he approached the coffee pot. "Sheriff, more trouble coming our way."

"Why do you say that?"

"Cora and some of her hands are headed in here."

"What now?" Gaynes rose from the chair.

The door opened, and Cora, Eli, and Jesse stepped inside.

"Hello, Cora. Didn't expect to see you in town," Sheriff Gaynes said.

"I have plenty to do, but I keep getting sidetracked because of McFadden."

"What's he done now?"

"His men showed up at the river when we were watering cattle. You know the river is on my land."

"I know."

"They started shooting, and the cattle got stirred. Some crossed over, confused by the noise."

"Did anyone get hurt?"

"Hurt and killed. Andy Quick is at Doc Hosner's, and Sheldon is dead."

"They killed Sheldon Bryant?"

"Yep, he caught a bullet in the chest. We'll bury him when we get done here."

"I'm sorry, Cora. McFadden has all those guns, and I only have a couple of young deputies."

"He kept my cattle, Sheriff."

"How many?"

"The men believe fifteen or so. You have to get them back."

Sheriff Gaynes recalled McFadden's recent visit with a request that felt more like a threat. If he were to confront McFadden, he might just order one of his gunhands to kill him. "Look, Cora, I'd like to help, but this situation is far beyond what any sheriff is qualified for. I have a family."

"Those men McFadden injured and killed have families, too. And they are our family."

"I know that, and McFadden does also, but he doesn't care."

"What about sending for the army?" Jesse questioned.

"I sent a wire, but it will take weeks for them to make a decision."

"We can't wait weeks," Cora uttered.

Eli stepped up to the desk. "Sheriff, you don't have to go to McFadden's alone. Jesse and I will ride with you and your men. We are Texas Rangers and can still work with the law."

Gaynes reached a hand to his chin, thinking. "Alright, I'll have to deputize you, though. A star on your chest might show legitimacy."

"Sure."

The sheriff reached inside a drawer and pulled out two badges.

"You should get one more," Cora said. "I'm going along."

"That's not wise."

"Those are *my* cows McFadden stole. I want to look him in the face when we ask for them back."

He put his hand again inside the drawer and turned toward them. "If you concur, say yes. Can I count on the three of you to adhere to the laws of the land and the constitution of the United States?"

Jesse affirmed. "I will."

"Yes, I will," Eli stated.

Cora frowned. "Yes, Sheriff, but when you go after him for murder, I want to be present."

"We'll see about that." Gaynes turned to his deputy. "Shep, find Willis and someone to watch while we're gone. I have no preference about who."

"Yes, sir."

"Let's get our horses, gentlemen—and ma'am."

∗ ∗ ∗

The sheriff guided them through the entrance to McFadden's ranch. When Cora recognized the location, she pulled her shotgun from the scabbard and laid it across the saddle horn.

"What intentions do you have with that?" Sheriff Gaynes inquired.

"Nothing if JA McFadden is peaceful, but I don't trust him, so I'm arming myself."

"I will do the talking, you hear? This conversation must be carried out according to the law.

"Do you think he will hand over my cattle?"

"That's what we are here to find out."

As they neared the ranch house, three cowboys marched onto the porch, and four additional men waited on the ground. Jesse could tell most were gunhands, so he adjusted his position to the group's left.

Eli noticed his movement, nodded in agreement, and steered his horse to the right side.

One of the gunhands hurried into the house as they approached.

"Is McFadden around?" Sheriff Gaynes asked as his horse came to a stop.

Jack Hagarty grinned and walked to the edge. "Maybe there's something I can help you with."

"Nope, I need the boss man. Now, where is he?"

"Don't get your underwear in a twist. He's coming."

Moments later, the big rancher stepped out, gazing over the men Cora brought with the sheriff. "Are you taking on more deputies, Sheriff?"

"McFadden, I'll first inform you that those two on the ends are Texas Rangers."

"I had heard the rangers would take anyone on for their dirty work, even known killers." He peered at Jesse as he put a cigar in his mouth and lit it.

"My understanding of the Texas Rangers is that they conduct investigations into a person's past before hiring them, ensuring their qualifications," Gaynes stated.

"But we know that's not always true."

"McFadden, I'm not here to debate rangers. I'm here because your men illegally acquired cattle from Riverview."

McFadden smirked and shook his head. "Hear me out, Sheriff. Witnesses swear that Cora's men started the fight at the river.

"What are you doing at the river? The river is Cora's property.

"Cora granted me permission to water my cattle there."

"Water cattle, yes, but you can't sit in wait for her to bring her cattle for water. It's irrelevant who started the gunfire. The fact remains that you have some of her cattle. So, if I were to examine yours, I bet I'd find about fifteen or twenty with Riverview's brand."

The big rancher turned his head to the left where Hagarty stood.

Jesse and Eli watched the silent interaction, wondering what McFadden had up his sleeve. Then the rancher gestured with a hand, and Hagarty backed from the porch's edge.

McFadden turned again to the sheriff. "No one has stolen cattle from Cora. Those cows sprinted across the river because of the gunfire. My men were merely rounding them up for Cora. She can have them back."

"I expect you to follow through, McFadden. You will have some of your men collect them and take them to the river—today.

"Of course, but I'm deeply disappointed in you, Sheriff. Your life could have flourished, though I perceive now how it is.

"I already told you I took an oath when I put on this badge. I'm going to do what's right."

"That's alright. You go ahead, Sheriff." Then he shifted his gaze to Cora. "Cora, my men didn't mean to create problems for you. We don't need your cattle. My men will return them today."

"McFadden, your actions have caused the death of four of my men," Cora said. "You should be put behind bars. If I had my way, you would be."

"Cora, answer this one question. Have you seen my daughter, Jenny?"

Cora paused before responding, recalling that Jenny had previously shared how badly McFadden treated her, but he was her father. "She's at the ranch and doing well."

"Thank you. Now, please tell Jenny that I consider this terrible move her choice and that if something happens to me, she will not get the ranch. Her inheritance is no more."

"I have a feeling Jenny doesn't care. She begged me to take her in to get away from you."

Stunned, the big man had not foreseen the reply.

Sheriff Gaynes wheeled his horse to leave. "McFadden, ensure this gets done by the end of today."

"Sheriff, you've made a grave error not coming to my side," McFadden muttered as the riders guided their horses away.

Chapter 52

Samuel took Jeremiah to the corral nearest the ranch house and set up a sawhorse for roping practice.

"Jeremiah, roping is as hard as you make it. So, don't give up if you miss at first."

"Maybe this is something I don't need to learn. I only want to herd the cattle."

"Why is that important to you?"

"Momma lost good men. I miss Sheldon a lot, and I want to make up for him."

"But remember, Sheldon had years of experience working cows."

"I know, but I have to start somewhere. I used to ride when my father was alive. After he died, I was too sad."

"Maybe we should try riding first."

"Everyone said I had to rope."

"Sure, cowboys need to rope, but every cowboy I know learned to ride first."

"Okay, then let's ride. Can I ride Sheldon's horse?"

"I don't see why not, but we'll ask your momma. We'll find out what cows she wants moved today. Maybe that's a good place to start."

They walked to the porch where Cora and Eli sat.

Cora stood as Jeremiah stepped onto the porch. "What are you doing today?"

"I'm going to herd cattle. Samuel will also show me how to rope."

Cora smiled. "I'm glad, Jeremiah, but don't do this if you're uncomfortable."

"Jeremiah wants to help, and we thought before learning to rope that riding should come first," Samuel said.

"I think that's a great idea. Just please be careful, son," Cora said as she reached and gave Jeremiah a hug.

He turned to leave, then spun around. "Oh Momma, can I use Sheldon's horse?"

"Sure. You can claim him if he works out."

"Does he have a name?"

"Sheldon called him Dusty."

Jeremiah smiled and turned away. "I like that."

"Samuel, watch over him. He hasn't been on a horse since Stuart died. They used to ride together a lot."

"I'll take care of him."

Jesse overheard as he stepped outside. "Samuel, do you mind if I go along?"

"No."

"What are we doing?"

Samuel turned to Cora for an answer.

Cora nodded. "We kept those cows brought back from McFadden's separate from the others. I wanted to be sure they hadn't contracted something before adding them to the herd. Two of the hands are tending to them, but it's time we brought them into the large corral for a close inspection. Do you mind helping with that project?"

"No, ma'am," Samuel said.

"I'll go along," Jesse said. "Eli, do you want to help?"

"No, I think I'll stay put. Doc will want to go with you."

Jesse smiled, peering at Cora, who seemed fine with Eli sitting beside her. "I'll see you later then."

Cora sat in the swing beside Eli as the cowboys rode away with her son. "I hope Jeremiah does alright."

"Jesse and Samuel won't let anything happen to him. Besides, that job should only take an hour or so."

"Yeah, you're right, though I worry about Jeremiah. He was close to Stuart before the accident."

"Jeremiah needs a father figure in his life."

"I know he does, and that's on me."

Eli turned to Cora. "I'm a man who generally works a job and then moves on, but when I saw Jesse again after all those years, I realized how much I had missed being around friends. I noticed how he interacted with Rebecca and then how he was determined to find Samuel."

"What are you trying to say, Eli?"

"Maybe...that I love you. When we rode in, and I saw you, I felt something stir inside I've never felt before around a woman. Have you noticed that I enjoy sitting and talking with you?"

Cora laughed. "At first, it seemed a nuisance."

"A nuisance?"

"Well, I didn't know you. Yeah, a nuisance, and you scared me a little because you wore that gun."

"I think now you understand why some of us still wear our guns."

"Yes, and I hate it. Stuart hated guns, too, and maybe that's what got him killed."

"I don't think so. I heard the story, and my bet is McFadden or his men did it."

"I try not to think that, but you are probably right."

Eli reached for her arm. "Now, back to us."

"Back to us, huh?"

"I meant it when I said I love you."

"Eli, I enjoy your company and believe I'm in love, too."

"But—"

"I must speak with Maggie and Jeremiah before pursuing a relationship. They should be okay with it first."

"Cora, I'm hoping for more than a simple relationship."

"What?"

"Marry me. Make sure your children are okay with it, but then marry me. I can't even imagine how life would be without you now."

"You don't know me that well, Eli."

"I know enough. I know I'm in love with you, and I know I can help you around this place. You need someone to help protect your children. Maybe you'll let me be that person."

Cora fixed her eyes on him. This man was serious. She never expected the day would come again when a man would look at her like Eli did at this moment. She drew closer and kissed him passionately, her breath evaporating as their warm lips drew together.

Cora peered down as they eased apart. "I loved that. It has been a long time for me."

"Yes, me too." He stared into her eyes. "So, do you have an answer?"

She turned her head, gazing toward the barn and the fields as far as she could see. Stuart would not want her to be alone. There may never be a day when she feels passionate about someone. "Okay, yes."

"What about your children?"

"I will work that out with them, but I must also think about myself."

"So, will you tell them right away?"

Maggie pushed open the door. "I already know. I was coming to sit with you, Momma, when I overheard. Sorry, I did not plan it."

"Then what do you think about it?"

"Momma, everyone here knows how you feel about Eli and how he feels about you."

"They do?"

"You haven't hidden it."

"Yeah, I suppose. I'm sorry."

"Don't be Momma. You're right. If you love someone, these chances don't always come. You should take it."

"What about Jeremiah? How will this affect him?"

"May take some time, but he'll be okay."

"Here they come," Eli said.

"What's going on?" Maggie asked.

"They are bringing in the small batch that crossed into McFadden's place."

"You want to check them out?"

"Yes, I do."

The hands herded the cattle into the corral as Cora, Eli, and Maggie strolled there to look them over.

When he had the last cow inside, Samuel rode through the gate and tied his horse to the fence. "There you go, ma'am. Jeremiah did a great job."

"He didn't seem timid?"

"Not at all."

Jesse ambled closer and slapped Eli on the back. "Any strange happenings while we were gone?"

Cora gazed at him, grinning. "Nothing much unless you count Eli asking me to marry him."

"Now, that would be strange."

"You and Eli?" Samuel asked. "Who could have imagined?"

Everyone hooted.

Jesse stared into Eli's face. "All I have to say is, it's about time."

Chapter 53

The ranch hands had finished breakfast and were saddling their horses for the day's work when the new ranch foreman, Rob Benson, entered the barn. "Hold up, men. McFadden wants a meeting in the bunkhouse."

"Wilburn already rode for the herd," Wash Seeley replied.

"Go and get him, and hurry."

"What is the meeting about?" asked Woodie Bosworth.

"What do you think? Like always, water."

"Maybe the boss will ride onto that ranch lady's land this time and do what needs to be done. Too many of our men got hurt at the river."

"Well, Woodie, we did shoot first."

"So, they got it coming."

Rob and the two men walked from the barn.

Tye watched as they left. "Howdy, I didn't come here to fight my friends."

Grant nodded. "Me either. I thought we'd be breaking horses. Now, McFadden has others doing it. All he wants is to fight with that woman for the water."

Howdy tossed his saddle on the rail. "He doesn't want her water, Grant. McFadden wants her land."

"For sure he does," Tye uttered. "Howdy, maybe we should think about leaving this place."

"Do you feel the same, Grant?"

"I do."

"Let's see what this meeting's about. If it appears things will get worse, let's hightail it after dark."

"Where to?" Grant asked.

"I'm thinking we should try Riverview."

"Are you crazy?" Tye responded. "We shot at those boys."

"I didn't hit anyone," Howdy said. "None of us did."

"They won't know that."

"We'll explain that we are leaving because we want no part of McFadden's war."

"We'll be changing sides, is all," Tye expressed.

"I'd rather be where Samuel and his pa are than these crazies."

A sound came from behind them, and they turned. Wilburn Capp tied his horse in a stable beside them. "If you boys are headin' out, I'm going with you. I worked for Stuart Rivers a few years back. Those folks were good to me."

"Why'd you leave Capp?" Tye asked as they left the barn.

"I went to see my dying mom. Guess I overstayed because Stuart hired someone else in my place. He was sorry but said there was nothing he could do. Maybe I can witness to Cora that you men disagree with McFadden's ways."

"That might help, Howdy," Grant said.

"Sounds good, Capp," Howdy replied. "Let's see what McFadden wants before deciding further."

"He wants more killers. That's what he wants," Grant spouted.

"Shush. We don't want anyone hearing us," Howdy said.

The three men and the elderly Wilburn Capp walked into the bunkhouse, where McFadden's men and gunhands sat in the chairs. They found a place to stand against the back wall as McFadden walked to the front.

The rancher turned and looked each of them in the eyes and took a puff from his cigar. "Men, I didn't want it to come to this. As most of you know, I've given Cora plenty of time and offered her a fair price, but time has run out.

"I rode to that ranch at least four times and to Clearwater to meet her twice. Cora Rivers has put up a wall against any negotiations. Now, it's time to force her hand.

"Tomorrow, we will take Clearwater. We will fire the sheriff and replace him with my choice."

"That ain't right," Tye whispered.

"Hush, Tye," Howdy said.

"We should have left with Samuel," Grant commented.

"Quiet."

"Now, men, I don't like war any more than you fellows," McFadden said. "But sometimes nothing else will alter an outcome, and I believe we are there.

"We will take the town, and I mean complete control. One man will run the hotel, and another will run the restaurant. We will gather the city council and persuade them to give us articles like water rights, land rights, and deeds."

"Won't the sheriff try to stop us?" Woodie Bosworth asked.

"He will," McFadden laughed. "But he will fail in his attempt. Gaynes doesn't have enough manpower or backbone to stop our progress and will soon learn that he does not have the town's support. Fear will see to that."

"What about those gunhands from Riverview?" Lane Hanson asked.

"We'll take care of them, but I prefer they don't discover our plans until we've assumed control."

McFadden peered around the room at his men. "Look, Samuel was pretty good with a gun, and I hear his father is too, but we have eight professional gunhands with us besides the rest of you. When this is all over, there'll be no more gunplay for land and water rights because I'll control the fine grazing lands and water in these parts. After that, nothing else matters."

"So, why are we waiting?" Woodie asked.

"Have you noticed I send out two men each day?"

Heads nodded around the room.

"These are my spies. They've watched how Riverview maneuvers. If Riverview follows their typical practice, later today or tomorrow, a wagon will go for supplies."

Woodie raised a hand. "How does that help?"

McFadden grinned. "Well, you see, Cora's daughter, Maggie, will be on that supply wagon with some other cowboy."

"That Samuel Stalls may come along," replied Lane Hansen.

"That could be, but we have a surprise planned, whoever is with her. We'll capture Maggie to ensure Cora's appearance in Clearwater."

"So you will bargain with Cora River to sign over Riverview?" Rob Benson asked.

"That is the second part of the plan, but first, we must take out Cora's gunfighters to level things, and then she will see the light. Isn't that right, Jack?" He spun to Jack Hagarty."

"That's right, boss. We've got it covered."

"I hope so, Hagarty, because everything rests on you and your men doing your jobs."

"Don't worry about us, boss. Worry about that Maggie woman and the sheriff."

"Speaking of the sheriff, you know what to do if he doesn't comply."

"I told you, McFadden, taking out a lawman will cost you."

"Then you have a payment coming. Do what you have to."

Howdy and the other two men stood against the wall, listening.

Why had they stayed here, Grant thought? They knew it was bad when McFadden called Samuel in and wanted him to kill the lady rancher's foreman. Getting away at this point might not be a straightforward task.

"We leave tonight," Howdy whispered. "Tye, you will saddle our horses and lead them outside to a safe place."

"Why me?"

"You're the fastest, and be quiet."

The meeting broke, and the cowboys rose from their chairs to return to work.

Rob Benson stood on a chair. "Hey, fellows, I'll signal you to come in with three shots to the air. When you hear that, don't delay."

Wilburn Capp found Howdy outside. "You're still leaving tonight, aren't you?"

"Yes, after dark, make your way to the barn and saddle your horse, and then wait for us."

"I'll be there."

Chapter 54

The empty wagon bounced as Maggie and Ellison McCarnnon straddled the bench seat on their way to town.

"You keep a watch, Ellison. Since McFadden tried stealing our cattle, I don't trust him."

"I think you're right, ma'am."

"Oh, stop with the ma'am. Just Maggie."

"Yes, ma'am. I mean Maggie."

"We've got to remember grain for the horses. I don't recall it being on your list."

"I'm used to Sheldon making it, but I promise I'll get better. Miss old Sheldon."

"I do, too, Ellison. Since Father passed, he's been like a father to me."

"Sheldon was like a father to all the hands."

Maggie smiled, knowing it was true.

Two horses rushed onto the road, blocking the wagon's path. Ellison drew the gun from his holster to point it when a bullet ricocheted off the wagon seat.

"What do you want?" Maggie pulled the team to a stop. "We've done nothing to you."

Hagarty rode up beside the wagon. "No, you've not done anything—yet. Tell your man there to get down."

Maggie fixed her gaze hard on the gunfighter. "You're just a bully."

"Make your man get down, or I will."

Maggie assumed Hagarty had no scruples against killing. "Ellison, better do what he says."

The cowboy stepped from the wagon, glaring at the gunfighter.

"Toss those weapons away," the gunman asserted.

Ellison threw the rifle into the tall grass ten feet from him and then unbuckled his holster, tossing it in the same location.

"Mister, you will take a message to the Rivers woman. Tell her we have her daughter and that she'll be waiting for her in town. As of today, McFadden runs Clearwater. If she wants supplies, they will come through JA McFadden. Tell her she can reverse these difficulties and have her daughter back if she agrees to sign over Riverview to McFadden."

"My Momma's never going to agree to those terms," Maggie declared, frowning.

Lane Hansen rode up closer. "She will, Maggie. Cora no longer has a choice."

Maggie turned to Lane. "You were working for McFadden all along, weren't you?"

Lane laughed. "Tingles down deep, doesn't it?"

"What I have down deep is the audacity to declare this. McFadden will never own Riverview."

"What makes you say that, little lady?" Hagarty asked.

"Everyone knows the trouble McFadden has brought us, but you should believe it's nothing compared to what's coming for the fat man."

"And there it is. They said you were a fiery tart. Only I didn't think you'd actually say it."

"What'd I say?"

"You just admitted those guns at your place will come looking for you."

Maggie knew she had said too much, but would they come to Clearwater? *Samuel! No, please don't come. They will kill you.*

Hagarty motioned to one of his men. "Jim, jump up there and drive the wagon. Let's get to town before that bunch becomes curious."

＊ ＊ ＊

Sheriff Gaynes looked up from the rocker when he spotted a wagon coming. Maggie Rivers sat on one side of the bench, but he didn't recognize the man driving the wagon. *New man?*

He stood to take a step toward them but heard a gun's hammer catch behind his head.

"Sheriff, drop that gun belt," Lane Hansen said.

"What is this?" Gaynes replied.

"They say there's going to be a new sheriff running things."

Deputy Willis Hobbs saw the gun pointed at the back of Sheriff Gaynes's head and hurried toward him, but Gaynes waved him back.

Willis turned, heading toward the courthouse to tell the judge or the other council members what he saw. When he reached the courthouse, two armed men stood waiting at the door.

"Drop that gunbelt, deputy," Archie Dolton demanded.

Willis loosened the belt and handed it to him.

"Now, get inside with the others."

When he entered the large chamber, Willis found several other townsfolk, scared and waiting.

JA McFadden soon appeared with five men, riding down a side street to the main. He turned his horse to the sheriff's office. Lane Hansen held a gun on Gaynes, shoving him to his knees.

McFadden dismounted and walked up beside them. "Sheriff, you should have taken me seriously. That was a colossal error on your part."

Gaynes declined to speak.

"You have nothing to say? No word of wisdom to offer before you die?"

"Haven't you killed enough men?" Gaynes retorted. "Why can't you leave folks alone?"

"The people are safe, but the town, well, it's a small part of what I'm after. All this time, I've been offering good money for Riverview Ranch, and Cora has refused me, but you haven't helped, Sheriff. I offered you a great opportunity. You could have survived with substantial gain, but your stubbornness has ended you."

Lane Hansen laughed.

Gaynes peered up from a kneeling position. "McFadden, if...if you want the town, that...that's fine. I'll retire and take my family away."

"But Sheriff, *time* has run out, and I'm afraid I must set an example so everyone knows that when I offer a bargain, I mean what I say!"

McFadden stepped to the side and gazed at Lane with a nod. The gunman raised his revolver and fired at the back of the sheriff's skull, and he fell dead.

The big rancher looked at Lane. "Well, the town needs a sheriff, so I guess you're promoted."

Lane reached down and rolled Sheriff Gaynes to his back, pulled his badge free, and pinned it on himself. "Yes,

I'm the new sheriff. Always wondered what it'd feel like to be a lawman."

"Don't get too settled behind that badge," came a voice behind them.

Turning, they saw Hagarty walking up. "We sent a man back to Riverview, just like you requested, McFadden. Won't be long until they know about Clearwater and that we have the daughter. I suspect they'll be coming."

McFadden tensed. "Well, that's what we wanted, right? Hagarty, where are you keeping the townspeople?"

"At the courthouse."

"Good. Where's the daughter?"

"Still holding her in the wagon."

"Bring her to the jail and put her in a cell. That jailhouse will be no simple place for them to break her free."

"Yes, sir."

"Then you can place your men in the best places for firing, up high, behind cover, or wherever seems suitable."

"Will do."

"What about me, boss?" Lane asked.

"You'll watch over the jail. I'll send another man. You two will keep the daughter secure until Cora signs the papers."

"Yes, sir. Can I have Grant Boyd?"

McFadden appeared annoyed at the request. "Grant's left. He and those other two from Arkansas and old Wilburn rode out during the night."

"Oh no. Traitors."

"My bet is they've left the country by now. I'll send you another gunhand. I want her kept safe."

As Lane turned toward the jail, a man in a suit walked up to McFadden. "JA, what's going on here?" asked Ennis Bentley.

"Well, can't you see, Councilman, we're cleaning up your town's mess?"

"How is killing the sheriff cleaning up the town's mess?"

"Gaynes failed to follow, and that's what happens when folks won't respect the plan."

The councilman stared at the sheriff's body on the ground. "This ain't right."

"Ennis, if you want to see what's right..." McFadden touched his protruding vest where a small gun lay inside.

"No, I don't."

"Get on to the courthouse where others are waiting. How many more are still walking around town?"

"I...I don't know. People ran when they saw what was happening."

"Go on now. We'll find them." He turned to Lane, who now stood on the porch. "When the other man comes to the jail, let him watch while you and Hagarty check every house and business. Some townsfolk are hiding, and we want them all in one place."

"Yes, sir."

Lane looked down the street, grinning. "Hagarty's coming with the daughter now."

"Alright."

Hagarty had tied Maggie's hands behind her back at the ambush. "She's hellfire and torment, sir."

"I know. Thought she would shoot me once."

"I wish I had, then none of this would have happened, Maggie said."

"But your momma was smart enough to appreciate a good neighbor."

"Your opinion, but mine is that you are responsible for my father's death. Shooting you would have been an honor for all those who died at your hands."

"And yet, I'm still standing."

"But your time is running out."

McFadden laughed. "No, honey, as you can see, I have the upper hand."

"You won't be laughing for long."

"Put her in a cell! Kill anyone who comes near that jail."

Lane took Maggie by the arm and pulled. "Come on, Ms. Hellfire. We got business inside."

McFadden turned to Lane. "You will not touch one hair on that young woman. Do you hear me? Put her inside a cell. Feed and give her water.

"I'm only funning, sir."

"I'm not. She's my advantage."

Maggie grinned as Lane walked her toward the jail.

McFadden gloated at the fact that he had thought of taking the daughter for leverage. *I expect that ranch will be mine before tomorrow's sun goes down.*

Chapter 55

Eli and Jesse stood near the corral, looking over a horse. They turned when they heard hooves sounding from the entrance lane.

"I don't recognize them," Eli said.

"I do," Jesse replied. "Those are friends of Samuel's. They came with him but then kept working for McFadden."

"Wonder if that rancher showed them out?"

"I doubt it. They're cowhands, not gunslingers."

"Let's see what they have to say."

Jesse raised a hand as they drew near. "Hold up, men. I know you fellows. You've been working for McFadden, but what brings you to Riverview?"

"We quit him," replied Tye Morgan. "The man is crazy."

"I'm sure there's truth to that, but why did you come here?"

Howdy Millard removed his hat and wiped the dust from his face with his bandana. "We messed up, Mr. Stalls. We should never have hired on with that man. Samuel realized it early and got away. We should have followed him out. Where is Samuel?"

"Punching cattle."

"Jesse, I'll have someone fetch him," Eli said.

"Mr. Stalls, do you think we'd be wasting our time talking to the Rivers woman about jobs?"

"I don't know, but I'll get her, and you can find out for yourselves." Jesse strolled toward the house.

Eli stood watching them. "When did you men come to terms with McFadden being a madman?"

Tye laughed. "We knew that a while ago. The ranch lady offered him all the water he wanted, but still, he wouldn't leave her alone about the land. He's obsessed with it."

"Jesse called it greed."

Grant Boyd peered at the porch where two women stood talking to Jesse. "Is that Jenny, McFadden's daughter?"

"That's right. Jenny and Nick Lambert showed up not long ago."

"Well, I'll be. I wondered what happened to them."

"Even McFadden's daughter wants nothing to do with him," replied Tye.

"Here comes the boss lady," Grant said.

Cora stepped up beside their horses, chin lifted with a narrow gaze. "Jesse said you men are looking for work?"

"Yes, ma'am," Howdy responded.

"I got to tell you, I'm hesitant knowing who you worked for. That man has caused me much trouble."

"Ma'am, I know our resume has a stench about it from where we came from, but I can assure you all three of us are good men." He looked up and saw Samuel riding toward them. "Ask Samuel. He's known us since we were kids in Booneville."

"Men change," Cora said.

"Not us," Howdy said. "We needed jobs was the only reason we stayed."

"I recall seeing you and that one at the river." She pointed to Grant.

"We didn't hit anyone with our bullets, but we had to make it look good," Grant replied.

"We were already talking about leaving then," Howdy said.

Cora shook her head. "That's been a few weeks ago. Seems your leavin's a bit slow?"

Howdy doffed his hat nervously. "Ma'am, McFadden plans to take over Clearwater. He met with his men yesterday to unveil a plan. When we heard this, we couldn't stay. He's gone mad."

"I'll give you men a try, but if I see anything that says you're still in cahoots with McFadden, you're gone."

"Yes, ma'am."

"Eli, would you mind getting these men settled in? You can put their horses in the stables for tonight."

Samuel stepped up to Howdy and grabbed his horse's reins. "I got their mounts, Eli. Take them to the bunkhouse."

Eli turned to find Jesse staring down the lane again. "What do you see now?"

"Someone walking this way."

Samuel spun to catch a view. "That's Ellison. He drove the wagon to town with Maggie."

Ellison gasped for air as he reached them. "They took...took Maggie."

"Who took Maggie?" Samuel asked.

"Those gunhands, Lane Hansen and Jack Hagarty."

"What would they want with her?"

"Ransom," Jesse said.

"Ransom for what?"

"Samuel, my guess is they will use Maggie to force Cora to sign over the ranch."

"We never understood all of McFadden's plan, but we know they are taking control of the town," Howdy said.

Samuel peered back toward the barn where Howdy stood. "How did you know about this?"

"We heard they would take the young woman at the meeting, but we couldn't warn you any sooner."

"That young woman is to be my wife."

Jesse smiled as he drew closer.

"When did all this happen?" Eli asked.

"A while ago," Jesse said.

Cora stepped up to Ellison. "Did they hurt my daughter?"

"Not while I was there, ma'am. I tried to stay behind, but they forced me to toss my weapons and leave. They wanted me to send a message."

"Well, we got it. Now I'm going after her."

"That's what they want you to do," Eli said. "McFadden will make you sign the land and ranch over or kill you and take it."

"He's got my daughter!"

"And we're going to get her back."

Cora gazed at Eli as tears streamed down her face. "Can you?"

"I promise we will do everything possible to get Maggie back safely. Don't sign those papers unless it's the last resort."

Jenny hurried to Cora and hugged her close.

"Eli, they have a lot of guns," Jesse said.

"I know, but I believe we can plan better."

"So, how are we going to do this?"

"I'm reasonably sure they will think we are coming tonight since they have Maggie."

"Maybe we should."

"Jesse, we have to plan this well."

"You're hoping to use war strategies?"

"Yes. Samuel is a great shot, and so are you. If we can separate those main gunhands, we can pick them off."

"I don't know. That's a lot of guns to try to separate," Samuel said.

"We'll need a few distractions. Sheldon told me about some dynamite they kept on the place for tree stumps."

"Dynamite!" Samuel said.

"Yes, but I don't know how much, and if it's leaky, then it's volatile and worthless."

"But we don't know where they are holding the people," Jesse said. "By now, McFadden has collected the townsfolk as leverage like he did Maggie."

"That's why we should ride in after dark and check things out," Eli explained. "They probably have the people together in one place. How many structures in town do you think could hold them all?"

"The church," Samuel said.

"And the courthouse," Jesse added. "Maybe the hotel."

"Good assessment. Now we need to speak with Cora's men," Eli said. "They should know what to expect and have a choice whether to get involved."

Howdy overheard them. "We'll help."

Samuel gazed at his old buddy. "Are you sure?"

"This has to stop. Men around here got to work, but those like McFadden take all the fun out of it. Yes, we'll help. We don't like seeing women getting hurt."

"Thank you, Howdy," Eli said. "We'll see about getting some grub for you men, then have a talk. Follow me."

Cora had gathered everyone behind the house after supper. Howdy, Tye, and Grant sat on the porch and listened.

Wilburn Capp had ridden in after Samuel's friends and Cora hired him.

Eli stood before them. "I've never been a leader, and wish Jesse would do this. But I reckon it's fallen to me."

"You've got a good plan," Jesse said.

Still unsure, Eli commented, "We're sending out men on reconnaissance tonight. That's a military term, which means we'll survey the town and then decide from there our best strategy. We need to learn where they are holding the people and where the gunmen are."

"So, do you have a plan?" asked Dolph Coker.

"Maybe, but strategies often changed depending on the circumstances. I think we will hit Clearwater in the morning early, but if we find something in town that tells us to alter our plan, we will. Do you men understand that they have Maggie?"

Heads nodded.

"The goal is to get her back unharmed. McFadden wants to trade Maggie for ownership papers to Riverview. Do any of you want to work for McFadden?"

The men mumbled and shook their heads.

"We'll get Maggie back," Andy McGrew said.

Cora nodded. "Yes, we will."

"Is there another way from here to town?" Eli asked. "McFadden will have men watching the main road."

"Simpson road," said Ellison McCarnnon. "You got to cross the river onto the Simpson place, but that's one way."

Eli peered at Cora.

"That's the best way," Cora said, "though it's longer."

"How much longer?"

"Five or six miles."

"I will need a guide tonight, Ellison."

"Yeah, I'll take you through."

"Good. So, in the morning, well before daybreak, all you men and women who want to fight will take the Simpson road on horseback. Wagons will be too noisy. Be sure to carry your weapons and as much ammo as you can. McFadden will have secured the hardware store."

"I can get you to the back of that store," Ellison said. "Maybe we can break in and gather some ammo."

"We'll give that a look over."

"Tell them about the dynamite," Jesse said.

"Dynamite!" Dolph Coker said.

Eli turned to the men. "Dynamite is not for everyone, so Jesse and I will take care of this part."

"What about the townspeople?" asked Julian Stokes.

"We believe they have them gathered in one place. Don't worry. We will take care not to harm anyone. The plan is to use explosives to cause distractions. Using dynamite might be the best way to overcome those guns and distract them so we can free Maggie."

"Who's going after Maggie?" Samuel asked.

"You are."

Samuel slowly nodded as he thought about the request. "What about Hagarty?"

"We can take care of him," Jesse said.

"No! I will do the honors."

"Nuh-uh! Samuel, your job is to get Maggie. That's it. You'll more than likely have gunhands to tend with wherever she is being held."

"My guess is Hagarty will have her, and he knows I will come for her."

Jesse zeroed in on Samuel. Gunfights were the kind of thing he had hoped his son might avoid. A man of God called to preach had no business in gunfights. If he were to kill someone, it would follow him wherever he goes. Somehow, he knew he must intervene. Hanna would never forgive him if Samuel killed a man or took a bullet.

"Hey, fellows. Thanks for coming to Riverview and agreeing to help," Samuel said to his friends.

"Sure," Tye replied.

"I might need your help to free Maggie," Samuel said. "Can I count on you?"

"Sure can."

"Be happy to help," replied Howdy.

"Yeah, we'll help you get Maggie," Grant offered.

"Thank you."

"Alright, folks. Get some rest," Eli said. "Sleeping will be short tonight."

* * *

Samuel slipped away to the barn to saddle his horse. When Sadie was ready, he stepped behind the barn to pray.

"Lord, I don't want to kill that man Hagarty, but it seems they've left me no choice. Show me your way. Please keep Maggie safe and help us find her and set her free."

When he had finished praying, he walked back to Sadie. Jesse stood inside, saddling his horse.

"Samuel, it was news tonight about you and Maggie getting married," Jesse said. "I thought maybe someday that might happen."

"But if she dies tomorrow, it won't."

"This is not over yet."

"I know."

"Hey, about your marrying Maggie. I think your momma would want you to marry at Booneville?"

"Maybe."

"When you see Maggie, ask her about it."

"No. When you see Cora, ask her. I figure she will want her daughter married nearby, not in Arkansas."

"I suppose it doesn't hurt to ask. Now, we better get these horses outside. Eli will want to leave."

"It's gonna be a long night," Samuel declared.

Chapter 56

The reconnaissance group left their mounts at the edge of town and crept closer. A piano echoed from the saloon as they came to the end of the street.

"Whiskey will keep some of them busy," Eli decided.

"But not all," Jesse said.

"Right. We should split up. How much time do we give ourselves to check them out?"

"Only about an hour," Jesse replied. "If anyone's not back in an hour, we should assume they are prisoners."

"Sounds right. Then Jesse, take the south end of town, and I'll take the north. Samuel, someone said there's an alley running down the middle of town. Find it, but don't cross the main street because they might see you. Gather what information you can and meet back here.

"We got to find out where they're holding Maggie and the townspeople. My guess is they won't be together."

"What do you want me to do?" Ellison asked.

"Stay here, out of the way."

"I'd like to go with Samuel since them taking Maggie is sort of my fault."

"Alright, but stay close to him. Let's go quietly."

They split up and started for their places.

* * *

The alley was dark as Samuel and Ellison strolled through. Chickens squawked inside a pen as they walked by.

From inside a house, a dog yapped, sending a spurt of fear up Ellison's spine. "We're gonna get caught."

"Quiet. The only thing that matters is finding out where they are holding Maggie and the townsfolk." Samuel fixed his eyes inside a shed, believing he had caught movement. If one of McFadden's men had hidden there, things could turn. "Hold up."

"Why?"

"Someone's in that shed."

They ambled to the side of the lean-to.

Samuel pointed his rifle into the dark space. "I know someone is in there. Come out, or I'll start shooting."

An elderly man with a beard wearing trousers and suspenders stepped where Samuel could see him.

"Charlie, what are you doing here?" asked Ellison.

"Hiding out."

"Charlie runs the livery stable."

"Where are they holding everyone? Samuel asked.

"Some in the church. They took others to the mercantile. Old man Stuart has a large room where he stores merchandise at the back. I figure that's where they are holding them."

"They brought a woman in on a wagon."

"Yeah, Cora's daughter, Maggie."

"Do you know where they have her?"

"In the jail. They got gunfighters guarding it."

Samuel nodded. "Ellison, stay here with Charlie."

"Where are you going?"

"To get Maggie."

"You can't go against all those guns alone in the dark."

"Ellison is right, mister," Charlie declared. "I saw some of those men shooting. They are mighty fast and accurate with a gun. There are two or three of them at that jail all the time."

"Samuel, all we need to do is report to Eli. Tomorrow, we'll get Maggie back."

"What about the town?" Charlie asked.

"We're going to take it back," Samuel replied. "Maybe you should come with us."

"Nah, I'll be safer here when the bullets fly."

Samuel pointed his rifle the way they came. "Then I suppose we should head back and tell Eli."

Chapter 57

Cora led her men down a south road to the edge of town as the sun presented the first glimpses of light. "Dolph, dismount and see if you can find Eli and those other men."

"No need, Cora," came a voice in the early morning darkness. "We're right here."

Four men walked from the shadows.

"Eli, what do you know?" Cora asked.

"They are holding the townsfolk in two places, the mercantile and the church."

"What about Maggie?"

Eli hesitated.

"Tell me."

"They got her in a jail cell with two or three armed men, all gunhands, watching over her."

"Where's the sheriff?"

"He's dead."

"Oh, no. Poor Gaynes."

"Charlie, the man at the livery, said they killed Sheriff Gaynes right off."

"Are you sure Maggie is still alive?"

"Yes. McFadden still believes he can leverage Maggie and the town to get your ranch."

"I'll give it to them if that's what it takes."

"I hope you don't have to," Eli said.

"So, how do we do this?"

"We need your men to climb up quietly on the roofs of the houses and businesses. We believe they will be safer up high. That's where they'll shoot from." Eli turned to the men. "Don't start firing until you hear the explosions. Jesse and I will set off several dynamite blasts from various places around town. There will be a little time between the blasts, so be patient. Our goal is to lure some of McFadden's men toward the explosions. When they get close, we'll take them out. If you're on a building near an explosion fire when you see McFadden's men."

"When will you get Maggie?" Cora asked.

"When the detonations begin, we expect this will distract some at the jail. Samuel and his buddies will try to get her out."

"Alright then," Cora said. "Let's find our places before daylight."

* * *

Not wanting to damage homes or businesses, Jesse pressed a stick of dynamite into a wooden box filled with household items inside an old building behind the saloon. The blast would be the first of three. He lit the wick and ran toward the church, hoping to free those inside.

The blast boomed moments after he lit the fuse, sending an inferno and scattering the building in fiery pieces on the ground.

McFadden's men ran toward the blast, and Jesse opened fire on them. The sound signaled Cora's men, who waited on the roofs, to follow suit. Three of McFadden's men took bullets as they ran into the saloon for cover.

Jesse gazed up and spotted Julian Stokes. "Keep them penned."

"Yes, sir."

Jesse hurried toward the church as another blast went off on the opposite side of town. He ran to the boardwalk and hugged the wall of a dress shop. Three men crossed the street, running toward the explosion.

Turning, he spotted Samuel cross the street, his friends following behind. *Lord, watch over my son, please.*

* * *

McFadden sat up in the chair when he heard the blasts. He had kept three gunhands nearby, believing the gunmen at Cora's had enough experience to try to pull something. If they were to capture him, they would abandon his bargaining for land.

He walked from the hotel's office. "Wash, what's happening?"

"Two blasts, one on each end of town. Our men are checking it out."

"No, don't do that. That's what they want you to do."

"Sorry, boss. Too late."

Gunfire sounded at the end of the town.

"How many men we got left?" McFadden asked.

"I don't know. Got to be some at the jail."

"Wash, get over there, and bring that woman to me."

"Yes, sir."

Wash Seeley stepped from the hotel onto the porch. Slithering down the boardwalk, he moseyed toward the jail, eyes open for Cora's men. Two buildings from him, he spotted men outside the jail at the edge of an alleyway. He raised his weapon and fired.

A bullet ricocheted off the brick beside Grant's head. "Get down, Tye. Someone is shooting from across the street."

"Yeah, and now the jail will know we're here. It's up to Howdy and Samuel."

"Guess we better be ready when the blast goes off."

"Blast," Tye said. "I thought they were coming in from the other side. Maggie's in there."

"Nope, they're blasting in at the back. Samuel said there was an empty jail cell at the backside. When they light the dynamite, we have to be fast getting in the front door. Samuel and Howdy are going in the back way to get her out. All we have to do is distract those gunhands inside."

"Yeah, I heard you. Gunhands. That won't be easy with bullets flying at our backside."

"I know, but we have to get Maggie out."

* * *

Samuel called to Maggie through the window. "Cover yourself with a mattress. We're blasting in."

"I'm so glad you came. Hurry," Maggie said.

He laid the dynamite on the windowsill farthest away from her.

"I sure hope this works," Howdy said.

"All we need is to knock a large hole in the wall. Either way, Grant and Tye will barge in, shooting."

"Samuel, those men must know we're behind the jail."

"Maybe not when Tye and Grant shoot at the door."

"Yeah, it could work."

"Okay, the cell door is unlocked," Samuel said. "We only need to grab the key and open Maggie's cell."

"Samuel, *you* get the key, but remember, those men will be ready for you."

"Well, here goes." Samuel lit the wick, and they ran to the side of the building. A few seconds later came a blast, tossing bricks from the window and crashing more inside.

"Wow!" Howdy said.

Samuel peered from the other side of the building. "Let's go."

As shots rang out at the front of the jail, Samuel and Howdy climbed over crumbled brick amidst floating dust until they came to Maggie's cell. The door to the office flung open, and a man shot at them, but Samuel returned fire. He fell dead, blocking the door open. "Help me, Howdy."

"They dragged him inside the jail portion and closed the door.

"Maggie, are you alright?" Samuel asked.

"I'm fine."

"We need the key."

"Lane is in there with another gunhand. Please be careful."

He eased open the door to the office. Lane had turned the desk on its side at a corner, giving himself cover as he fired at the front door. The other man had taken a position by the front window. Grant and Tye had made little headway, but at least they were a distraction.

Lane turned, spotting Samuel, and fired two rounds, one glancing off the wall, the other finding home in a wooden plank.

Samuel spotted the keys hanging on the wall behind Lane's concealment. "Howdy, get low and take out that man at the window."

"What are you gonna do?"

"Something stupid."

"What?"

"Now."

Samuel pulled the door open wide. "Lane, I'm here for Maggie."

Lane's eyes widened as Samuel dove into the room. The gunman spun to Samuel, firing wildly. Then Samuel's bullet found Lane's chest. He fell forward, drooping over the desk and gasping for breath. "Well, I...I...suppose you...get the girl."

The other man lay dead on the floor.

Samuel grabbed the key off the wall and hurried to Maggie's cell.

When the cell door opened, she reached out and kissed him. "Thank you."

"You're not angry with me for killing a man?"

"I understand now that sometimes killing is necessary. This was self-defense, though I hope the stench of blood doesn't travel with you to wherever God calls you."

"Does that mean you'll leave the ranch?"

"Yes, after we're married."

He took her in his arms and kissed her.

"Samuel, those boys need us," Howdy said.

"Uh, yeah, coming."

Through the window, they could see the dead bodies in the street.

"Where are Tye and Grant?"

"I don't know."

"Watch Maggie. I'm going out through the back."

"Samuel, if Hagarty is alive, he will look for you," Maggie said.

He moved toward the door. "I hope someone else has taken care of him."

When he reached the outside corner, he spotted his two friends on the side of the building, hiding behind a wagon. "What's going on, fellows?"

"Grant's hit real bad," Tye said.

"Where's the shooters?"

"Across the road. We hit one of them, but another came."

"Tye, we need to get him inside."

"I know, but they'll shoot again."

"Howdy!" Samuel called out.

Howdy cracked the door. "Yeah."

"We're going to bring Grant inside the jail. He's wounded. Give us some cover."

"Wait a minute, and I'll help," Maggie said.

After a moment, Howdy replied, "Alright, we're ready."

"Here we come," Samuel said.

Tye took hold of Grant's legs, and Samuel held his torso. Howdy and Maggie fired two shots as the men carried Grant's injured body. As they reached the door, Samuel spotted Hagarty across the street with his gun pointed at them. Then, as quickly, he lowered it.

"Samuel Stalls," came a voice. "I think our time has come."

"Hagarty," Maggie said.

"Time to end this," Samuel said.

"But why you?"

"I'm faster than Pa and Eli, and I can settle this once and for all. That rancher will have nowhere to turn once his key man is dead. The question is, will you forgive me?"

"Yes."

"Really?"

"Yes, I will."

"Then I'll be right back."

"She wrapped her arms around his neck and pulled him down, and kissed him. I love you. Come back to me, cowboy."

Samuel nodded and walked out the door.

As he stepped into the street, he saw there were three men. One man on each side of Hagarty. "So it takes three of you now."

"We plan to get the job done, but if you're worried, I get first dibs. These fellows get their fair shot if I go down."

Then, from the left side of the street, Jesse marched and settled beside Samuel. Eli came walking from the other side and found his place on the right side.

Samuel grinned. "Nothing wrong with balancing things, right?"

Hagarty frowned but remained sure of himself, knowing Samuel was his. He motioned with his hands for his men to spread out. "I'll take you anyway and add another notch to my gun handle."

Samuel turned to Jesse. "Why did you step out to help? You should have already left for Booneville. You've got Momma and Rebecca to care for."

"You're my son, Samuel. I can't leave until I know you are safe. Someday, you'll have a kid and understand."

Hagarty shook his head. "Ya'll gonna jabber all day, or are you going to draw?"

Samuel turned his attention to the gunman, gazing into his eyes. "Like you said. The first draw is yours."

Hagarty gave a one-sided grin and then reached for his gun. In an instant, Samuel discharged a bullet before the gunfighter's weapon departed the holster.

The two other men were no match for Eli and Jesse. Three men lay dead in the street.

"Look around," Jesse said. "Might not be over."

"Where's that big rancher, McFadden?" Eli questioned.

"Right behind you. Turn slowly and look at me!"

McFadden stood about fifteen feet away on the boardwalk, holding a shotgun. "Everything was going fine until you rebels rode into Clearwater. I had it all planned, and it would have worked. But you—"

"No, you, McFadden!" came a soft voice. "You brought this on yourself, and now you've lost it all."

McFadden shifted his eyes and saw Cora holding a rifle.

"You lost Jenny," Cora said. "She wants nothing to do with you."

Not far behind the ranch woman stood Jenny, shaking her head.

"I gave my daughter everything!"

"Everything but love. That's all she ever asked for. You've lost her forever, and now you'll lose your ranch and be in jail for the rest of your life. The army is on the way to Clearwater. Because you killed Sheriff Gaynes, they will take over here."

The rancher's eyes widened. "No, I do business with the army." He laughed. "They can't do anything to me. They need their beef and horses."

"I'm sure other ranchers can fill their needs."

McFadden's face tightened, gripping the shotgun. He spun toward Cora. "This is your fault. He raised the shotgun and aimed at her—but it was too late. Cora's Winchester sounded, knocking the rancher to the ground."

Blood from McFadden's chest poured on the porch as Cora walked up. "This was for all those bodies lying in the street and for those who died at my ranch, including Stuart. I know you had him killed."

"Cor...Cora, I...I'm sorry." Then, his eyes no longer moved, and his breath faded.

Jesse and Eli ambled to the porch.

"This is a sad day," Jesse said. "So many dead."

"But better days lie ahead," Eli remarked. "Ranching in these parts will again be normal."

"Is Maggie alright?" Cora said.

"Yes, they have things under control at the jail," Jesse said.

"Let's find the doctor so he can tend to the wounded. After that, I will take a long rest at the ranch."

Eli turned to Jesse. "Yeah, that's the best idea I've heard today."

Chapter 58

Jesse stood before Samuel inside the bunkhouse, tying his bowtie. "I received a wire from your momma, and she gave her blessings. She asked me to discuss you and Maggie visiting the ranch before you head west with the wagon train."

"We should have time. We're meeting the wagon train at Independence in the spring."

Jesse pulled down on Samuel's coat. "You look so grown. I want to tell you how proud I am of you."

"You weren't so proud of me that day you saw me shooting my gun and not helping with the horses."

"I was worried what you might get into with that sort of weapon, and still am. Maybe you becoming a preacher will allow me to rest better."

"I've got to carry my weapons on our trip, you know."

"My advice is to keep a low profile. The more folks know about you, the more they will expect when it comes to that gun. Always try to stay clear of other folk's struggles."

"Yes, I understand."

"Alright, I'm going in for some punch. You should come in soon."

"I will."

As Jesse left out the door, Howdy turned to Samuel. "Wish Grant was here to see this."

"I'm sorry he didn't make it. Is Tye coming?"

"Yes, but he's spending time with that rancher's daughter while his arm heals."

"Jenny? I bet he's milking that since Nick didn't stick around," Samuel uttered.

"Nick's not the marrying type, and then Cora made Eli the new foreman. I suppose Nick felt he should move on and find a place better suited. Jenny told him she was staying around and maybe becoming a partner with Cora."

"So she's getting the ranch? I thought McFadden said she wouldn't."

"Seems he never set that up legally before he died."

"Tye and Jenny. That has a ring, but what about you, Howdy?"

"I don't know many women that would have me. So, what are you doing after the wedding?"

"Pa wants us to head back to Booneville and spend time with Momma. She wants to meet Maggie before we start west."

"I heard you and your pa talking. Are you really going to be a preacher?"

"Looks that way. I know it will make Momma happy."

"Will you find one of them churches out West?"

"I hope so. Folks traveling west will want a preacher along, but I'm hoping to find a proper town where a church needs a preacher, and folks want us."

"You never know. You might get out west and decide to pan for gold."

"That's not in the plans, but who knows?"

Howdy sat on the bunk beside his friend. "Samuel, what if I tagged along to Booneville?"

"Sure. What's on your mind?"

"I want to see my momma," he chuckled, "and if Anna Clemens or Berta Wyman aren't married, I might look at getting hitched."

"Maybe you should first find a job."

"Yeah, but it won't be with Bartlett. I hear he got himself ten years."

The door opened, and Jesse stepped inside. "Time for you, Samuel. You are not getting cold feet, are you?"

"I'm coming. Howdy, and I will be along in a minute."

"Don't make us wait."

"I'll be right along. Howdy, can you give me a few moments to pray?"

"You aren't sure, are you?"

"That's not it, but I want God's blessings on our marriage."

Howdy started for the door and paused. "You taught me a lot, Samuel, and I'm proud to be your friend."

"I'm proud to be yours."

Howdy nodded and grinned and walked outside.

Samuel kneeled beside the bunk to pray.

∗ ∗ ∗

Eli, Jesse, and Howdy were waiting in the ranch house, finishing their punch.

Jesse turned and saw Samuel come in. "Hurry, son, they are starting the music."

"I'm here," Samuel replied.

"I've never been in a double wedding before," Howdy commented.

"Well, you didn't think Eli could run this place without Cora, did you?" Jesse asked.

"Things should be better with McFadden out of the way, and if another like him comes along, Eli will handle it."

Eli turned, overhearing Howdy. "I'm not marrying her to be in gunfights. I'm marrying Cora because I love her. This is my first true love for a woman."

Jenny pushed through the door. "We're waiting for you, gentlemen. Follow me."

When they had settled behind the crowd, Jenny turned to them. "The best man for each groom will walk down the aisle first."

"I thought the woman walked down the aisle, and the men waited," Eli said.

"That's right, but since Cora sprained her ankle to get to the street where McFadden was, we're turning it around."

"I didn't know that," Jesse said.

"Her ankle is not that bad," Eli said.

Jenny stared into Eli's face. "When she woke up today, there was swelling, so yes, it is."

"Okay, I believe you."

* * *

Beside the preacher, Maggie waited. Cora sat on a chair, awaiting the ceremony.

Musicians played guitars and a mandolin as the preacher gave the go-ahead to Jenny.

"Jesse goes first, and then Howdy."

The two men walked down the grass aisle to the front and found their places. Samuel and Eli followed to their rightful positions.

The music ceased as the preacher stepped up beside the couples. "Today is a beautiful day for a wedding. The sun is shining, and there are smiles on people's faces across this place. God will today join *two* fine couples in matrimony…"

Hearing the preacher made Samuel realize that he would have the job of marrying folks in the future. God laid many responsibilities upon a preacher, but none more critical than explaining the word to others. As Samuel ventured into this new role, he knew he must take to heart everything the Lord showed him so he may reveal it to his people.

He set his eyes on Maggie. She was beautiful. Her wish to follow him wherever he goes to preach was something he could not grasp. He supposed that was love, one remarkable aspect of human nature God had instilled in people.

The preacher called on the couple to turn. Samuel peered into Maggie's hazel eyes. The veil over her face could not prevent the breathtaking beauty beneath. Those same eyes had captured him that day he spotted her on the porch at the mercantile.

Nearing the end, the preacher asked him and Eli a question. "Do you, sirs, take the woman as your lawfully wedded wife?"

"Yes," the men replied in unison.

"Ladies, do you take your man as your lawfully wedded husband?"

Cora and Maggie shouted together, "Yes!"

"Then, by the powers invested in me, I pronounce you man and wife and man and wife. You may kiss the brides."

Samuel rolled back the veil over Maggie's face and hair and kissed her. "I will love you always."

"And I will love you more."

"Never."

"We'll see."

The preacher tapped Samuel on the shoulder. "I think they want the couples to head back down the aisle toward the house."

"Sure," Samuel said. "This is the part I don't like."

"Oh, come on," Maggie replied as they started walking. "The fun part is we get to eat cake."

Chapter 59

Samuel purchased a wagon and team for the return trip to Booneville and the journey westward. Maggie wanted to take many of her things, and Samuel had to remind her they would return before joining the wagon train.

"Then why are we taking the wagon? We could ride our horses to Booneville."

"I have a few things to gather and can't carry them back on a horse."

Cora sat watching the newlywed couple. "Are we witnessing their first skirmish?"

"Might be, but I bet it's not their last," Jesse declared.

"Surely not because of Maggie. Would have to be Samuel." She grinned.

"I don't know. I just bet Maggie wins more."

"You've learned my daughter well since you've been here."

"Hey, not to change the subject, but what about Doc? Is he sticking around?"

"Looks that way. I made Eli my new foreman. Or I should say, he made himself foreman. Marrying me comes with privileges, you see. Doc wanted to be here for Eli. War buddies, I guess."

"Eli will do you well as foreman."

"Yeah, I know. I wish that Mexican would have stuck around. He was a hard worker and fine at rounding up cattle."

"Sacho loves to track, and there's no job for him here. When the Army showed up, he knew the sergeant, and they asked him to get back to the fort and track some murderers. But it sounded like that troupe's staying to keep order in Clearwater until the town hires a new sheriff."

"Sadly, that may be a while, Jesse. I can't see anyone around these parts applying for it."

Eli stepped outside with a cup of coffee. "I hope the army doesn't up and leave prematurely. There will be gunhands coming for the job. They'll have to sift through some bad men."

"Well, they'll have you to help them. You can spot those easily," Jesse said.

Samuel and Maggie walked to the porch.

"We are ready," Samuel said.

Jesse raised from his chair. "Are you sure?"

"Yes."

"So, you are taking that wagon and team home?"

"I have to gather some of my things."

Cora stood and walked to Maggie. "Please be careful. You've not traveled away from home this far. That trail will be dangerous."

"Samuel warned me."

Cora hugged Maggie and kissed her on the cheek. "I love you, daughter. Now, before you leave, find Jeremiah and say bye to him. Let him know you're coming back soon."

Eli reached to shake Samuel's hand. "Grateful to have met you. Travel safe, and tell your mom and sister I said hello."

"I will."

"Jesse, it's been nice seeing you again," Eli said. "Maybe someday I'll get to your ranch again."

"Well, I'll see you here in a few months. Cora wants six young horses in the spring. If Hanna and my brothers have kept the ranch secure, I have some very nice colts."

"I'm sure they have," Cora said. "I hope Hanna will come with you. She sounds like a jewel."

"She is and keeps me on the right path for sure."

"We'll get our horses when we return," Samuel said.

"They will be fine here," Cora replied. "Now, you folks need to be on your way unless you plan to camp on Riverview."

Maggie and Samuel walked toward the horses.

Jesse followed, waving. "Cora, I'll send a wire when we get there so you know."

"Thank you. I enjoyed your time here. Bye now."

Cora and Eli watched as the wagon turned to leave.

"I like the Stalls family," Cora said. "Though I never knew anyone was so fast with a weapon as you and Jesse."

Eli smiled. "Well, Samuel is much better. A chip off the old block. And it's good that he is moving away from that life, or gunfighters will come calling."

"I hope that young man sets his mind to preaching and caring for my Maggie."

"He will."

"Momma, Maggie said she would see me soon," Jeremiah said, "but I know she will leave again, and I will miss her."

Jenny overheard them. "Jeremiah, Maggie will always be your sister, but you can think of me as a sister if you want to, and you can visit me at the ranch anytime."

Jeremiah reached and hugged her.

"I believe everything is going to work out," Cora said.

"Somehow, I perceived that," Eli replied.

"Yeah, uh-huh."

Chapter 60

The travelers reached Jesse's ranch in three weeks of hard journeying. It pleased Hanna to see Samuel again after many months and to meet Maggie. After a week at the ranch, Hanna came to love and appreciate her new daughter-in-law.

Jesse spent much of his time back working with his horses. Several needed new shoes, and Samuel lent a hand to that task.

"I've got a lot to catch up on around here," Jesse said. "I wish you could stay longer."

"We have to reach Independence by spring, so we hope to return to Clearwater early to give Maggie more time with Cora and Jeremiah."

"I know you can't stay longer, but I can wish."

"Momma said Rebecca had gotten pretty good with the horses when she was down with that leg."

"Yeah, Rebecca will be a great help. Still, I'm considering hiring a couple of fellows to have around here. Eli and Doc were my first choice, but—"

"I know you don't have them. So, make sure whoever you hire isn't someone who worked for Bartlett."

"Men can change, Samuel. That's something as a minister you might deal with."

"I know, and I have lots to learn."

"What about a church?"

"My goal is to find an existing church or build one."

"Well, if you're considering building, why not here? I could help you."

"Pa, your hands are full caring for the ranch and training horses. Besides, I've prayed about this. Something tugs at me to travel west. I can't explain it except to say that God is drawing me in that direction."

"Then stick with that feeling because God won't let you down, although there may come times when it seems he's steered you wrong. When that happens, keep standing on what he said. God fulfills his promises even if it takes many years."

"That sounds like good advice."

"So, did you hear Momma when she told about Kendall looking into taking horses to Montana by rail?"

"That's an interesting opportunity."

"I want to visit with him more about that. I thought maybe we could take a trip to Montana and check it out. It would be worth it if we could find buyers for our horses."

"I'll keep in touch. Maybe one day you will visit where we live."

"I hope you write often, especially for your Momma's sake, Samuel. Children leaving home hit women harder."

"I suppose so."

"Now, we better get to supper. I want to spend some time with you and Maggie tonight before you leave."

"Yeah, tomorrow's the day."

"I know it is, but I hoped you'd change your mind," Jesse said as they approached the porch.

"Sorry, Pa. Like I said, we have to get there so Maggie has plenty of time with Cora and Jeremiah before we make our trip to Independence."

"That western trail will be grueling. Your Momma and I will pray for you."

"Thanks, Pa."

✳ ✳ ✳

Following breakfast the next day, Maggie and Samuel said their goodbyes and set out on their way.

When they were gone, Jesse rode away to check out the horses in the field. He roped a bay mare and brought her to the round pen to work with.

I've traveled so much in the last few months that I've forgotten how much I love this part.

He slapped his leg with the rope, and the horse trotted around the pen.

"Jesse. Jesse. Come," came a loud voice.

"What? I'm busy," Jesse replied.

"Jesse, come."

"What is it?" he called out. "Why can't Rebecca help you, Hanna?"

"Please come. I need you."

He walked from the pen and hurried into the house. Hanna sat at the kitchen table, crying. "What's wrong now?"

"This." She handed him a piece of paper.

Dear Pa and Momma,

I love you and know you'll think I'm too young to leave home. Maybe I am, but I have to. You know how much I want to be a writer, but I can't write at the ranch. My stories are on the trail with a wagon train. So I'm with Samuel and Maggie. Please don't blame them. I've been hiding in the wagon since early this morning. I'm not sure how far they will travel before I tell them. Pa, please don't come after me. I'll be okay with them and wire you from Kansas when we arrive.

Love, Rebecca

"Not again," Jesse said. "How did we miss this when we raised them?"

"You have to go after her!" Hanna said, tears streaming.

"This time, I can't, Hanna. Work here must prevail."

"But it's our daughter."

"Hanna, Rebecca is with our son and his wife. She is safe with them. You know where she is, and that should mean something."

"Oh Jesse, what are we going to do? All our children are gone."

"I'm going to remind you like you've often reminded me. We're going to pray and believe God. He will take care of them."

Hanna rose from the table and hugged him. "Thank you for assuring me. Letting Samuel go hit me hard, and now, my last child is gone, too. The hardest thing, will be not knowing where they are or what is happening. That will be like looking at darkness."

"Rebecca said she would let us know when they arrive. Samuel assured me he would write and wire whenever they could."

"I guess I'll have to live with that."

"No, you can pray. I've heard that God will offer visions to his prayer warriors. Trust the Lord to reveal things to you."

Hanna nodded. "We'll do this together each night before we lay down to sleep."

Maggie gazed at Samuel as he drove the wagon along the trail. "So, do you have any ideas where we might end up on our journey?"

"I thought a lot about Colorado. Someone recently struck a large vein of gold there. So, mining camps will spring up with a surge of newcomers. Might be a good place for a church, and I also wondered about Oregon. Though a might further, I hear there are established towns. Maybe a church in one of them needs a pastor."

"I love the thought of Oregon if it wasn't so far."

"Yeah, we need to pray for direction."

"Samuel, I read that Indians on the way to Colorado are giving the pioneers problems when they cross their land. They burn wagons and sometimes kill folks with arrows. That's scary."

"Yes, and there's risk everywhere, but no matter where we wind up, we will settle into that place and do God's work."

"As long as we follow his will, everything will work out."

"We will pray about it."

"Samuel, it's getting dark. Why don't we stop and camp?"

"I thought that the horses need rest."

"How far have we come today?"

"I'd say close to thirty miles. Under those trees looks like a great place."

"Oh yeah. There's a stream just down a piece," Maggie said.

Samuel guided the team beneath the large oak trees and called to them to halt. "Good horses."

"I need to stretch," Maggie said as she set her foot on the first step.

"Help me down!" came a loud voice.

"What'd you say?" Samuel asked, peering at Maggie.

She shook her head. "I said nothing."

Their eyes widened as Samuel reached behind the wagon seat for his rifle. He hopped down and started toward the rear of the wagon, rushing around the corner with his weapon in hand.

They found Rebecca staring down at them from beneath the wagon's cover. "Well, aren't you going to help me, brother?"

Maggie stood staring, her hands on her hips. "This better be good."

Author Information

Michael is a writing enthusiast who enjoys creating action-adventure stories influenced by his childhood, which included farming and ranching, hauling hay by hand, raising colts and calves, the difficulties of breaking and training horses, and everything that comes with hard living. As a teenager, he discovered the love for trail riding with large groups and traveling to rodeos with family.

As for inspiration, there's none better than the Western writers of the old West movies for actors like John Wayne, Alan Ladd, Roy Rogers, Henry Fonda, James Stuart, and others. These old West movies included great plots with action heroes and love stories, leaving audiences hungry for more. These were all huge influences on Michael's writing career. But what often seems missing that he tries to incorporate in his stories is true Christian inspiration. His stories are always clean and fashioned around the consequences of deeds done and a message of hope.

More to Come

Find these fine books at Amazon.

PRODIGAL TRAIL
Jesse Stalls Series
BOOK 1

This is where the story begins.

Those long days and nights on the cattle drive are a breeze for Jesse Stalls compared to the mistakes he has to live with. Jesse longs to leave home and the family farm. At eighteen years old, he can't wait to see what the world offers away from Booneville. He and his friend, Billy Cantrell, purchase Colt .45 revolvers while waiting for a cattle drive to come along.

After months on the plains, the cattle drive from Omaha ends at Fort Worth. Jesse finds himself in a gunfight with a man named Max Toliver. When the smoke clears, Toliver lies dead. Jesse takes a bullet in the shoulder but finds he's tagged as the latest fast gun.

The journey brings Jesse face to face with Mexican bandits who've abducted three women. During the conflict, he meets a beautiful young woman, Hanna Elrod. Their relationship grows, but Hanna soon realizes that Jesse struggles with the gunfight lingering at the center of his thoughts. As his faith plummets, she keeps praying, refusing to give up on him.

Prodigal Trail is the saga of a young man's determination to leave home on an adventurous journey that turns treacherous. Can the woman Jesse's fallen in love with persuade him to lean on God and his loving earthly father? Or are his trials too overwhelming, even for her? How many must die by Jesse's gun before he realizes the answer he needs is God?

Find it on Amazon.

CURIOSITY OF LAURA STONE
Laura Stone Mysteries

An unimaginable homecoming. A father's bizarre death.

Is coming home too overwhelming for this passionate journalist?

Laura Stone took six years away from the family farm to work on her education and career in journalism. The journey home should be only for a short spell and then back to Boston, except something about her father's passing seems amiss.

Then, after hearing the sheriff's peculiar account, she decided to stay to investigate what the law failed to accomplish.

While remaining at Santa Fe, Laura's greatest homecoming surprise is meeting a man who teases her emotions. An obstacle, however, stands in the way of her happiness, for he boasts an outdated concept of marriage.

Will Laura discover the truth about her father's demise? Is romance brewing for this journalist from Boston?

Find it on Amazon.

For more information about books from this author, visit https://mspanhanksbooks.com/.